Smith is a killer, a paid assassin. Hired by the Enterprise, an American shadow agency, and trained by folks who know how to take a talent for killing and turn it into an asset.

The first kills settle an old score.

The next job is to remove an unwanted Central American political figure. It's not a mission. The mission is to stay alive. It's not a calling. It's a matter of life and death.

Smith would love to retire. But there's always one more job. If Smith can live that long.

Smith is a killer, a paid assassin. Hired by the Enterprise, an American shadow agency, and trained by folks who know how to take a talent for killing and turn it into an asset.

The first kills settle an old score.

The next job is to remove an unwanted Central American political figure. It's not a mission. The mission is to stay alive. It's not a calling. It's a matter of life and death.

Smith would love to retire. But there's always one more job. If Smith can live that long.

Smith

Timothy J. Lockhart

STARK HOUSE

Stark House Press • Eureka California

SMITH

Published by Stark House Press
1315 H Street
Eureka, CA 95501, USA
griffinskye3@sbcglobal.net
www.starkhousepress.com

ISBN-13: 978-1-944520-23-6

Book design by Mark Shepard, SHEPGRAPHICS.COM

First Stark House Press Edition: June 2017

FIRST EDITION

DEDICATION
To Anne

ACKNOWLEDGMENTS

Thanks to all of my fellow readers, writers, and editors for their
invaluable advice and encouragement, especially:

Elaine Raco Chase
Carmel Corcoran
Steve Dowdy
Peggy Earle
Annette Freeman
Guy Holland
Lisa A. Iverson
Charles H. Jackson
Dena L. Jackson
Raymond Leach
Chikako Mori
Rick Ollerman
William Ruehlmann
Erica J. Smith
Warren L. Tisdale
Cina L. Wong
Bonnie Xie
Harry Zhang

and of course Gregory Shepard and
the rest of the fine folks at Stark House Press.

Smith

Timothy J. Lockhart

CHAPTER ONE

Smith shifted the rifle, squinted through the scope, and centered the crosshairs on the target. This one looked much like the last two—a man in his mid-20s, fit, and fairly good-looking. But unlike the last two this man was drunk and getting a blow job.

The target perched naked on the edge of a hot tub. Two women and another man sat in the tub, steam rising around their nude figures in the moonlight. The kneeling blonde giving the blow job might or might not be pretty—Smith couldn't tell from the back of her head—but her movements showed she was definitely enthusiastic.

The target leaned back with his eyes closed. He looked as though he were about to come. A few seconds earlier the scope had shown the three onlookers, each with a drunk-happy expression, watching closely.

Prone on the hillside above the target's house and about a hundred yards from the hot tub, Smith considered the irony of killing the man at this moment. While having sex, he was also dying for sex—literally. Just as the other two had although they'd been engaged in mundane activities when Smith closed in on them. One mowing his lawn, the other dozing in the sun. The first never finished the lawn, the second never woke up.

Smith hadn't been able to tell any of the three why they were being executed. Doing so would have been pleasant and certainly fair—the sporting thing to do, really—but Smith wasn't willing to compromise success of the mission for the momentary satisfaction of looking into the targets' eyes and explaining things.

The devil could explain in hell.

Meanwhile, two shots to the head—one to kill, one to make certain. Smith inhaled, crooking the index finger over the trigger as the shooting instructors had taught.

"Goddamn it!" that one sergeant had kept shouting into Smith's ear on the Fort Jackson range. "Squeeze the fucking trigger, don't yank it!"

The South Carolina sun had made sweat drip into Smith's eyes, blurring the target and making it hard to keep breathing properly. But Smith and most of the other recruits had kept trying day after hellish day of boot camp until they could hit the target more often than not.

Although Smith didn't usually wear shooting gloves, this uninsulated pair was thin and didn't interfere with the shooting routine drilled into the bone six years earlier. Smith exhaled half a breath and then squeezed the trigger so gently that predicting the precise moment of firing would have been impossible.

And as the classroom instructor had said, whacking at the projected schematic with an ancient wooden pointer, the firing pin hit the base of the cartridge, igniting the primer that set off the propellant, and the bullet rocketed down the rifled grooves of the barrel, quickly becoming supersonic.

The rifle kicked Smith in the shoulder, and the *crack!* of sound rang in both ears. Smith kept looking through the scope as a black hole appeared in the target's forehead and his skull jerked forward from the explosion of brains and blood out the rear.

Dead. Yes, surely, but in contrast to TV and movie shooters, a professional takes no chances. At least none that don't have to be taken.

Smelling the familiar acrid odor of burned gunpowder, Smith worked the bolt to eject the brass casing and chamber another round as the target's companions began reacting to the effect of the shot. The man and one of the women screamed while the other covered her eyes with her hands.

The busy blonde reacted last, pulling her head back and looking up at the dead eyes of the man she'd been pleasuring seconds before. Then she too began to scream.

The sound of the second shot made them shut up for a moment. A second hole appeared millimeters from the first, and the target's head jerked again although less violently this time.

The blonde thrashed backward, and the target's body slid into the bubbling water. As the water turned frothy pink, then red in the glow from the recessed lights on the tub's inner walls, the dead man's friends scrambled out, slipping on the wet surfaces.

Only one of them was still screaming, but now the others were shouting at each other, and Smith thought one of the shouts included the word "police." Even if the witnesses weren't calling the cops right now, they soon would.

Smith had expected to feel ecstasy or at least satisfaction at completing this difficult triple mission, but the actual feeling was one of numbness—a draining of emotion. Smith had focused on the mission so hard and long that the future was hazy, indistinct. No clue about what to do next.

Except escape. That was the immediate task, and it was time to start.

Smith was on the military crest of the hill, a few yards lower than the actual crest. Retrieving the ejected casing and crawling to the back side of the hill took only moments.

As the shouting died down, a neighbor called across the fence on one side of the large lot. Smith rapidly disassembled the rifle, acutely aware of the seconds ticking by. Working by touch in the darkness under the trees, Smith stowed the parts in their fitted case.

Smith didn't plan to use the rifle again, but the same Remington Model 700—the civilian version of the Army's M24 sniper rifle—had killed the mower. Although that hit had been in a different state, there was no point in helping the police use ballistics to link the two events to her weapon. Smith would dispose of the rifle components just as the parts of the pistol that killed the sleeper had been scattered in trash bins across three counties.

Smith clicked the case shut and began moving down the hill, stepping quickly and quietly but not running through the underbrush still common in this lightly developed neighborhood. Walking might create the appearance of someone searching for the shooter instead of the shooter fleeing the scene.

But being seen wasn't likely. Dressed in black boots, pants, and long-sleeve shirt and wearing a black watch cap, Smith was sweating lightly in the midsummer California night but blended into it like one shadow cast on another.

At the bottom of the hill Smith paused just inside the tree line. Across a shallow ditch lay a two-lane road that needed repaving. The rental car was parked on the other side, already headed in the direction of the airport.

Smith didn't see any headlights. That wasn't surprising on this back road at almost midnight and was the third reason for choosing the road. Good access to the target and the exit over the hill were the first two.

Then Smith heard the siren. It was on the other side of the hill, somewhere in the web of streets that led the target's house. A few seconds later a second siren joined the first.

A flashlight beam probed the top of the hill. That must be the neighbor. The witnesses were probably too scared to do anything but wait for the police. Well, they wouldn't have long to wait.

Smith pulled out the key and stepped into the ditch. Just then the glow of headlights appeared to the right. Smith could get across the road before the vehicle arrived but might be caught in the lights.

Smith dropped flat in the ditch. There had been enough rain recently to soak the bottom, and Smith cursed at having to lie in the mud.

The vehicle went by—a car or light truck from the sound, nothing bigger—and Smith rose enough to check the road. All clear.

Smith sprinted across the road and unlocked the car. Having previously turned off the dome light, Smith entered and started the car in darkness. After the headlights came on, no one could see the driver's face very well. Smith checked the rear-view mirror and pulled onto the road.

The trip to the airport would take about 40 minutes at normal speed, and Smith didn't drive faster than that. The nondescript car wouldn't attract attention unless it was speeding.

At the first big intersection a motorcycle cop zoomed into the middle of the road and stopped green-lighted traffic while an ambulance went by. Smith was pretty sure where the ambulance was going.

Smith was at the head of the line of stopped vehicles, and the cop was staring into the car. Smith sat still, keeping gloved hands out of sight and maintaining a neutral expression, not looking right at the cop but not looking away either. After the ambulance passed, the cop waited a moment, still staring at Smith, then waved the car forward and went back to his motorcycle.

The watch cap must've caught his attention, Smith thought. Shit! Should've taken that off.

Smith drove on, taking deep breaths but not removing the cap or wiping away the sweat until through the intersection and well away from the cop.

To discard pieces of the rifle, Smith made three quick stops on the way to the airport, each time turning off the main road and going a couple of blocks to some closed and dark business that had a large trash bin out back.

At the second stop Smith smashed the scope—reluctantly and only after again admiring its fine craftsmanship—so that no one who found it would be tempted to keep it. After the third only the case was left, but Smith didn't want to throw it into a bin containing any of the parts that fit the case.

Near the airport Smith pulled into an all-night service station, choosing the island farthest from the cashier's window. Smith topped off the tank as an excuse for stopping and to streamline returning the rental car.

Smith paid at the pump with the same credit card the rental was on, one purchased along with a fake driver's license from a dealer in such things. A dealer who claimed to sell only quality goods and charged accordingly.

But it was worth every penny, Smith thought, to be able to do the job without worrying about leaving a trail. To be able to remain free, anonymous, and—best of all—alone.

Smith changed clothes in the restroom, afterward wrapping the boots, watch cap, and gloves inside the black pants and shirt. The mirror above the sink reflected red eyes and white lips in a pale, strained face.

Well, it was done now. Completely done. All three men dead, simply, cleanly, neatly. No evidence left behind as far as Smith knew. At least not enough to lead police to the killer.

Smith knew there was no perfect crime, let alone three, but apparently the detailed planning and careful preparation had paid off.

And luck—don't forget the vital element of luck. You couldn't count on it, but you had to have it to pull some things off. Smith had seen that many times in the desert and now had seen it three times back here.

Smith also knew you could press luck too far—use it up until you were naked and defenseless. Then you had to face whatever the luck had shielded you against. Usually that was the last thing you ever faced.

Back at the car Smith turned away from the cashier to put the bundle of muddy clothes into a trash barrel, pushing the bundle down as far as it would go and covering it with crumpled newspapers and oil-stained paper towels. Then Smith retrieved the rifle case and did the same thing with it, being careful to smear any fingerprints that might have been left on the latches and handle of the case.

Smith drove the rest of the way to the airport and found the rental-return area. Smith parked and handed the key to the attendant. He was a pimply young man who, Smith noted with relief, was too sleepy or stoned to pay much attention to his late-night customer.

Of course it was actually early morning now. And it would be almost noon when Smith got back east.

Home. Get undressed, crawl into bed, and sleep for a week. Sleep until this time and the other two times were just unpleasant memories. Okay, bad memories—but surely not as bad as the recollection of the horrible night that started things. No, that would always remain the worst memory of all.

Smith grabbed the carry-on from the back seat and moved briskly toward the terminal. Halfway there a man carrying a small black bag emerged from a row of cars and walked in the same direction.

Smith glanced at the man, who was tall and trim with a pale, hawk-like face. He was looking straight ahead, so Smith merely edged away and kept heading for the terminal.

"Nice job." The man kept his voice so low that even if other people had been around, no one but Smith would have heard the remark.

Smith was startled but tried not to show it while thinking rapidly of what an innocent person would say. "Excuse me?"

The man looked at Smith and smiled. A cold smile, reptilian, with no mirth in it. "You heard me. And you know what I'm talking about— that guy in the hot tub."

Smith stopped and frantically looked around to see if there were any possibility of escape. Ducking into a row of cars and trying to run seemed the only way, and Smith knew the odds were poor at best.

Who was this man? To know what he knew, he must be a plainclothes police officer even though he wasn't talking like one. Smith didn't know whether he was armed, but given the situation, it seemed likely.

Nevertheless Smith was about to drop the bag and run when another man, a short, stocky black guy, stepped out in front of Smith. He wasn't carrying anything and bent his knees and spread his arms slightly as though preparing to make a tackle. He must be the other one's partner, Smith thought.

Smith looked at the tall man, who smiled that cold smile again. "Plus the other two earlier. All good, clean hits."

Smith fought the panic that was like being strangled with strong, cold hands. Caught. They seemed to know everything, and there was virtually no chance of escape. Still, Smith wasn't going to prison. Not if there was any way to avoid it. Death was preferable to rotting in a cell for the next half-century or longer.

Smith swung the carry-on at the tall man, who dodged it easily but had to step back to do so. Then Smith threw the bag at him and began sprinting for the closest row of cars.

The tall man used his bag to bat Smith's to the ground. "Go!" Now loud, his voice echoed off the concrete and metal. The short guy ran to intercept Smith, moving very fast for someone built like a wrestler.

Smith made it past one car, then another, but the runner caught up at the third. He grabbed a shoulder and twirled Smith around. Pinned against the side of a vehicle, Smith twisted and bucked, trying to get free, but the man was so strong that only Smith's head could move freely.

The man laughed softly, his face close to Smith's, and Smith could smell his dinner on his breath. Something with onions. The smell combined with tension and fatigue to make Smith's stomach surge. I wonder how he's going to like me puking on his shoes, Smith thought.

"No need to fight," the man said in a raspy but surprisingly gentle voice. "We caught you fair and square."

Smith was too choked with fear and nausea to say anything. The tall man walked over to them, carrying Smith's bag as well as his own. He set the bags down and pulled a pistol from his pocket. "I was pretty sure we'd have to do it this way."

Smith's eyes grew big as the man put the pistol up to Smith's arm and fired. Smith felt a sharp, painful sensation like being jabbed with a knife. For some reason there was no blood.

But there had to be blood, even from a small-caliber bullet. As Smith stared at the entry wound, the world grew dark. Within a few seconds everything was completely black, and Smith slumped into the short guy's arms.

The tall man looked around, didn't see anyone. "Come on. We've got to get out of here." He picked up the bags. "Can you make it to the car?"

The stocky man lifted Smith easily and motioned with his head for his partner to lead the way. "Sure, doesn't weigh much."

Then he looked down at Smith's face. "You know, for a big, bad killer, she's really pretty small."

CHAPTER TWO

Smith woke up naked and alone. The naked part was immediately obvious—she was lying on a concrete floor and felt its cold roughness all along her body. The alone part became obvious when she opened her eyes and looked around, trying to ignore the hammer pounding on the inside of her skull.

The room was large, maybe 20 feet by 20 feet with a high ceiling. The walls and ceiling appeared to be made of metal painted a dull gray. There were no windows, but the ceiling lights were on, casting a harsh glare that didn't help her headache. Besides Smith, there was nothing in the room but a sink and a toilet, both made of stainless steel, and, on the floor, a roll of toilet paper.

Smith sat up, groaning. Along with the pain in her head, her mouth tasted of vomit, and thirst burned from her lips to her stomach. Together they were almost enough to make her forget the throbbing in her arm.

Smith looked at the arm. There was a purple bruise but no blood or bandage. Then she understood—tranquilizer gun. So she'd probably been out for hours and might be far away from where the cops had arrested her.

Or were they cops? They hadn't said they were and hadn't acted like it either. But who else would know about her, what she'd been doing? Who else would have tracked her to the airport and confronted her that way? Who else would have locked her up?

At least she assumed she was locked up. Well, she'd check that in a minute. Right now she had more pressing business.

Smith stood, swaying so badly she almost fell. Keeping one hand on the wall, she walked slowly over to the toilet. After relieving herself Smith splashed her face with water several times and rinsed her mouth, rubbing an index finger over her teeth. Then she drank from her cupped hands until she couldn't drink anymore.

Feeling a little better, she looked around again. The room—too cold for nudity to be comfortable—was clearly a cell. She'd seen plenty of them at various places in Iraq, but there she'd been on the outside looking in.

And sometimes, not always but more than once or twice, the prisoners had been naked. Now that she was in that situation, she had more sympathy for the men who'd cowered—or occasionally stood—in front of her, using their hands to cover their genitals from the eyes of the

American whore in Army camouflage.

Remembering how the Americans and Iraqis had monitored those prisoners, Smith assumed she was being watched even though she couldn't spot a camera. She shivered, partly from the cold and partly from fear as naked as she was.

She couldn't see a door either, but she knew there had to be one. Moving more steadily, she walked around the room, keeping her fingertips on the wall—partly for support but mostly to feel the crack where the door was set into the gray metal.

She finally found it although the crack was so slight it was almost invisible. But she couldn't find any button or panel that might open the door from the inside even if it were unlocked—and she was sure it wasn't.

Smith pushed on the door, but it didn't move. She pushed harder with no more result. She turned around and mule-kicked the door with the bottom of her foot. That made her foot hurt, but it didn't make the door move. The door was as solid as the rest of the room.

Smith clenched and unclenched her fists. Without tools she wasn't going anywhere. Not until someone let her out.

She drank more water from the sink, used the toilet again—giving the finger to whoever might be watching her do it—and sat on the cold floor, leaning against the equally cold wall. She hugged herself in an effort to keep warm, and waited.

◻   ◻   ◻

After what seemed like two or three hours, the door opened. It swung inward, and the tall, hawk-faced man entered. He was followed by the short, stocky guy, who was carrying a metal folding chair. The door shut as silently as it had opened.

The short man opened the chair and placed it in the middle of the room. The tall man sat and looked at Smith. The short man stood against the wall and looked at Smith.

Smith noticed that the short man had a pistol on his belt. The tall man didn't appear to be armed. The short man must be backup in case she was able to overpower his boss. Sure, fat chance of that, she thought. With her unarmed and still shaky from being caught, drugged, and waking up here. No, she wasn't going to be able to fight her way out of this.

But she was going to act as though she weren't afraid. She stood, trying to ignore both the stiffness from the cold and being naked in front of two strange men.

Naked just as she was when... she clenched her fists again and forced herself to tamp down the panic that threatened to engulf her. After the moment passed she leaned against the wall and crossed her arms, trying to look calmer than she felt.

"Well?" Smith looked at the tall man, who said nothing. Although his deep-set eyes seemed to be studying her, she didn't think he was interested in her body. Not in that way.

She glanced at the short man, who also seemed to be studying her. The two of them might have been sizing up a race horse. Or a prize fighter. Whatever they were doing, she hated it. Their appraising stares made her feel like a piece of meat on display in a butcher's window. She wanted to ask for her clothes, but she'd be damned before she'd ask these guys for anything.

"Like what you see, boys? I assume you've seen a naked woman before, but maybe I'm wrong about that."

The short man smiled at the dig, and the tall man nodded slightly. "Good," the tall one said. "You've got some spirit left. That's what we need—among other things."

"Who is 'we'?"

"I am the Assistant Director. My colleague is the Sergeant."

"He's military? Then why isn't he in uniform? And you're assistant director of what?"

"The Sergeant was formerly in the military, and his duties are still... shall we say, 'martial' in nature. I am the Assistant Director of the Enterprise."

"That doesn't tell me anything. What the hell is the 'enterprise'?"

"The organization we serve—the organization for which we hope to recruit you."

Smith's mouth opened in surprise. After a moment she caught herself and closed it. "Then you're not the police?"

The short man chuckled. "No," the tall man said. "Far from it. In fact, the police would try to stop us if they knew what we do."

The man seemed to enjoy being cryptic, and Smith didn't know whether to believe him. "What do you do?"

He permitted himself a slight smile, the same cold smile she remembered from the airport. "We kill people."

Smith stared at him for several seconds. The room was very quiet, and she could hear herself breathing. "You kill people."

"Yes. We do a few other things, but primarily we kill people."

"Why? Are you with the Mafia?"

"No, of course not. We're a perfectly legitimate business—on paper. We're legally organized as a corporation, we have revenue and expenses, and we pay taxes on our profits. But making money is not our main goal."

"Killing people is."

"That's right."

Something about him made Smith more conscious of the room's chill, and she hugged herself again. "You get paid for that... service?"

"Yes. Our clients pay us rather handsomely. Of course, we have significant expenses. Carrying out a mission to kill someone can be quite costly—especially if it's done right. And we always try to do it right."

"These clients—they're criminals? One group of drug dealers wanting to wipe out another?"

"Oh, no, nothing like that. Our clients are a few agencies of the federal government. One agency in particular, and I'm sure you can guess which it is."

Smith stared at the man again. "You're kidding."

He frowned. "Certainly not. I never make jokes about our work. We perform a valuable service for the government—invaluable, in fact." He leaned forward, looking closely at her. "Have you ever heard of Executive Order 11905?"

Smith wondered if the man were trying to make her feel stupid. "No."

"That order forbids the federal government from engaging in what's called 'political assassination.' President Ford issued it—rather foolishly, I might add."

"Really? It sounds like a good idea to me."

The tall man frowned again. "Well, it's not. Assassination is a valuable tool—granted, one to be used sparingly. But killing the right person at the right time can do a lot to advance our national-security interests."

Smith wasn't in the mood to debate the assertion, so she said nothing.

He seemed pleased that she hadn't challenged him. "Unfortunately, Carter and even Reagan affirmed the policy, and no other president has challenged it. Not even the second Bush or Barack Obama although their administrations figured out ways to get around the order."

Smith thought for a moment. "That's why you're a company, not part of the government."

"Yes. Of course the order also says federal employees can't conspire in assassination, so our clients never give us direct orders. They just imply everything would work more smoothly if certain people weren't around to cause trouble."

"And you make those people... go away, so to speak."

Now the man smiled again. "Exactly. I see you're a fast learner. That's what we assumed after reviewing your records."

"My records?" Smith told herself to stop asking questions that made her sound like a third-grader.

"Yes, your Army records. Your IQ is superior and you handle weapons well, especially the rifle. We can teach you the rest of what you need to know."

"To kill people."

"Yes. We think you have an aptitude for it. Don't we, Sergeant?"

The short man pushed himself off the wall. "Yes, sir. She sure took out those three guys without any trouble. And that's with no special training or backup."

Smith stared at him and then at the tall man. "If you're not the police, how do you know about those three men?"

The tall man leaned back in his chair. "Because you told the Army what they'd done, and the Army told us. We have a highly classified program in place to identify military personnel coming off active duty—and people in certain other circumstances—who have the talents we need and a motivation to work with us." He glanced at the short man, then looked back at Smith. "We were pretty sure you'd try to handle the problem the Army wouldn't handle for you, and it turned out we were right."

Smith didn't speak, thinking about what he'd said.

"Your killing those three men proves you're right for this job and gives you a strong reason to join our little group."

"What reason is that?"

The man made a slight gesture. Opposite the door a slot opened in the ceiling, and a large video screen slid down. Its black surface turned blue as the power came on, and soon moving pictures appeared.

The images were green and grainy, obviously taken with night-vision equipment. A slight shaking of the frame indicated that the camera had been placed a considerable distance away and fitted with a strong telephoto lens.

In the video a figure dressed in black belly-crawled through weeds. Smith could just make out the rifle in the figure's crooked arms. After a few seconds the figure stopped and brought the rifle up to peer through its scope.

The camera panned down a hill and framed the back of a house.

Smith felt the chill again and knew what was coming. The camera zoomed in to focus on the hot tub.

The dead man was still getting a blow job from the blonde, and the other three were still watching.

The camera lingered on the scene a few seconds, then panned back to Smith, shown closer now. She watched herself pull back from the scope and glance around to make she was alone on the hillside. Despite the poor quality of the video, Smith recognized her face and knew a jury would too.

The camera held on Smith as she squinted through the scope again, lining up the first shot. When she squeezed the trigger, the camera caught the muzzle flash and showed the recoil.

The camera stayed on her through the second shot and then swiveled back to the hot tub. That night Smith had watched only a few seconds of this scene before picking up the ejected casing and crawling back over the hill.

Now she stared at the screen as the target slumped lower in the reddening water. Visibly panicked, the four nude figures scrabbled out of the tub, the blonde in the rear, and dashed for the sliding glass door that led into the house, their screaming and shouting loud enough on the video that it must have aroused the entire neighborhood. They fought each other to throw the door open and get inside, the last two knocking each other down and falling through the doorway in a heap.

Then the screen went dark. The tall man turned to Smith. "Would you like to see it again?"

"No."

"Do you know why we went to the trouble of making that video?"

"I can guess—to have leverage over me?"

"Exactly. We knew about the first two men you'd killed, but we didn't have much in the way of proof. However, I think this video would convince any court, don't you?"

Smith didn't answer.

The man gestured again, and the screen slid silently back into the ceiling. "So what it comes down to is this. You agree to work for us, or we'll turn you and the evidence over to the police."

"And what if I tell the police about you—blow your cover?"

He laughed, and it was as cold as his smile. "What would you tell them? You don't know our names or the real name of our organization. You don't even know where you are. We have a plausible story about how this video was made, one that will hold up in court. And we have a prosecutor sympathetic to our cause who's looking to make a name for himself."

He studied Smith for a moment. "I realize your Army service and your explanation about why you killed the men might earn you some points with members of a jury. But I don't think they could overlook your taking the law into your own hands, appointing yourself judge and executioner for three of your fellow soldiers."

"Just as you break the law by killing people the government finds... inconvenient."

"Not just inconvenient—threats to national security. But doesn't the similarity between your actions and ours argue in favor of your accepting our offer? Especially when the alternative is spending the rest of your life in prison, perhaps even being executed if you're convicted in Texas for that second hit."

Smith was silent for several seconds. "I'd like some time to think about it."

"Very well—but not too much. For our cover story to be convincing, we'd have to turn you over to the police very soon. I can give you an hour."

"I could think better if I had some clothes to wear and something to eat."

"Certainly. We took your clothing so you couldn't try to harm yourself in some way. I assume there's no chance of that now."

Smith knew they'd really taken her clothes to intimidate her, wear her down, just as she'd seen her fellow soldiers routinely do to prisoners in Iraq. But she knew it was pointless to argue. "No, I'm not the suicidal type."

"Good." He looked at the other man and nodded. The short man went to the door, which opened as he approached, and went out. Less than a minute later he returned with Smith's clothes.

"Get dressed," the tall man said, "and the Sergeant will bring you some food. I'll be back in an hour."

"All right."

After the men left, Smith began pulling on her clothes. Halfway dressed, she suddenly thought of the Wicked Witch turning over the hourglass and cackling at Dorothy—one of the most vivid memories Smith had from her short, unpleasant childhood. But this was real life, not some movie where her friends would rescue her.

Not that she had any friends. Not now. The three dead men had seen to that.

CHAPTER THREE

Sitting in the chair they'd left, Smith finished the small salad and started on the turkey sandwich. The clothes and food made her feel better—so did getting off the floor. Her head and arm still hurt but not as much.

As she took another bite of the sandwich, tasting mustard instead of mayonnaise, she wondered how they knew what she liked. Obviously they knew quite a lot about her. Even what had happened in the desert.

Well, they would, wouldn't they? After all, they had the enormous weight of the U.S. government behind them. All the money, information, resources. They could do anything.

But what was she going to do? Killing people in combat was one thing. She had no problem with that. It wasn't necessarily easy, but you knew the enemy would kill you if he could, so killing him was fair as long as you followed the minimal rules.

Assassinating someone was different. Even snipers shot only at people in uniform or at least only at armed combatants. But shooting an unarmed man—or woman? Someone who wasn't fighting you? That was completely different.

But was it? Was it really? What if the unarmed person had the power to kill thousands or even millions of people? What if that person had already killed people? Or done something almost as evil?

Like the three men she'd killed. They deserved to die, she told herself. Maybe not for what they'd done to her—although that was bad enough—but surely they deserved to die for what they'd done to Laura. And what that had driven Laura to do.

So killing them was just, at least in her eyes. But how was that different from assassination? None of them had been armed. One was even asleep.

She shook her head. It was all so complicated. How could anyone know the right thing to do? She'd hoped that once she'd ended those three, she might be able to go on with her life. Get some sort of job, live quietly, try to forget the past.

Now it seemed the people of this strange organization, this "Enterprise," as they called it, weren't going to let her do that. Her choices were stark: agree to kill for them—call herself what perhaps she already was—or rot in prison for the rest of her life. And she knew that wouldn't be very long.

She'd told the Army shrink she wasn't suicidal, but she knew she couldn't, wouldn't, let herself live if she were locked up like an animal forever.

Smith took the last bite of the sandwich and drank the last of the iced tea the Sergeant had brought with the food. She felt much better now, dressed, warm, full. She knew that sensation was part of the psychological game they were playing with her, but still it felt good. Much better than lying naked on cold concrete with that awful pounding in her head.

She put the plate and glass on the floor. She glanced at the wristwatch they'd returned with her clothes. The hands on the old-fashioned face—her grandmother had given her the watch for high-school graduation, and it was the only expensive piece of jewelry she'd ever owned—told her it was 2:27, but she didn't know whether that was early morning or mid-afternoon. She'd lost all sense of time in this place. Another part of the psychological game....

A few minutes later the door opened and the tall man entered.

"Feeling better?" He smiled his wintry smile.

She knew he knew the answer, but she said it anyway. "Yes, I am." She hesitated, then added, "Thank you."

"You're quite welcome. Are you ready to see the Director?"

"The Director?"

"Yes, to give him your answer. He always likes to handle the final decision personally."

Smith thought about that. She couldn't see any reason not to talk to this "Director," and if she tried to refuse, they'd probably make her talk to him. "Okay."

"Good. Please follow me." The door opened as he stepped toward it.

She was getting out of the room—out of her cell! She forced herself to keep from smiling. Instead she flexed her hands and thought about how hard she was going to hit the tall man outside and how fast she was going to run.

She couldn't believe he was turning his back on her. But as soon as she walked through the door, she understood. The short man was there, and now he had the pistol in his hand, hanging loosely at his side.

He nodded. "Hi. I know you won't get any foolish ideas. Just follow the AD."

AD? Oh, the Assistant Director, Smith thought. What a silly little fraternity they had here, with their mysterious ways and clubhouse titles. And, of course, keeping her naked for so long. She wasn't overly modest, but she did like to choose whom she let see her nude.

She looked at the short man and then at his pistol, figuring the odds. He could shoot her before she took two steps toward him. She relaxed her hands and turned to follow the tall man.

He led the way down a corridor that, except for its shape, looked exactly like the room she'd been in. None of them said anything, and the only sound was that of their footsteps echoing from the metal walls.

After several yards the tall man stopped and knocked on what appeared to Smith to be just another section of the wall. She heard a muffled voice say, "Come." A lock clicked, and the door swung open.

The tall man stepped back and motioned Smith inside. She hesitated. Although she didn't consider these two her friends, at least they were now somewhat familiar, and she didn't know who—or what—she'd find inside.

But she had no choice. She squared her shoulders and walked into the room.

It was the same size as her cell, but contained a metal desk instead of a sink and toilet. There were two metal chairs, one on each side of the desk. On the far side of the desk a man sat, working on some papers. He rose as she entered.

The man was of medium height and middle-aged, not fat but carrying a few extra pounds that told her he did a lot of desk work. He was completely bald, had a friendly face, and was wearing a dark suit, a white shirt, and a necktie selected by someone with good taste in ties.

"Hello. Please sit down."

Smith sat. The man remained standing, studying her carefully.

"How are you? Rested and fed, I hope?"

"Yes. But also a prisoner."

"For the moment." The man resumed his seat, still looking at her. "However, you hold the key and can choose freedom if you like. Or you can go on being a prisoner—in someone else's care of course. I believe the Assistant Director explained all this to you?"

"Yes, he did."

"And do you have any questions? I'm sure you do."

"The first one is why me?"

The Director leaned forward and put his hands on the desk, lacing his fingers together. "Good question. Lots of reasons. You're smart and know how to take orders. You're in excellent physical condition. You know how to plan and how to be patient when executing a plan. All those things are very important in our line of work."

"Thanks."

"You're welcome, my dear, although—"

Smith bristled. "I'm not your 'dear,' so please don't call me that."

The Director paused. Her comment surprised him, and he was a careful, thorough man who tried to avoid surprises.

The silence lengthened as he took a long look at the young woman on the other side of the desk. Her tomboy appearance and direct gaze reminded him of his daughter, Elizabeth. How long had she been dead? Eight, no, nine years now. A drug overdose—so foolish, so wasteful.

Maybe if the Company hadn't sent him overseas so much... maybe if he'd been home more.... But he knew it was futile to dwell on the past, no matter how many memories—a few bright but most dark, some very dark—crowded in to keep him awake at night.

By now Elizabeth would have looked something like the young woman across the desk. The young woman he was recruiting to kill people.

He remembered what their family priest had said about hell. He hoped the old man was wrong.

"Pardon me. That was a polite expression when I was growing up, and sometimes I forget times have changed."

Smith made no reply, but he saw her settle a bit in her chair.

"I was going to say I wasn't trying to compliment you. I was just stating the facts. And I won't insult your intelligence by denying that we've been looking for a female recruit. Obviously, there are places women can go and things women can do that men can't."

This courtly older man is trying to tiptoe around something, she thought. "Do you mean I'd have to fuck some targets before killing them?"

The Director frowned at her profanity. "I wouldn't put it that way, but, yes, such intimacy is a distinct possibility. We don't anticipate it will be necessary in most of your assignments. However, we play to win, as the saying goes, and we can't afford not to use every resource at our disposal."

Smith reflected on that. She didn't like hearing her sexuality described as a "resource." Also, she wondered if she could go to bed with someone she didn't care for. Especially now.

The Director interrupted her thoughts. "There's one other reason, perhaps the most important of all. To put things as bluntly as you do, I'll say you don't mind pulling the trigger."

Her face grew hot. "It's not like I enjoy it—or even that it means nothing to me. I just do what I'm told."

The Director looked at her. "Come, my—come, now. You know that's not the whole truth. Yes, you were following orders in the Army. But sometimes you go beyond what you're told. For example, nobody told you to shoot these last three."

"They deserved it! Not just for me, but for—"

The Director held up a hand. "Calm yourself. No one is blaming you for anything. We know what Williams, Kolenko, and Bugatti did. And what happened to your friend. They would have kept on that way if you hadn't stopped them."

Hearing their names like that made her fall silent. She wondered if she'd done the right thing. Before she'd had no doubt, but now for some reason she did.

Just because someone else knew about it and might turn her in? No, there was something more. She didn't want these people to think she was nothing but a rabid dog, attacking blindly, senselessly.

Smith gave herself time to slow her breathing. Then she looked at the Director. "So if I came to work for you, I'd have to kill political enemies of the United States?"

"That's an oversimplification but essentially accurate. Yes."

"I'd be specially trained to do that? The Army taught me to shoot and some simple hand-to-hand stuff, but that's about it."

Sensing that her resistance was softening, the Director smiled. His expression reminded Smith of the father she hadn't seen in—how long? Almost ten years. Her big, handsome father who'd smiled this way... when he wasn't drinking.

Or coming to her room late at night. Pinning her to the bed, breathing whiskey fumes in her face, and trying to run his callused hands under her t-shirt.

She was just big enough and old enough to keep him from doing what she knew he wanted to do. And she'd never told anyone except her best friend. Laura....

She swallowed hard and tried to focus on what the Director was saying.

"Yes, of course we'll train you. Our course will make your Army training, useful as it was, look like kindergarten. That's what military training essentially is when it comes to killing individuals in a targeted way."

"Where would I live?"

"In or near a large city. You'll have to go places quickly, often on civilian transportation."

"Anywhere I like?"

"Yes, within reason. For obvious reasons you can't continue to live where you live now."

"How about Northern Virginia, near Washington, D.C.?" She'd been stationed there for a couple of years and liked the area.

"An excellent choice. It will suit your cover story very well. Plus, as you might imagine, we have an office there, so your living nearby will be convenient."

She was sure he was thinking only of the convenience of the Enterprise, but she didn't express the thought. She doubted she could play a better verbal chess game than his and didn't want him to prove she couldn't. Instead she asked, "What would be my, uh, cover story?"

"We'll set you up as a defense consultant who travels frequently and often unexpectedly. You'll also pose as an Army reservist who gets called up a lot for special duty. Have you kept your uniforms?"

"Yes." She didn't know why. She'd thought she'd never have anything to do with the Army again. But she hadn't been able to bring herself to throw the uniforms away.

"Good. That will simplify things. Plus help our budget a tiny bit. Our resources are considerable but not unlimited, and I try to save the Enterprise's money when I can. It's the career bureaucrat in me, I suppose."

His reference to his career made her wonder. "Why do you use only titles, no names? And why are you so mysterious about everything? Like where I am, for instance?"

"For the simple reason that you can't tell what you don't know. Whether to an enemy if you're captured or...."

"To the police if I decide not to join. Or later to quit."

"Correct. Although you'll soon know enough about our work that we can't allow you to quit."

"You mean—"

"Yes, I'm afraid so. Once you sign on with us, you're ours until you retire, which, depending on how many missions you perform and how successful you are, could be in as little as five years. Certainly no more than ten."

Assuming I live that long, she thought. "And if I do try to quit?"

The Director looked her in the eye. "Then, unfortunately, you'll become the target of a mission assigned to one of your colleagues."

Both to confirm his meaning and to hear how it sounded, Smith said, "You'd kill me, just like that." She snapped her fingers.

The Director nodded. "If necessary, yes. Just like that." He paused. "We've done it only twice since I became the Director, and I don't want to do it again. But if I have to, I will."

Smith realized that despite his paternal air, the Director meant exactly what he said. He'd have her killed if she tried to walk away.

She thought some more, but she knew the decision was already made. In a way, they'd made it for her.

"Okay." She stood and held out her hand. "I'm yours."

The Director stood, smiling broadly, and took her hand. "Excellent! We thought you'd agree, but one never knows. We're delighted to have you on board."

As Smith stood there, shaking hands with her new boss, she wondered what she'd gotten herself into. Being a soldier was one thing, but being an assassin? That was something else altogether.

She also wondered if she'd regret her decision and, if so, how soon. She didn't know the answers, but she did know life was going to be very interesting from now on.

Wasn't there some Chinese curse about that? She tried to remember, and after a moment it came to her: "May you live in interesting times."

CHAPTER FOUR

The desert was very hot. The sun wasn't bad when they went for the day's first run at 0500 and not too bad when they went for the last one at 1800, but it was a blazing ball of fire for the 1100 run and nothing but white heat when they did calisthenics for the Sergeant at 1500. She was glad she wasn't prim enough to mind being soaked in sweat in front of the others.

There were five of them, five students. There was Smith, not surprised to find herself, once again, the only woman in a group. Lee, a former Marine, judging from his bicep tattoo of a bulldog wearing a drill instructor's hat. Dietzler, pale and thin with a penetrating stare. Mori, compact, quiet, watchful. And Wright, a rangy Australian with a friendly face and ready smile.

Smith wondered if any of the others' names were real. The Director had talked to her about hers.

"We know your real name from the records, of course. And we know when you began using Smith. I suppose you thought that would help cover your tracks while you... carried out your mission?"

Smith nodded.

"Not a bad idea although you should've picked something that sounds less like an alias. Still you had the wit to choose a last name that begins with the same letter and sounds something like your real name. You're probably getting used to it."

"Yes. It seems to fit who I am now." Someone completely different, she thought, from the idealistic young woman who'd raised her hand and joined the Army six years ago. Only six? It seemed like a lifetime.

"Well, keep it then. To the extent you've left any 'Smith trail' in the last couple of weeks, we'll clean that up. In fact, we've already started."

She was sure they had. She was also sure they'd tucked that video safely away in case they decided to turn her over to the police.

They were housed in a Spartan barracks—empty but for the five of them—on a remote corner of a dusty military base. Smith didn't know the name of the base or even what state it was in although the desert terrain told her it was somewhere in the Southwest. There was a lot of flight activity by a wide variety of aircraft, most fixed-wing, so the base must be Air Force. She figured the golf course was probably nice.

A fence with razor wire across the top separated their area from the rest of the base. In addition to the barracks, their compound contained a small chow hall, a well-equipped gym, the instructors' quarters (which even from the outside looked much more comfortable than the barracks), and a two-story building with offices and classrooms. That was it.

Six days a week the Sergeant woke them at 0455 by slinging an empty metal trashcan down the puke-green tiled hallway. "Get up! Get up! Rise and shine! Feet on the floor and out the door!"

They had five minutes to use the latrine and get into their olive-drab shorts and t-shirts and black running shoes before forming up outside for what the Sergeant called their "wake-up run"—three miles along the perimeter road on the back side of the base. That early there was very little traffic. In fact, there was very little daylight, just a golden glow in the eastern sky. For almost the whole length of the run they could see a few stars still twinkling in the crisp desert air.

When she heard the Sergeant shouting, Smith groaned and burrowed deeper into the plain but warm covers, wondering if she could lie in bed just one more minute. But she'd been a few seconds late once, and the Sergeant had added a mile to the run, telling her classmates they had Smith to thank for the extra exercise.

Wright had just laughed, but Dietzler had cursed her in a tight, low voice. Smith said nothing but returned Dietzler's stare with one of her own until he shut up.

Each of them had his own room, and Smith had her own latrine as well. But there were no locks on any of the doors.

Not knowing these men well and still having nightmares from the desert, Smith always put a metal chair a couple of feet inside the bedroom door before going to sleep. Someone coming in at night wouldn't see the chair, and the sound of the door hitting it would wake her up.

Unless the person was careful and opened the door very slowly. But she didn't let herself think too much about that.

Smith checked the walls and ceiling of the room to see if she were being watched or listened to. She didn't find a camera or any bugs, but that didn't mean they weren't there. She remembered the blank walls of her cell... wherever that was.

She'd gone to sleep and awakened here. More use of the tranquilizer, she supposed, or maybe they'd drugged her food. They seemed to do whatever they wanted. And why wouldn't they? They were holding all the cards. She was just trying to stay out of prison. She knew that later on she'd be trying just to stay alive.

All five students were still in their 20s and in good shape, but the Sergeant exercised them as though he wanted to sweat every ounce of excess fat from their bodies. He wasn't brutal about it, but he pushed them to the limit of their endurance—almost past it.

Smith's body-fat percentage dropped so low she stopped getting her period. She knew that sometimes happened to athletes, so she didn't give it much thought.

In fact, she didn't have time or energy to think about sex, and the male students seemed feel the same way. They were always so busy and usually so exhausted they didn't crack the crude jokes or make the clumsy passes she'd endured during her Army days. And maybe the thought of what would happen if they flunked out of training kept them focused on their work.

In a way it was a relief. Still, she wanted to feel like a woman again, not just a cog in a machine, especially one operated by this so-called "Enterprise."

Smith and Lee knew the exercise drill from their boot-camp days although this regime was ten times tougher than basic training had ever been. Dietzler endured it stoically, seemingly determined to show the instructors he could take whatever they could dish out. Mori panted to keep up during their long runs but somehow managed to do just enough to pass. Wright smiled through all but the worst of it, making Smith think he'd probably been in the Australian military at some point.

She wasn't as certain about Dietzler's past. For some reason she thought perhaps he'd been in prison. Maybe that's why he was so pale. And maybe he'd acquired that stare from standing in the prison yard, warning others away with his eyes.

Of course she never asked him. The AD had made it very clear that none of them was to discuss anything personal with any of the others, and each of them knew the AD had ways of finding out if they broke that rule.

So she could only speculate about what Mori might have done previously. On the rare occasions when he spoke she noticed a slight Japanese accent, which made her think he'd probably immigrated to the United States as a child.

She also noticed that the first two joints of his left little finger were missing, and she remembered reading that members of the Yakuza, the Japanese Mafia, sometimes cut off their finger joints as penance for having made mistakes. But she didn't know whether Japanese-American gangsters did that, and she wondered if he'd lost that part of his finger in some sort of accident.

Regardless, Mori didn't seem to belong with the rest of the class, and Smith wondered why the Enterprise had recruited him. She found out when they began their martial-arts training.

Their instructor was a woman a few years older the students. She was as slim as Smith, and her auburn hair was cut even shorter than Smith's dirty-blonde mop. She always wore a plain white t-shirt and loose white pants that ended just above the dragon tattooed on one ankle and the tiger on the other.

The instructor said to call her "Jay." Smith thought that was an odd cover name for a woman until she figured out the instructor meant the letter "J." Maybe an initial? Smith shook her head—she'd probably never know.

At the beginning of the first lesson Smith thought she and J, being the only women in the compound, might become friendly. But Smith quickly learned that J was going to be harder on her than on the male students.

She doesn't want to be seen as having a double standard, Smith thought as she lay flat on the mat where J had thrown her. Or maybe she's just one of those women who don't help other women. Smith had known plenty of them in the Army.

"What's the matter, girly? Can't take it?" Standing with her fists on her narrow hips, J glared down at Smith. "Don't tell me you're the only pussy in this class—that would be just too ironic."

"No, ma'am," Smith said as she got to her feet.

J pushed her face close to Smith's. "Don't call me 'ma'am.' I work for a living, like the Sergeant. Besides, what you really mean is 'bitch,' isn't it?"

Smith didn't back away. "Yeah, that's what I mean."

J grabbed Smith and hurled her back onto the mat, making her wince with pain. "Too bad. You can't call me that either. Now get up and let me show you how to fight. It might save your life someday."

Smith had thought she knew something about hand-to-hand combat, but J showed her how little she knew. J showed the same thing to all the students except Mori, who'd studied martial arts and sometimes could beat J. After a couple of weeks she made him her assistant instructor. Then the other four students had two people kicking their asses instead of only one.

After six weeks of training Smith could sometimes beat Lee and Wright. She never beat Dietzler—he fought dirty, gouging at her eyes and trying to bite her. She pointed this out to J, who merely shrugged and said, "This isn't a tea party, Smith. Deal with it."

So Smith dealt with it by kicking Dietzler in the balls. He lay groaning on the mat for almost five minutes while the other students watched. J said nothing, but Smith thought she saw a gleam of respect in the woman's eye. After that Dietzler tried just as hard to beat Smith, but he stopped trying to hurt her.

Smith never beat Mori or J although she was finally able to throw them once in a while. Mori doled out an occasional "Good!" on her progress, but being thrown seemed to piss off J, who'd immediately bounce up and throw Smith ever harder.

The hard physical training made Smith ache all over, and she wondered what she'd gotten herself into. To ease the muscle pain, she began taking a hot shower right before falling into bed. One night she reflected that at least she was able to shower alone and not in front of a bunch of criminals in some women's prison. Fellow criminals, she forced herself to add, determined not to add hypocrisy to her own crimes.

Their firearms instructor was a one-eyed man who went by the name of Houston. Judging from his accent, maybe he was from there. Or maybe—Smith was beginning to think anything was possible in the strange world of the Enterprise—he was descended from the family of Sam Houston.

Whatever. Despite having only one eye he was the best shot Smith had ever seen. Looking like a pirate in his eye patch and rumpled black clothes, he held the weapons gently in his big, hard hands. Smith thought he caressed them as he would a woman. Then he would point the pistols and rifles toward the targets and shoot the hearts out of them. Every time.

Houston showed the students how to stand and crouch and lie and breathe and sight and squeeze. Smith and the others were already good shots, but he made them better ones. He also showed them how to disassemble, clean, and reassemble every gun they used—and to do it more rapidly than Smith would have dreamed possible.

"Knowing how to take care of your weapons is just as important as knowing how to shoot." Houston walked around the table, peering one-eyed over their shoulders as they worked with rags and rods and gun oil. "More important sometimes. Not all shots are difficult, but you can't fire a jammed weapon."

Houston also taught the students how to throw knives and fight with them. "Always have a knife with you—always. There'll be times when you can't afford the noise of a pistol, even with a silencer. Which, by the way, don't work nearly as well in real life as they do in the movies."

Houston flicked his hand, and the knife he'd been holding thudded into the wooden target 10 feet away. "Be good with a knife, and you get to keep both eyes." He gave the students a crooked grin. "That's one lesson I learned too late."

Smith found she liked knife-fighting. At least until Houston cut her.

That afternoon she and Houston had been fighting for a while, and she was getting tired but didn't want to admit it. They circled each other, each looking for an opening. Houston saw one and lunged, slicing into her side.

She stepped back and twisted her neck to look down at the crimson stain spreading low on her t-shirt. The pain didn't kick in for a few seconds, but when it did, it burned as though Houston had jabbed her with a branding iron.

"That's not bad," Houston said. "In real life you'd be dead. Now you'll have a scar to remind you not to leave your left open. Go get the kit, and I'll sew you up."

Smith stared at him. She was the one bleeding, but she had to fetch the medical kit? What kind of shit was this? She started to speak, then saw Houston looking at her. She gritted her teeth, clamped a hand over the wound, and went off to find the kit.

The Assistant Director was their tradecraft instructor. He taught them how to tail a person in a car or on foot and how to spot and shake off a tail. He taught them how to use invisible inks and dead drops and how to search a suitcase or room without leaving any sign. He taught them how to implant and use electronic bugs and tiny cameras.

He even taught them how to read lips. "You'll have to practice to get good at it, but it comes in handy. Say, if you're in a noisy bar or restaurant, and your target isn't close by."

The intense tradecraft training puzzled Smith. "I thought we were just going to kill people. Why do we need to know all this spy stuff?"

The AD paused, looking at the other students in the classroom before giving Smith his cold smile. "First of all, you'll learn anything and everything we care to teach you. You know what the alternative is, don't you?" He stared at Smith until she nodded.

"Second, what I'm teaching you will help you escape after you carry out a special mission." He always referred to assassination as a "special mission" as though they were astronauts preparing to destroy an earth-bound asteroid instead of people they'd never met.

"Okay, but I don't understand why we're training for 'special missions' with only guns, knives, and bare hands. Surely the intelligence community has more sophisticated weapons—drones, even lasers and poisons, things like that."

"Of course. But what would happen if you used them? That would point a finger right at the CIA, and the whole purpose of the Enterprise is to deflect attention away from the U.S. government. If you use guns or knives to kill, anyone could've made the hit—after all, most of your targets will have lots of enemies, not just us. The last thing we want is to leave a trail that makes people think only some James Bond type could have done it. Understand?"

She thought about that for a moment. The reasoning made sense even though it also made their missions harder. But she already knew that the Enterprise wasn't concerned about whether their work was easy or hard. Just that it was successful.

"Yes. I get it."

"Good. Now pay attention and see if you can get this next lesson."

□   □   □

The AD taught some of the tradecraft course in the classroom but much of it outside, both on and off the base. From being able to walk around the base and in the town nearby, Smith figured out where they were: an Air Force base in Nevada, the one used to flight-test all types of stealth fighters and other high-tech aircraft.

The one that wasn't supposed to exist but obviously did. Just like the Enterprise.

"Pretty weird, huh?" Smith said to Lee on a bright fall afternoon when they were following the AD—or trying to—on foot through the faded, sun-blasted town. "I mean, to be here, doing what we're doing, in a place that doesn't officially exist."

"Yeah." Lee smiled at her. "But we're alive. And not in prison."

"For how long?"

"I don't know. Look, he's ducking down that alley."

"Wright will pick him up coming out on the other side."

"Yeah, if he comes out. But he won't if he finds an open window or some other way to disappear."

They quickened their pace, but when they reached the entrance the alley was empty. After a moment Wright came into view on the sidewalk across the street at the other end of the alley. There was no sign of their instructor.

"Shit!" Smith looked up at Lee. "I'm sure this'll cost us some extra homework. Probably about a hundred pushups as well."

"Well, what else are we going to do? It's not like there's a bowling alley next to the barracks."

"And you say we're not in prison. Yes, we are—they just don't call it that."

"Well, what if we are? Do we have a choice?"

She knew the answer—the only answer. "No, not really."

"Right. So let's keep looking for the AD."

"Okay. Maybe we can find the prick before he gets back to the base."

He put a hand on her shoulder and gave her a quick squeeze. "Good! Now come on."

Smith almost flinched when he touched her. She'd never liked being touched unless she initiated the contact, and she knew that was one reason some people considered her aloof, even cold.

I'm just not a hugger, she'd thought more than once, letting it go at that. She'd never tried to figure out why physical contact with other people bothered her. Since leaving home at sixteen she'd enjoyed sex—on her own terms—and thought that was all the contact she needed.

She knew Lee's gesture was meant to be friendly, so she said nothing.

As they began retracing their steps, hoping to find the AD before he got back to his car, Smith looked over at Lee. In a rugged sort of way he wasn't bad-looking. And he'd always been kind to her—as kind as one could be in their closely monitored and controlled environment, where their instructors and schedule worked together to discourage personal interaction of any kind among the students.

She wondered if Lee would ever want to touch her in another way. She wondered if she'd want him to. And whether she'd let him.

CHAPTER FIVE

They trained like that for four months, getting no time off except Sundays, when they were so tired and sore they did little but rest. Although she didn't consider herself particularly religious, one Sunday Smith thought about asking for permission to attend services at the base chapel, but no one else seemed to want to go, and she could imagine the look on the AD's face if she made the request. So she said nothing and simply offered up a silent prayer that she hoped God would hear even though it was coming from her.

The training was so intense that Smith knew she couldn't have taken it if she hadn't already had Army basic and advanced training. The other students seemed to feel the same way, drawing on what they'd learned previously to summon enough strength and endurance to get through the hellish days—and many nights, designed to accustom them to operating in the dark. It helped that there were only five students and almost as many instructors. Still, Smith never would have believed how much training the Enterprise crammed into only a few months.

At the end of the course the AD presented them with what he called the "final field problem." Wearing civilian clothes, each student had to find some way other than walking to get to the nearby town, locate his or her assigned instructor in some public place, simulate killing that person by hand, and escape back to the base, again not on foot.

The AD made clear that a student couldn't pass the course without passing this last test. He didn't say what would happen to any of them who didn't pass, but by this point he didn't have to. They all knew they'd learned too much about the Enterprise to be allowed to return to their previous lives.

The night before the field problem Smith lay awake, staring at the ceiling in the darkness and wondering if she should try to escape. Once she even got up and went to the window to gauge whether she might be able to make it out of the compound.

She saw the Sergeant strolling by the barracks, seemingly outside for some fresh air. But she noticed how he kept scanning the area—obviously keeping watch for any student who might try to run. And although she had made no sound or any other sign that might have attracted the Sergeant's attention, she was sure she saw him glance up at her window as though reading her thoughts.

She sighed and went back to bed. But her eyes were still open when the Sergeant sounded the alarm that began their last day.

Smith learned later that Lee had been assigned to "kill" J. He hid in the back of a FedEx truck that had made some deliveries at the base, rode into town, and found J in a motel bar. He stole a knife from the motel's coffee shop. Then, pretending to be drunk, he weaved through the bar, keeping his face averted, and was able to touch J's side with the flat of the blade.

J silently acknowledged the kill, and Lee stumbled out of the bar. He dropped the knife in a trashcan, stole a car, and drove back to the base, where the gate guards had his name on a "special access" list that required a code word instead of a picture ID.

Dietzler had Houston. Dietzler went to the base golf course, took the car keys of a showering golfer, and drove into town. He found Houston reading in the public library and simulated breaking the instructor's neck. Then he drove back to the base.

Smith drew the AD.

My usual luck, she thought. The hardest one to track and kill. She wondered whether the pairing was intentional or simply the result of chance. Not that it mattered—in either case she had to pass the test to survive.

She decided to go low tech, stealing a bicycle in the family housing area and riding it to town. Locating the AD took almost all day. She finally found him in a barbershop, getting a shave.

With his torso covered by the barber's cloth and his lower face covered by lather, he was hard to recognize—undoubtedly his objective—but even through the window Smith could see his lanky legs and familiar West Point ring. Plus who else would think of such a clever way to hide in plain sight?

She wondered where and how he'd hidden earlier in the day. Very possibly she'd seen him before without recognizing him. If she had, she was sure he'd laughed to himself about it, and the thought strengthened her determination to beat the AD at his own game.

Only one barber was on duty, so Smith knew that if she came through the front door the man would speak to her, drawing the AD's attention. She went around back and used a bobby pin to pick the lock on the rear entrance—something the AD had taught her in the tradecraft class. As the lock clicked open she allowed herself a moment to savor the thought of using that lesson now. She didn't think the AD would appreciate the irony as much as she did.

She came in quietly through the storage room, where she found a heavy glass bottle of hair gunk. She snuck up behind the barber and knocked him out with one blow of the bottle.

The AD threw off the cloth, but she had the straight razor to his throat before he was able to get out of the chair.

"I win." She spoke softly, her mouth close to his ear, and couldn't keep a mocking tone out of her voice.

"You sure? Look over here." He flicked his eyes to the right.

Smith glanced down and saw the pistol in his hand, the muzzle pointing straight at her head.

She didn't flinch. "Okay, it's a Mexican standoff, but that still means I win. I only have to kill you, not avoid being killed."

"Yes, but you weren't supposed to hurt any civilians. You broke the rules."

Angry, she nicked him with the blade, making a line on his throat that seeped red. "And you weren't supposed to be armed. There aren't going to be any fucking rules when I'm doing this for real."

The AD paused. He'd never liked this girl with her smart mouth and impertinent questions. But she was bright and capable and kept up with the men, even outperforming them on occasion, especially when it came to shooting.

He knew the real reason he didn't like her was that even though she didn't flaunt it, her sexuality was always there, always simmering just below the surface. A continual distraction to the male students and, although he hated to admit it, to him as well.

His memory of how she'd looked standing naked in front of him hadn't faded a bit after all these weeks. And he watched the surveillance videos of her, especially those of her showering or changing clothes, much more than he did the videos of the men.

He told himself that watching the students at all times was something the instructors had to do to know the students as well as possible and be able to train them to the limit of their abilities. But he knew that line of reasoning, sound though it might be, didn't explain why he watched the videos of Smith over and over.

When the Director had ordered him to recruit the girl, he hadn't liked the idea. He understood the reasons for bringing a female operative into the Enterprise, but he thought the negatives—especially the temptation she would pose whenever she worked with the men—outweighed the positives. Still, orders were orders, and he did what he was told.

Now he wished he'd tried to persuade the Director not to go through with the plan. He put his free hand to his throat, drew the hand back, and looked at the blood staining his fingers. "I see your point. All right, I'm going to pass you."

She took the razor away and stepped back. The AD got out of the chair and dropped the cloth on it. He studied his neck in the mirror that ran across the back wall.

Smith said, "As Mr. Houston told me once, 'That's not too bad.'"

The AD glared at her before pulling a tissue from a box and pressing it to the cut. He raised his chin and watched in the mirror as the gauzy paper reddened. "Don't think I'm going to forget this, Smith. I owe you one."

His voice was tight and cold and a chill ran through her. But she wasn't going to let him know that. "All right. Anytime you're ready."

He replaced the bloody tissue with a fresh one and stared at her in the mirror. "Oh, I'll be ready. But what about you?"

She was about to answer when the barber groaned and moved slightly on the tile floor. She glanced down at him and looked back at the AD's reflection. For a moment they stared at each other in the mirror. Then, by unspoken agreement, both of them left through the back door.

After biking back to the base Smith learned that four of the five students had been successful. Mori had used his bare hands to "kill" two recent graduates of the school who'd returned to assist with the final field problem—the pair being counted as equivalent to one instructor.

But Wright hadn't quite managed to kill the Sergeant—in fact, Wright hadn't even surprised him in the hardware store where Wright found him.

Smith never learned what mistake Wright had made, whether it might have been letting the Sergeant overhear Wright speaking to someone in his Australian accent or trying to sneak up on the Sergeant in a bright, open space.

Regardless, the Sergeant used a metal yardstick to deflect the thrust Wright made with a screwdriver. Then the Sergeant spun Wright around and twisted one of his arms behind his back while whispering in his ear.

The Sergeant let Wright go before many people started to stare, but Wright knew he'd failed the test and therefore the course. He left the store quickly, trying to get back to the motorcycle he'd stolen.

But the Sergeant stopped him. Wright wasn't coming back.

Smith had liked the long-limbed Australian with his bright smile and quick wit. She would miss Wright—she thought everybody would in their strange and now deadly world. She realized that what had happened to him could have happened to any of the students and that his fate was a lesson to each of them.

Smith didn't know exactly what the instructors had done to dispose of Wright, and she didn't ask. She just shivered even though the barracks wasn't cold. Shivered and, despite feeling ashamed of the thought, was very glad it had been Wright and not her. Not this time.

The two graduates stayed for dinner, which because of Wright was even quieter than the rules demanded. Afterward, drinking the beer the AD had authorized—their first alcohol since beginning training—Smith asked the former students what their lives had been like since graduation. She knew her question was out of line, but she thought that under the circumstances she might get away with it.

The two men were pleasant, and one seemed mildly attracted to Smith, but they told her very little and nothing revealing. Their answers were vague and always followed by questions about her—her experiences before being recruited by the Enterprise, what she thought of the school, and so forth.

For some reason, perhaps simply natural caution or perhaps the inescapable influence the Enterprise was having on her, she found herself being as guarded as they were. She was relieved when Lee flicked on the TV in the corner and gave them something to focus on besides each other.

"Maybe we can catch the news," Lee said, his "ay-yuh" New England accent still sounding strange to her after all these months. "See what's going on in the world since we all became monks."

"You must be a monk," Smith said, "if you think I'm one." She instantly regretted the remark but didn't try to take it back.

Lee smiled. "Sorry, Smith. 'Nun' then. How's that?"

"More correct but not more fun."

Lee and the two graduates laughed, and Smith was pleased to have covered her embarrassment with a quip. Then the announcer introduced a story that showed the president talking tough about nuclear weapons in the Middle East, and they quieted down to listen.

The thought crossed Smith's mind that there might be a job for one or more of them in the Middle Eastern situation. Looking at her comrades, she could tell the same idea had occurred to them.

After the president made some veiled threats that sounded exactly like those he'd made on several previous occasions—but never carried

out—one of the graduates said, "What a wimp! The ragheads know
he isn't going to do anything but talk."

"So does the rest of the world," the other one said.

Lee, always quiet, a tendency probably reinforced by his Marine training, said nothing. Smith also remained silent but mostly because she was
surprised to hear fellow members of the Enterprise talking so disre-
spectfully about the person who was, in fact if not in law, their com-
mander in chief.

Smith saw the AD closely watching the four of them, a narrow
white bandage noticeable even against his pale skin. When her eyes met
his, he turned away.

□   □   □

The next morning they graduated.

Smith felt tired, mentally as well as physically, more tired than she'd
ever been in her life. But she'd passed the course, done everything required of her. She'd never been in better shape—she could run 10 miles
carrying a loaded backpack, crank out 200 sit-ups and 75 pushups in
minutes, and do 12 chest-to-bar pull-ups.

And now she was a trained killer.

The Army had taught her how to shoot, even how to fight a bit with
a knife or bare hands. And in a way the Army had made her a killer—
although certainly not as the Big Green Machine had intended.

But the strange, silent people who made up this thing, this "Enterprise," had taught her how to kill coldly, ruthlessly, remorselessly. How
to shoot someone at long range, short range, and point-blank range.
How to kill someone with a knife, whether thrown or thrust into the
body.

How to kill someone with her bare hands, either by sharply twisting
the neck or by strangulation. Even—and this was something she'd never
heard of before—how to kill someone by shoving a sharp pencil
through the roof of the mouth.

They'd also taught her how to trace and find and track her prey. How
to close in without arousing suspicion. And, at least theoretically, how
to get away without being caught.

We'll see about that last part, Smith said to herself. She suspected that
much of the evasion and escape training had been merely to give her
and her fellow students some degree of confidence that they could survive their first mission, thereby encouraging them to carry it out instead
of deserting.

Smith wasn't a quitter, but she would have quit this madness in an instant if she could. If she hadn't essentially been held prisoner at the Enterprise compound on the base and if she'd had any money and any means of transportation.

And if they weren't sure to catch her and either have her locked up in a much worse place than this or....

She didn't like to think about that second possibility. She certainly didn't love her life at the moment, but she was equally certain she didn't want to die. She was going to keep looking for a chance to get away from these people, and she was going to take the first chance she found.

As Smith had expected, the AD didn't organize any sort of graduation ceremony for them. The students reported to their usual classroom, where the Sergeant, J, and Houston were already seated in the back. The AD came in a few minutes later and looked at the students.

"Well, you four made it. I'll confess that at times I had my doubts. We usually lose two or three from every class of five."

Smith thought he was looking straight at her.

"Once we lost all five. But congratulations—you did well."

Smith was astonished. She had never before heard the AD compliment anyone about anything.

"First, you accomplished your mission. Second, you survived. That's what we want you to do in the field. But remember the mission always comes first."

The AD paused, looking at them one by one as though to gauge their reactions to his words. The students said nothing. One or two shifted in their seats.

"Very well. I think you'll be pleased to learn the Director is here to congratulate you in person."

The AD opened the classroom door and the Director entered. Everyone stood at attention until the Director told them to sit down.

He made a short speech about how tough the students' training had been, how they'd probably questioned whether they'd done the right thing by coming to work for the Enterprise, and how they undoubtedly wondered what their lives would be like from now on.

"I'm sure you'll find your assignments interesting and challenging. And I hope you'll enjoy your time off between assignments. Remember to use that time to stay in shape and hone the skills we've taught you."

He paused, looking at each of them in turn much as the AD had. "Don't let yourselves get soft. We've lost some good people that way."

Although his tone didn't change, Smith thought she saw a flicker of sadness in his eyes, but it was so quick she couldn't be sure.

"For obvious reasons we don't give out diplomas and we don't take pictures at this ceremony. But know that you've earned the thanks and respect of every member of our team."

He called the students up one at a time and shook hands. As each stood self-consciously in front of him, the Director said some simple words of congratulations and thanks.

That was it. They were done. The four remaining members of Smith's class stood looking at one another—Mori with a rare smile, Dietzler frowning as he always did, Lee looking as though he wondered what he'd gotten himself into, and Smith struggling not to show the mixed emotions she felt. Then she thought about how Wright would have looked standing there with them, grinning at them all and giving her a wink.

After a moment she shook her head. In this business you couldn't afford to dwell on the past. You couldn't afford to do a lot of things. Maybe you couldn't even afford to have a close connection with another person.

You had to focus on the present and plan for the future—whatever there might be of it. If you didn't, you'd be dead.

Smith kept her face blank as she turned away from the others.

CHAPTER SIX

There was a short reception in the mess hall. They ate pieces of a sheet cake that had "Congratulations!" written on it and chatted with the instructors, who treated them not as equals but at least as junior partners in the Enterprise.

J went so far as to give Smith a smile—a first—and wish her good luck. Smith mumbled something back, not sure what to say to this woman who'd treated her so roughly and seemed to enjoy it. Smith was more comfortable accepting good wishes from Houston and the Sergeant—they'd treated her roughly too but only because their jobs demanded it.

The Director shook her hand but didn't say much beyond the usual things. Smith thought he looked at her strangely, almost from a distance even though he was standing next to her. She tried to hide her doubts and seem pleased to have graduated. She liked this kindly older man and wanted him to feel proud of her and her fellow students.

Afterward the students packed their meager clothing and personal gear. Then the AD drove them in a van to the base air terminal, from which they were to fly to military bases close to where they were going to live.

At the terminal the AD parked the van and turned to look at them. "Goodbye—or perhaps I should say, 'See you later.'"

Or maybe "*Hasta la vista*, baby," Smith thought. She glanced at Lee, and his expression told her he was probably thinking the same thing.

"Get yourselves settled and start a routine. We'll get in touch to see how you're doing." The AD paused. "And of course we'll let you know when we have work for you."

"What about weapons?" Dietzler asked.

"Good question. We'll bring you firearms so you can stay in practice on a range. Don't forget what the Director said about staying sharp."

Mori flew to the West Coast, Dietzler went to the Midwest, and Lee and Smith headed East.

Smith slept for the first two hours of the flight to Andrews Air Force Base near Washington, D.C. The plane was only half full, and she had a row to herself. When she woke, she got up to use the latrine.

As she walked past Lee's seat on the aisle, he glanced up from a magazine and smiled. He held up a fist, and she tapped hers against it. Neither of them spoke.

During the rest of the flight she ate one of the box lunches the crew distributed and read a Daniel Woodrell novel. The girl who was the protagonist in the country-noir seemed eerily familiar—the world viewed her as tough, but she herself wasn't so sure.

The plane landed after nightfall. In the terminal an obviously curious Air Force major gave them bulky sealed envelopes with their names on them and the keys to a rental car. He told them where the car was parked, and waited for them to say something that might give him a clue about their status and mission. They said nothing but "Thanks."

The major had handed the keys to Lee, but as he and Smith walked to the car Lee held them out to her. "Here. You know this area better than I do."

They opened their envelopes in the car. Smith's contained the papers for the car, a map to her new residence, and the keys for it. Lee's contained printouts concerning a hotel reservation in Northern Virginia for that night and a flight to New York the next day. It also held a set of keys and a map to his new apartment in Brooklyn.

Smith started the car. "Want me to drop you at the hotel?"

"Sure. Maybe we could get some dinner first."

She paused, then looked over at him. "Okay. You like Vietnamese?"

"Whatever suits you."

"I know some places in the Vietnamese part of Arlington—'Little Saigon,' they call it."

"Lead on, Macduff."

Smith was pretty sure the *Macbeth* quote was really 'lay on' but decided not to mention it. She didn't want to make him feel stupid—she knew he wasn't—and sometimes she felt like a nerd because she liked reading so much. But reading gave her great pleasure, and sometimes it almost compensated for spending so much time alone. She put the car in gear and pulled out of the parking lot.

They didn't talk much on the way to the restaurant. A couple of times Smith was tempted to turn on the radio, but Lee seemed comfortable with the silence, so she tried to be as well. After a while she was, and she felt herself relaxing for the first time in months.

The slim, elegant hostess looked at the two of them and led the way to a quiet table in the back. Lee held Smith's chair for her, the first time anyone had done that in a long while, and she smiled at him.

"This is nice," she said. "Thank you for suggesting it."

"Thanks for agreeing to come. I didn't know whether you would."

"Why? Do I seem that unfriendly?"

"No, but you do keep to yourself. Even more than the rest of us, I mean."

For some reason the words stung. "Oh, really? Well, maybe this shit we're in doesn't make me very friendly. I mean, they can kill us anytime they want."

"Yeah, but they've got no reason to." He paused. "As long as we perform for them."

"'Perform' is the right word. It's like we're trained animals."

"We're not animals, we're soldiers. Just in a different war."

She thought about that. Maybe he was right. Maybe they were soldiers, more draftees than volunteers, but soldiers just the same.

Instead of replying, she studied the menu. After a moment Lee did the same. The waitress arrived to take their orders.

After she left they fell into silence again. The silence was still comfortable, as it had been in the car, but now she was aware of Lee studying her, seeming to look at her hair and eyes and mouth in turn. When she looked back, he shifted his gaze to the other diners, a faint smile on his lips.

Smith's wine and Lee's beer arrived first. She held up her glass. "To success in battle."

Lee grinned and clinked her glass with the beer bottle. "Success."

After they drank he said, "You've never told me what you did to become part of our merry band."

She put her glass on the table and slowly took her chopsticks out of their paper wrapper. "No, I haven't. You know the AD's rule."

"Sure, but he's not here now." Lee waited, but she didn't reply. He sipped his beer. "I stole."

She looked at him. "Stole what?"

"Pistols. From the Marine armory where I was assigned. At that point I'd been in the Corps long enough to think I knew all the rules and which ones I could break. Anyway, I sold the guns, sold them to a civilian who probably supplies criminals. Like the guy in *The Friends of Eddie Coyle*. Have you read that book?"

"No. Is it good?"

"I think so. I've read it twice, and it's even better the second time."

Smith was pleased they had something in common besides the obvious, but because she wanted to hear his story, she didn't change the subject. "So what happened?"

Lee sighed. "I got caught. On my third run, my last one—at least that's what I told myself. Even as dumb as I was then, I knew I'd be caught if I kept doing it."

"Probably hard to turn down the money though."

"Yeah, but looking back, I think I was after the thrill more than the money."

The waitress returned with their food, which kept Smith from making a reply. But she knew what Lee was talking about. She knew from the desert how you could become addicted to the thrill of beating the odds, the high of taking risks, especially when you didn't have to.

When the waitress had gone, Lee said, "Anyway, the NCIS investigators were a little better than I thought, and they stopped me as I was driving away with a trunk full of M9 Berettas."

"What did they do to you?"

"Court martial. Sentenced to ten years at Leavenworth. After I'd done six of them the AD showed up to offer me a deal. At that point I'd have made a deal with the devil to get out of there."

Smith took a bite of her spring roll. When she'd swallowed, she said, "I think you did."

Lee looked up, chopsticks poised in midair. "Maybe you're right."

"Of course I did the same thing. Not that I stole, but I did make a deal."

"And what sentence did you get out of?"

"Life—or worse."

"Worse? You mean—"

She looked into his eyes. Dark brown. She'd never noticed before. Quite a bit darker than her medium brown. "Yeah, that's what I mean."

"Then you must've...."

"Right. I must have. I did. But I don't want to talk about it."

Lee was surprised. They'd all signed up to become killers, but Smith was already there. In one of the few conversations Lee had with him, Dietzler claimed he'd killed a man, but Lee didn't know whether to believe him. Dietzler seemed like someone who'd lie about things in an attempt to impress others. Still, who knew? Maybe he had done it.

But he did believe Smith. She'd never tried to impress him—in fact, she didn't seem to care what he thought, and that was beginning to bother him. Or, more accurately, thoughts of her were beginning to bother him. He kept replaying images of her running beside him in her snug shorts and t-shirt, matching him stride for stride, her face flushed from the exercise.

She certainly didn't look like a killer, this petite young woman with her pretty face and slim figure who smiled—when she smiled, which wasn't as often as the women he was used to—with her bright eyes as well as with her mouth. A mouth he'd thought of kissing more than once.

Although his own looks and personality had enabled him to kiss a lot of women over the years, something about Smith had held him back from making a pass at her. She was reserved, self-contained. Not unfriendly, as she'd asked him, but... what was the right word? Self-sufficient. That was it. Like she didn't need anyone else and therefore didn't particularly want anyone.

But he was beginning to want her and wondered if he could make her want him.

Suddenly aware that he'd been silent for several seconds, Lee said, "All right. I respect that. Maybe you'll feel comfortable enough to tell me someday."

"Maybe. We'll see."

He gave her a slow smile, and she was glad to see he wasn't offended. Maybe she really would feel that comfortable with him. Someday.

"Okay," he said, taking another drink of beer. "Then let's talk about something else. Where are you from?"

She didn't want to answer, didn't want to reveal anything about her personal life, partly because of the rule but also because she'd become used to living inside herself, not trusting others. Still, he'd shared something with her, so she felt she should reciprocate. It won't hurt to come out of your shell a little, she thought. Besides, it would be rude not to answer such a simple question.

"Nowhere, really. My father was career Army, so we moved a lot. I've lived all over—Alabama, Texas, Washington, the D.C. area mostly but the state too."

"Never overseas?"

"Not as a child. My father did two tours in South Korea and one in Germany, but he didn't take us with him. Or maybe my mother just didn't want to go. They didn't get along very well, and it'd be hard to move to a foreign country with three kids."

"I guess so. Which of the three are you?"

"Oldest. My little sister came next and finally, after a few years, my brother." The boy Dad always wanted. The thought still hurt even after so many years.

"Where are they?"

She paused. Another question she didn't want to answer. But it was too late to stop, so she plunged ahead. "My sister's dead. Killed in a drunk-driving accident when she was sixteen."

Remembering their father, Smith could imagine why Becca had turned to booze and boys—lots of both—but she didn't tell Lee. "My brother is married, has a couple of kids. They live in Dallas."

"And your parents?"

"They split up. Dad always had a woman—or women—on the side, and Mama finally got tired of it. Or maybe she just waited until all of us kids were out of the house. Anyway, both of them live in Florida now, but they never even speak to each other. Dad remarried. Mama's on her own. I try to get down to see her every spring. She spends Christmas with my brother's family."

"And you don't?"

"No. I don't think I ever believed in Santa Claus—the elves, reindeer, all that shit. If I did, I stopped pretty quick."

Conscious of talking far more than she was used to, Smith continued eating. Perhaps sensing her mood, Lee did likewise.

Neither of them said anything for a couple of minutes. Then Lee said, "Thanks for telling me that. I wondered about your background. All I knew was that you'd been in the Army."

"Yeah, just like dear ol' Dad."

She hadn't meant to sound so bitter. Hoping Lee hadn't noticed, she said, "Well, that's my fascinating life story. Now tell me yours."

"Okay, but there's not much to tell. I'm from a little town in New Hampshire—lived there all my life before I joined the Marines."

"A Yankee with a Southern name, huh?"

"Hmm, you're right. 'Lee' would probably go better with that accent of yours."

"Probably. But I've gotten used to 'Smith.'"

"Just like I've gotten used to 'Lee.' I guess we'll get used to a lot of things before ...." She held up her hand. "Don't think that way. No one can predict the future."

"Maybe you're right. I hope you are." He drank some more of his beer. "Anyway, I'm a twin—fraternal. My sister's name is Amy. We were very close growing up, but I haven't seen her for a long time."

"Because of prison?"

Lee looked uncomfortable. "Yes, that and now this. But...."

"What?"

"The truth is I don't know where she lives."

Smith waited, giving him time.

"My mother died when we were fifteen—sleeping pills. She'd been depressed for a long time, and it was probably suicide. She didn't leave a note, so we don't know for sure."

"I'm sorry. That must've been hard for you."

"Yeah, it was. But it was years ago." He paused a moment before continuing. "After that my dad started drinking too much, and my sister and I started getting into trouble. Skipping school, shoplifting, things like that. Finally I got caught in a stolen car—hell, let's be honest: I got caught in a car I stole."

"A bad boy, huh?" She hadn't meant to sound teasing, but it came out that way.

He smiled that slow smile she was beginning to like. "Yeah, I guess. Anyway, to stay out of juvie and just to get out of that little town, I got my dad to sign papers saying I could join the Marine Corps at seventeen. Amy went off to college the next year, but she never finished. My dad wrapped his car around a tree driving home drunk one night, and that ended school for her."

"So you're an orphan."

"Yep. With no close relatives other than Amy. She stayed in our hometown for a while after Dad died but moved away while I was in prison. I found out because my letters started coming back. Maybe she was embarrassed to have a jailbird for a brother. I don't know where she is now, but one of these days I'll find her. Here." He pulled out his wallet, extracted a picture, and handed it to her.

Smith studied the photo. "She's very pretty. And I can see the family resemblance. You have the same eyes, the same mouth."

"I think they look better on her."

"Oh, don't sell yourself short. You didn't come out too badly." As she gave the picture back to him, she thought about what he'd told her. "It sounds like neither of us is from the All-American family."

"No, I guess not." His smile was gone now, and even in the low light she could see the serious look in his eyes. "If we were, we probably wouldn't be doing this job."

Neither of them said much after that. Lee insisted on paying the check even though Smith offered to split it.

"No, thanks," he said. "This'll make me feel like it was a date, the first I've had in years."

Smith blushed and was angry with herself for doing so. "It wasn't a date."

"No, I guess not. But I did have a nice time."

She paused before saying, "Thanks. I did too."

She drove him to his hotel and pulled up in front. A valet opened her door before she could tell him not to, and Lee looked over at her.

"Want to come up? They'll park the car for you."

She knew what he meant by coming up, and she was flattered. But the day had been long, and she was tired. On top of that she didn't know if or when she'd ever see him again.

Most of all, she didn't know whether she was ready to be with a man again. She'd left some part of herself in the desert—they'd taken it from her—and she didn't know whether she'd gotten it back yet.

Or if she ever would.

"No, I better not." Seeing his disappointment, she added, "I do like you, Lee. Maybe another time, okay?"

"Okay." He hesitated a moment before leaning over to kiss her on the cheek. She almost pulled back but then was glad she hadn't. His gesture made her feel more feminine than she'd felt in a long time.

"Stay safe, Lee. I hope we see each other again."

"I hope so too." He got out and retrieved his bag from the back seat as the valet closed Smith's door. He bent to look at her. "Good luck on the job."

"Thanks. You too."

He nodded and shut the door. Walking into the hotel, he glanced back at her and waved.

She lifted her hand, then dropped it onto the steering wheel. Pulling away from the hotel she said to herself, "Well, that's it. Now I'm alone again."

She wasn't quite as relieved as she'd thought she would be.

CHAPTER SEVEN

The AD didn't call with her first assignment for over two months—so long that she'd kidded herself once or twice that he might never call. But whenever she saw the knife scar on her side or opened the suitcase of weapons they'd given her to train with, she knew she was just marking time until the phone rang.

She spent a lot of that time shooting on the ranges of nearby military bases and gun shops, varying her routine so she wouldn't become too familiar anywhere, and taking the same approach to her intense workouts at several local gyms. Training by herself quickly became boring, but because she knew her life would depend on how well prepared she was, she kept at it.

Finally the phone did ring. The AD, typically omitting the usual polite preliminaries, told her to go to Central America and kill a man. Juan Jesus Hernandez, a self-proclaimed communist who headed a labor union and was said to harbor presidential ambitions. His increasing popularity with the common people indicated he might be able to achieve those ambitions.

No, the AD said. The U.S. government was not going to let this man become *el presidente* of Honduras, a country where America had important interests.

By now Smith knew better than to ask the AD what those interests might be in a third-world nation where over half the people lived in poverty. A place where the ragged children begging in the street were more numerous than the pigeons shitting on the statues of the country's great men that stood in the capital.

The CIA never has its agents pose as journalists—at least theoretically. So to avoid any suspicion that she might be CIA, Smith was "Maria Tyler," a free-lancer working on a magazine article about how the capital, Tegucigalpa, was going to be the next Buenos Aires.

"Tegus" was becoming—slowly—a hot Latin destination for young, well-to-do American and European expats who wanted to prove how cool they were by living in Latin America even though they lived there much as they had back home. They listened to Latin music and watched Latin TV but did so on high-tech equipment most of their Latin neighbors couldn't afford, and they never realized how the shopkeepers laughed behind their backs at their broken Spanish.

The Enterprise had booked Smith into a medium-priced American chain hotel. With its carefully coordinated colors and Spanish-speaking maids, the hotel might have been in Miami or San Diego or even Des Moines, but the shacks Smith could see from her 11th-floor window reminded her of where she was.

And why she was here.

Smith had flown in a week earlier to become familiar with the layout of the city and the location of the target's home and office while ostensibly gathering material for her article. Through good planning by the Enterprise or, more likely, dumb luck, they had sent her to Honduras at a pleasant time of the year. In early February the rainy season had ended, but the foliage was still lush and green, and the temperature, although still warm, was about as comfortable as it ever got in this tropical land.

She had walked past Hernandez's condo building as he was getting into his bodyguard-driven car, window-shopped next to the restaurant where he was having lunch, and sat on a park bench across the street from his office while the bodyguard brought the car around for him at the end of the day.

Each time she had a different appearance. Not dramatically so, but enough to avoid being tagged as the same woman.

While she was living in her new home in Northern Virginia the Enterprise had sent a stylist to her to teach her how to wear wigs and falls and how to change the color of her hair—even how to change it quickly in an emergency. A few days later a makeup artist had appeared to show her how to make her face look fuller or thinner, her eyes lighter or darker (including with the contact lenses the woman gave her), and her skin tone match whatever hair color she had that day.

Smith had never paid much attention to such things. With her oval face, high cheekbones, and clear skin, she'd never needed much help from makeup. And she disliked fussing with her hair, which is why she wore it short.

She proved a poor pupil for the stylist. Finally the frustrated woman put down her comb and looked Smith in the eye. "Honey, you better pay attention to this stuff. I work with the girls out at Langley, the ones who go overseas a lot, and I don't think all of them come back. If you know what I mean."

Smith did, so she nodded.

"What I'm trying to teach you could save your life someday. You should practice this just like shooting a gun or talking into a lipstick radio or whatever it is you people do."

Smith laughed. "Well, I don't have one of those radios, but I see your point. Can we go over that quick-coloring thing one more time?"

The woman smiled and showed her.

Feeling chastised, Smith was a better student for the makeup artist. And now, watching the labor leader, she was glad of those lessons.

Her surveillance showed her that the Enterprise's plan—her shooting Hernandez in the street near his home or office—wasn't a good one. At least one of the two bodyguards, both big men who looked alert and moved quickly despite their size, was always with the labor boss. Smith might be able to kill the target, but her chances of killing both the target and his bodyguard du jour weren't good. And her chance of getting away afterward was even worse.

Not nearly good enough to bet her life. Smith wasn't eager to carry out this mission, but she was eager to come home from it.

So she came up with another plan, remembering what the Director had said to her about using her gender if she had to.

Smith noticed that Hernandez usually had lunch at a small, family-owned restaurant near his office. Once when he was there she had gone in and asked directions in her basic Spanish—as much as the tutor the Enterprise had sent had been able to cram into her in a few weeks. While listening to the manager explain how to find a place a few blocks away, she'd seen that Hernandez had a table at the rear of the dining room. Both he and his bodyguard sat with their backs to the wall, Hernandez closest to a corridor that appeared to lead to the back of the restaurant.

And probably to a back door, Smith thought. He's smart and careful, so I've got to find a way to make him think he's safe with me, safe enough for us to be alone.

The next morning, a Saturday, she called the AD—on a land line, not her mobile—and explained her plan.

"A bit elaborate for a simple job," he said. "Don't you think?"

"What I think is that this is a better way to do it. At least if you want me around for more work."

He paused. "I hope that isn't a threat to leave our little group."

"I'm not that stupid. But doing it in the street could get me killed along with him. Plus it'd attract a lot of attention, which would be bad for my escape. My way will be quiet and discreet. And look like a quarrel, not an assassination."

"All right. Give me a little time to make the necessary arrangements. Contact the embassy, and unless you hear from me to the contrary, assume you may proceed on Wednesday."

Smith spent Sunday researching Hernandez. She'd been briefed but not in detail, the theory being she didn't need to know much about him to kill him. Now, to make the new plan work, she had to know a lot more about him—and a lot more about his union and its involvement in politics.

She'd brought her laptop—an ordinary-looking machine that was actually very sophisticated and could send and receive encrypted e-mail that not even the NSA could crack—and was able to find a good bit of relevant information on the internet. Unfortunately, most of the websites were in Spanish, and her grasp of the language wasn't strong enough for her to translate all of the information into English, at least not as quickly as she needed. But she skimmed the sites to learn what she could, making entries in the sort of long, narrow notebook that reporters carry.

On Monday morning Smith telephoned the U.S. embassy and asked to speak to a staffer named Elena Castillo. Before Smith left on her mission the AD had given her Castillo's name and phone number, saying she could call Castillo if she needed anything in-country or ran into any trouble.

The AD had said Castillo was attached to the embassy's commerce section, but Smith had learned enough about "the game" to know she was probably CIA. Smith also figured someone—the AD? one of his contacts at Langley?—had probably given her code name to Castillo, which was confirmed when the woman immediately took her call.

"Hi, Ms. Castillo. This is Maria Tyler. I'm an American journalist doing a story on Juan Hernandez, the labor leader, and thought you might be able to give me some background."

"Ah, yes. Señor Hernandez is often in the news these days." Castillo's voice was warm with a trace of a Spanish accent.

To enable Smith to make her cover convincing, the Enterprise had also briefed Smith on journalistic techniques and jargon. Smith didn't know how much Castillo knew about her or her real mission, so she decided to stay in character. "I'm doing the piece on spec, so there's no deadline, but to keep my expenses down, I'd like to finish it as soon as possible."

"I see. Well, my schedule is full for today. How about three tomorrow afternoon at Café Dulce? Do you know it?"

Smith was surprised Castillo wanted to meet somewhere outside the embassy. "Yes, I've passed it. Would that be better than your office?"

"Well, the coffee is better anyway. And we're less likely to be interrupted."

"That sounds fine."

"I'll bring along a package from your uncle. I've been told it's supposed to arrive in the diplomatic pouch tomorrow morning."

Now I understand, Smith thought. The AD let her know he sent me something, so she wants to keep things unofficial. Avoid having me sign in at the embassy and be seen there. Smart move. Just like the AD's sending the package that way instead of using an overnight service that would create a paper trail and go through customs.

Smith knew a real journalist wouldn't receive anything in a diplomatic pouch, so Castillo had to realize that Smith wasn't what she said she was. But Castillo's training must have included a lesson on not being too inquisitive when a fellow American was under cover.

Both of us are acting, Smith thought, and each of us knows the other is too.

"Good. I always enjoy hearing from Uncle."

"All right. I'll see you then."

When Smith walked into the café she saw why Castillo had chosen it. At that hour of the hot afternoon the place was empty except for a bored waiter, who glanced up from his newspaper on the counter when Smith came in, and a stylishly dressed woman sitting alone at a small table.

Looking at the woman—attractive, 30-ish—Smith wished she'd worn something nicer than khakis and a sleeveless top. She'd been in the country long enough to make the adjustment from the winter weather back home. Annoyed with herself, she pushed the thought away and went over to the table.

"Ms. Castillo?"

"Yes." The woman smiled. "You must be Ms. Tyler. Please call me Elena."

Smith wondered if Castillo's name was as fake as her own. "Okay. And I'm Maria."

"A lovely name. Well, please sit down. Would you like some coffee?"

"Sure, that would be great."

"*Café con leche?*"

Smith preferred her coffee black, but she said, "Sure," and Castillo raised a hand.

The waiter came over, and Castillo ordered in rapid Spanish. As he walked away Castillo said, "I have your package in my purse. Is yours big enough to hold it"

Smith shifted in her chair. "Uh, I don't have one. With me, I mean."

"All right. If you don't have anything to put the package in, I'll give it to you outside."

"I guess I should've thought to bring a purse, but I usually don't carry one. Just a wallet in my pocket."

"You travel light." There was no tone of disapproval.

Smith relaxed a bit. "Yeah. I mean, yes, I do. I learned that in the—uh, on my last job." She was afraid Castillo might ask her what that job had been, but again the woman refrained from asking questions. At least none that Smith didn't want to answer. "So what can I tell you about Señor Hernandez?"

"Well—" Smith broke off as the waiter arrived with two coffees.

"Aren't we having lovely weather?" Castillo asked.

"Huh? Oh, yes. Yes we are."

As the waiter departed again Castillo said, "You can never tell in advance who speaks English or how much. A good thing to remember as one travels around the world."

"Yes, I'm sure it is. Thanks for the tip."

Castillo studied her. "I take it that you haven't done much work abroad."

Not like this, Smith thought. Not playing a part. "Is it that obvious?"

"No, not necessarily. It's just that I've been in this job for a while, so maybe I've learned to spot some things. But a certain naïveté can be useful, especially for a pretty young woman trying to get close to a man. To interview him or... for any other reason."

Smith said nothing. To cover her silence she drank some coffee and was surprised at how good it was.

"We women have to use all the tools at our disposal. It's the only way to level the playing field. Don't you agree?"

Smith wondered what Castillo would think of her plan to deal with Hernandez. "Yes, I do although sometimes I wish things were different."

Castillo nodded. "Maybe one day they will be, but of course we must live in the present." She paused. "I see you're not a chatterbox. That will serve you well as long as you know when and how to speak."

"I'll remember how you do it and try to follow your lead."

Castillo smiled again. "Ah, I see you already know what to say. I think you will do fine with Señor Hernandez. Let me tell you what we know about him."

She pulled a page of notes from her purse and began to give Smith the highlights on Hernandez. Born poor and grew up that way. Smart but not well educated. Self-conscious about his lack of schooling. Got rich—by his country's standards—as a union leader. Ruthless, he fought his way to the top of the country's labor movement. There were rumors, which the U.S. government believed, that he'd personally killed two men and had at least a dozen others killed.

"To put it as plainly as he would," Castillo said, "no one fucks with him. And now he has his sights set on the presidency. If he's elected, we're pretty sure he'll nationalize the major industries, including those in which U.S. companies have investments. And we also think he'll be a thorn in our side just like Castro and Chávez."

"I see." Smith looked up from her notes. "What about his personal life?"

"What do you mean?"

"Is he married? No, wait, is he straight?"

"Yes, very machismo, in fact. And, yes, he's married, but his wife and children live on his estate in the country. He's seldom seen with them. He has a large condo here in town and is known to entertain women there... sometimes more than one."

"Interesting. Does he have a particular girlfriend?"

"No, not at the moment." Castillo looked at her. Then she leaned toward Smith and spoke softly. "Is that how you plan to get close enough to interview him?" She put no additional stress on "interview."

"Yes."

"Well, he likes gringas, especially blondes, so you're in luck there."

"Thanks. I think."

Castillo laughed—a bit grimly, Smith thought. "That will make your job easier. Although I'm quite sure it will still be difficult enough."

Smith made no reply.

Castillo waited, sipping her coffee. When the silence lengthened she said, "Well, I suppose that's all. I should get back to the office." She left some money on the table, and they went outside.

The street was busier now than it had been when Smith arrived. The air was still warm but not as hot as it had been, and people were going back to work after their long lunch break.

"I appreciate your taking time to meet me." Smith didn't know whether she should offer to shake hands, so she kept her arm at her side.

"*De nada, mi amiga.*" Castillo embraced her, putting her lips next to Smith's ear. "Here you are." She slid a small package into Smith's hand

and stepped back.

"*Gracias.*" Smith didn't think she could smile convincingly, so she didn't try.

"Most probably I will not see you again. Good luck with your project."

My project, Smith thought. Well, that's one way to put it. "Thanks. I can use some luck. Well, goodbye."

"*Adios.*"

Castillo turned and stepped down the street, weaving among people coming the other way. In less time than Smith would have thought possible, she lost sight of Castillo in the crowd.

CHAPTER EIGHT

Back at the hotel Smith examined the package, which was a flat rectangle about eight inches long. The package was wrapped in brown paper that bore a diplomatic stamp. She tore off the paper and saw a cardboard box sealed with transparent tape.

Smith used nail scissors to cut the tape, and inside the box she found a scuffed black leather sheath containing a nail file. There was also an unsigned computer-printed note: "Hope this is what you need. Good luck." Typical of the AD, she thought. Terse, almost curt.

Although some attempt had been made to age the nail file in the same way as the sheath, the file still looked almost new. It also looked ordinary, a shiny silver blade ridged for filing and having a small hook at the pointed end. The broader end was fitted into a short black plastic handle.

But using all her strength Smith could barely flex the blade, and the inside edge of it was razor sharp, as she confirmed by testing it on her thumb. Sucking on the pearl of blood, the taste of pennies in her mouth, Smith reviewed her plan.

What she had in mind was dangerous but not as dangerous as trying to hit Hernandez with his bodyguards around. She thought the plan would work. Then she revised that thought: her plan had to work. Or she'd be dead, not Hernandez.

Smith ate dinner alone in the hotel restaurant and went to bed early. She had to be sharp for the work she'd do the next day.

But sleep wouldn't come, just as it hadn't come on the nights preceding the three "missions" Smith had carried out before joining the Enterprise. Finally she gave up, poured some bourbon in a glass, and sipped the drink in a chair by the window, looking out over the lights of Tegucigalpa.

This is a long way from home, she thought. From any of the homes I had. The kids I went to high school with are all asleep, most of them in their own houses with husbands or wives, children, dogs, all that. Tomorrow they'll get up and go to work or stay home and mind their little ones.

Tomorrow I'm going to work too. But my job is so different from theirs, a job no one would choose.

No one? She thought about that. How about someone who lived for the thrill of being on the edge? Someone who was eager, not merely willing, to put all the chips on the table, to make that ultimate bet?

The AD—yes, surely the AD. Probably Dietzler. Maybe even Wright, that poor, dead man who'd made her laugh. But not Mori. Nor Lee.

Lee. She wondered where he was and what he was doing. Wondered if he were with someone, a woman. Wished he were there with her or she were with him. Then she banished the idea, angry at herself for allowing thoughts of him to distract her from her job.

And what about her? If she'd had a choice, would she have chosen this... life? She didn't know. She liked to think she wouldn't have, but she'd essentially made her choice when she killed the first one back in the States. And reaffirmed it when she'd killed the second and the third.

So here she was, a well-trained but unofficial and very solitary assassin in a strange city in a foreign country, about to kill a man she'd never met. Not sleeping next to her own man in a little house in that drab Army town she'd probably never see again.

She wept then, cursing herself for doing it and trying to blame her tears on the whiskey working in her gut. But even as she cried she knew the real reason.

After a while she dried her eyes, splashed some water on her face—avoiding a glance in the mirror—and went back to bed. This time she fell asleep, and if she had nightmares, she didn't remember them the next morning.

Knowing she'd probably have a late night, Smith didn't get up until nine. She worked out in the hotel's tiny gym and then took a long, hot shower back in her room.

She dressed carefully, sliding into a red skirt that ended a couple of inches above her knees. She put on a snug white blouse and stepped into red pumps that matched the skirt. Her legs were bare but smooth and evenly tanned.

She put on simple earrings and one ring on each hand, careful to leave her left ring finger unadorned. Then she applied a touch of makeup and lightly sprayed on a subtle perfume.

Smith stepped back and looked in the mirror. She saw what she'd hoped to: a young, eye-catching professional woman.

She didn't know what the day—or night—would bring, but she tucked the nail file into her small black purse so she'd be ready for any opportunity. She had a gun, a Beretta 3032 Tomcat that somebody, she didn't know who, had left in a sealed package for her at the hotel on her second day in-country. But she'd decided not to use the little semi-automatic, so she put it where the AD had taught them was the best place to hide a pistol in a hotel room: taped to the inside wall of the closet, just above the door.

She made sure she had her notebook and a pen. Then she put on a lightweight black blazer and left her room.

In the hotel lobby she bought *The Wall Street Journal*, which she noticed was from the previous day, and the local daily paper. She folded the newspapers under her arm and headed for the restaurant where Hernandez usually had lunch.

She arrived there just before noon, but Hernandez wasn't in the restaurant. Her plan depended on meeting him there, so she decided to wait and see if he came in later.

Because she was by herself, the waiter tried to give her a small table near the front. She spoke to him in English, but he shook his head. "*No habla Inglés.*"

Using a combination of sign language and her halting Spanish, Smith asked for the table in the rear where she'd seen Hernandez sitting. The waiter shook his head again and said, "*Reservado.*" She was pleased but tried to keep her face blank.

She went to the four-top next to Hernandez's table and spread her newspapers and notebook on the table. She could tell the waiter wasn't pleased by her choice, but she ignored his frown and sat, opening the menu he handed her.

She ordered mineral water and a chef's salad, making the waiter frown some more. While she waited for her meal she scanned the local paper, pretending she understood a lot more than she really did. The waiter returned with her order. He offered her a small basket of bread, which she declined with a polite "*No, gracias.*"

She had almost finished the salad and the first section of the *Journal* when Hernandez and his bodyguard arrived. They went to their usual table, looking at Smith as they passed—the bodyguard obviously evaluating whether she might be a threat and Hernandez evaluating her looks in a different but equally obvious way.

Because her new cover was that she was writing a piece on Hernandez, she didn't pretend she didn't recognize him. She stood and stepped over to him before he could take his chair.

"Pardon me, Señor Hernandez. I don't want to interrupt your lunch, but perhaps you could spare a few minutes to talk to me after you have finished."

The guard moved a hand toward the inside of his suit coat, but Hernandez made a slight gesture and the guard froze. Hernandez looked into her eyes. "And why should I do that, even for a lady as lovely as you?" His English was good, the accent strong but understandable.

She smiled. "Because I'm an American journalist doing a story on you."

"What is your name?"

"Maria Tyler." She knew that if Hernandez checked, he'd find several magazine articles with that name in the byline. At least until she'd completed her mission. Suddenly she made the connection between her cover name and the old sitcom, and she wondered how anyone could pick a name so stupidly cute.

Fortunately Hernandez didn't seem to get it. "I do not know that name. Do you have any identification? Pardon me for asking, but a man in my position must be careful."

"Certainly." Smith got her purse and pulled out the fake ID that said she was a stringer for a New York paper. Hernandez examined it closely. "The picture does not do you justice, señorita, but identification photographs seldom do."

He handed the ID to his bodyguard, who looked at it while pulling out his phone. The guard punched in the phone number on the ID, handed the card back to Hernandez, and stepped away a few paces.

Hernandez gave the card back to Smith. "What sort of story do you have in mind?"

"What we call a feature. A profile of you, your background, your role in the labor movement. What you want to do for the people."

"And how I am a communist? Or am supposed to be?" He smiled for the first time. "I know I am not well-loved by your government."

Smith glanced at the guard, who was talking softly into his phone. "Well, I don't represent the government." She was surprised at how easily the lie came to her lips. Apparently she'd absorbed the training better than she'd thought. "I'm not saying my story will make you look perfect, but I'm trying to show people who you are and what you're really trying to do."

"I see. That would be a refreshing change from what most American journalists have written or said about me." He looked at the guard, who was now listening to his phone. After a few seconds the guard looked at Hernandez and nodded.

"Would you like to join me for lunch?" Hernandez's smile was brighter now, and she sensed he was trying to charm her.

"Thank you, but I just ate. However, I would love to ask you some questions. May I do that while you have your lunch?"

"Certainly. Please sit." He held out a chair for her. She retrieved her things, put them on his table and then smiled back at him as she lowered herself into the chair and crossed her legs carelessly, hiking the red skirt halfway up her thighs.

He was careful not to stare, but she saw him look at her legs as he took his own seat. So did the guard, more openly, as he joined them.

The waiter came over, and the two men ordered, not bothering with menus in this restaurant they came to so often.

"Would you like some coffee, Ms. Tyler? Or, if you are learning to relax here in our beautiful country, perhaps a glass of wine?"

"Yes, Señor Hernandez, a glass of wine would be lovely. Perhaps something white and dry."

Hernandez fired some rapid Spanish at the waiter, who nodded and left. Then Hernandez turned back to Smith.

"So, my dear, what would you like to know?"

Smith stopped herself from saying to her target what she'd said to the Director seven months ago. My God, she thought, was it only seven months? It seemed more like seven years.

"The real question is what would you like Americans to know about you and about your plans for your country?" She flipped her notebook to a blank page and held a pen poised over the paper. "I've done my homework, so I know your background—where you were raised and went to school and how you got started in the labor movement. What I want now is to learn things about you that perhaps no one else knows."

He leaned toward her. "Something personal? But surely your readers would not be interested in that?"

"Yes, they would. Something that makes Juan Hernandez the man he is—a man so many of his countrymen admire."

"And so many Yanquis hate." He laughed, and she jotted down the comment, assuming a real journalist would have done the same.

"Well, let me think for a moment." He paused, looking at the scuffed tile floor. After a few seconds he raised his head, running his gaze over the full length of her, lingering on the long expanse of her bare, toned legs and stopping at her face. She looked back at him with what she hoped was a playful smile.

"I love life. I always have. That is something my father taught me." Hernandez paused. "He was a bricklayer who never had much—just his wife and six children all crammed into a little shack. But he liked to eat and drink and laugh and even to work hard. He taught me to do the same." He paused again. "And to love, of course. Without love there is no meaning to life."

She jotted more notes, conscious of him watching her do it. Then she looked into his eyes. "And what do you love, señor?"

He held her gaze and started to answer but stopped short when the waiter arrived with a tray holding her white wine, a glass of red that the waiter placed in front of Hernandez, and a cup of black coffee that he put by the bodyguard.

Hernandez raised his glass. "*Salud.*"

Smith recognized the word and repeated it as she raised her own glass. The wine was excellent, much better than she'd expected.

Hernandez waited until she'd put down her glass. Then he said, "That is a very good question. One should know what he loves and why. I love my family, my country, and our people, in that order. I also love my job, which is trying to make things better for all three of them."

She was taking notes again. "Do you think you're succeeding?"

"Yes although not as rapidly as I would like. But I suppose that is in the nature of things. Do you not agree?"

She looked into his eyes again. "Sometimes things seem to move slowly. At other times we are surprised by how fast they move."

He smiled. "That is very true. I can see you are a wise woman."

The bodyguard lowered his cup to glance at his boss and then at her. She smiled back at Hernandez and shook her head. "No, just a reporter trying to do her job."

"Knowing who you are and what you are about is wisdom in itself."

She allowed herself an instant to reflect that she didn't know who she really was—certainly not in this parade of masks her life had become. Nor was she sure what she was doing. She was sure only that she had to do it or she'd have no need of masks. Like Wright.

To cover the brief pause she made a note and was about to ask Hernandez another question when the waiter arrived with two plates of steaming food and a basket of bread. Hernandez got a grilled fish with the head still on, and the bodyguard got *pollo con arroz.* Both dishes smelled wonderful. Having eaten lightly to remain alert and be able to move quickly, Smith hoped her stomach wouldn't growl while the men enjoyed their lunch.

"Let me describe the progress our union and others have made and what we must do to give our people a decent life."

"All right. But I hope you'll also tell me more about yourself." She knew men could rarely resist that invitation.

"I am not important—only our movement is important."

"Oh, that's a good quote." She jotted down the remark, wondering if he were really that modest. So far he didn't seem to be. "Please continue."

He did—at great length, telling her how "his" union had grown to be the largest in the country. He also told her, with obvious pride, how influential the union had become, using the large amount of money it donated to politicians and the threat of industry-crippling strikes to extract major concessions from the government and from large companies. She was careful to take good notes and relieved that she didn't have to ask many questions to keep him talking.

At first he spoke between bites of fish and sips of wine, pausing occasionally to wipe his lips with the snowy napkin. Smith noted that for someone who'd been poorly educated, he had good table manners. As he became more animated by what he was telling her, he put down his fork and interrupted his monologue only to sip from his second glass of wine.

He'd ordered a second glass for her too even though she hadn't quite finished the first one. Wanting to keep him talking and in a good mood, she didn't object. She put the almost-empty glass aside and took tiny sips from the full one, matching him about one drink in three.

As he brought his story up to the present, he asked her if she'd like dessert. She tried to decline but he pressed her.

"Are you worried about your weight? You do not need to be—if anything, you are too thin."

Normally she would have objected to such a personal comment from a near stranger, but she played her part. "Do you really think so?"

"Perhaps not for an American girl, but here we like our women more...." He smiled and moved his hands to indicate an hourglass shape.

"So you don't like slim women?"

"Oh, no, please do not misunderstand. I am merely describing a cultural difference. No, you are most attractive—and obviously quite intelligent."

She knew he was flattering her, but she took the comment as a good sign. "*Gracias*, Señor Hernandez."

"*De nada*, Miss Maria." He looked at his watch. "This has been a most pleasant conversation. I am sorry that I must draw it to a close—I have a meeting to attend soon."

"I'm sorry too. I have so many more questions to ask you. There's a lot more my readers would like to know about you."

"Just your readers?"

She didn't think she could blush on cue, so instead she looked down at her notebook and turned the page even though it wasn't full. "Well, no, not just my readers."

"I see. Well, then, we must arrange more time for you. Let me check my schedule."

He pulled a digital device from his coat pocket and began tapping. After a moment he smiled at her. "Ah, this is lucky. It seems I have no plans for this particular evening, at least none I cannot change. Please join me for dinner, and you can ask all the questions you like."

She looked into his eyes and hesitated just long enough to make him unsure of her answer. "All right, that would be fine. Where should I meet you?"

"I will pick you up at your hotel."

For a number of reasons she didn't want him to know where she was staying. "I have a number of things to do this afternoon, and I'm not sure when I'll go back to the hotel. It would be better if I meet you somewhere."

His expression told her he didn't like people disagreeing with him, but after a moment his face relaxed and he said, "All right. Meet me at La Cocina del Diablo at eight o'clock. Do you know this restaurant?"

"The Devil's...?"

"Kitchen. It is a very good restaurant with authentic Latin food. Also very popular, but because I know the owner they always give me a good table."

"Okay, I will meet you there at eight."

Hernandez and his bodyguard stood as she did, and she held out her hand to Hernandez. "Thank you for your time. I look forward to seeing you this evening."

He held her hand long enough for her to notice it. "And I look forward to seeing you again. *Hasta luego*."

That phrase she knew. "*Hasta luego*."

She could feel the men's eyes on her all the way to the door.

CHAPTER NINE

Smith had already asked the concierge at her hotel for the name of the best women's dress shop in the city, and she went there now. After trying on several cocktail dresses, she bought a simple but expensive black one and waited an hour while the seamstress shortened it. Then she went to a department store and bought a pair of black pumps with heels higher than she usually wore and lacy black panties with a bra to match.

Next she bought something she'd never worn before—a garter belt and black stockings. To save time later, she asked the saleswoman to show her how to attach the stockings to the belt, and the woman did so with a smile.

"These things are a nice present for you. Also for your man."

This time Smith did blush, feeling annoyed as well as embarrassed. She remembered how angry she'd been when the Director suggested she might have to seduce a target to get close enough to kill him. Now here she was, planning on doing just that, even though no one had ordered her to. The AD had even questioned the wisdom of her plan.

Maybe she wasn't as good a person as she liked to think. Most people probably weren't. Someone who'd killed three men in cold blood probably shouldn't think she was good at all.

And given where she was and what she had to do, maybe she should just stop thinking about things that didn't matter and get on with the job.

She paid for her purchases and went back to the hotel. She went online to buy a ticket for the first flight to Mexico City the next morning. Then she undressed, set her alarm for 6:00 p.m., and got into bed.

She was so keyed up about the evening to come she thought she wouldn't be able to sleep, but eventually she dozed off, and the alarm woke her. She showered and then dressed as carefully as she had that morning. The dress fit her well, and she was pleased with what she saw in the mirror.

Not bad for a tomboy, she thought. Maybe I have a girly side after all.

She didn't know how much time she'd have later—perhaps very little, even none at all—so she electronically shredded everything on the laptop that related to her mission and deleted everything from her mobile phone's memory. Then she packed her clothes and personal items in the single suitcase she'd brought and put it in the closet.

She glanced up at the Beretta, wondering if she were making a mistake. Maybe the AD was right—maybe she was over-complicating things. Perhaps it would be better simply to shoot Hernandez. Then she wouldn't have to do what she was almost certain she was going to have to do to make her plan work.

But her gut told her that although she might be able to kill Hernandez with a gun, that method would be too loud and too public for her to get away afterward. And she was determined to get away, not get killed herself or rot in some hellish prison where the guards would make what she'd experienced in the desert—as bad as that had been—seem mild by comparison.

Smith left the pistol where it was.

She went through the bedroom and bathroom carefully, looking for anything she might have missed. There was nothing to indicate she'd been there at all except the rumpled bed and a couple of damp towels. Her fingerprints were there, of course, and probably some DNA, but she knew the Enterprise had ensured that those clues wouldn't lead anywhere.

Smith glanced at her watch and saw it was time to go. She took a deep breath and headed for the door.

Before she pushed the button to call an elevator she hid her room key under the lamp that stood on a table at the far end of the elevator lobby. Maybe neither Hernandez nor his bodyguard would search her purse, but if either did, he still wouldn't know the name of her hotel.

Downstairs she went out into the warm, humid evening that smelled of engine exhaust tempered by the scent of the colorful flowers planted in front of the hotel. She didn't want to walk far in the heels, so she asked the doorman to get her a cab.

"With pleasure, señorita," he said, giving her an appreciative look.

The driver said yes, of course, he knew La Cocina del Diablo. He shifted lanes more aggressively and used his horn more often than the other drivers, all of whom drove as though in some crazy stop-and-start race, and even with the choking traffic he had her there in a few minutes. When she reached into her small purse for money, she touched the case of the nail file.

Inside she surveyed the crowded restaurant but didn't see Hernandez. She had timed her arrival to be just late enough to make Hernandez wonder whether she'd stood him up, and she hoped he hadn't gotten angry and left.

She pushed past a line of people waiting for tables, glaring at a man who pinched her ass and winked at her. Then she saw Hernandez and his bodyguard sitting on the far side of the bar. Hernandez saw her at the same time and smiled.

Smith walked slowly toward them, not exaggerating the roll of her hips but giving Hernandez time to look her over and giving the other men at the bar time to notice her and turn to look too. She smiled back at Hernandez, not exaggerating that either but trying to make it friendly and warm.

There were no empty seats at the bar, but as she approached, the bodyguard stood and gestured for her to take the vacated stool. She murmured her thanks in Spanish and sat, moving carefully on the high heels.

Hernandez leaned toward her. "You look quite elegant, Miss Maria. I hope you did not go to any trouble simply to have dinner with me."

"Well, I wasn't sure what would be most appropriate and decided not to take a chance on being too casual."

"Then please allow me to say that you chose very wisely."

She thought he'd want some reaction to the compliment, so she smiled again, telling herself not to let anything he said distract her from her job. She thanked him in Spanish and put her purse on the bar.

"Would you like a drink before dinner?" he asked.

"That would be nice." She glanced at the glass in front of Hernandez and saw it contained brown liquor, probably either scotch or bourbon. She knew men preferred to drink with women who ordered liquor instead of the conventional wine, so she said, "I'll have whatever you're having."

He motioned for the bartender, who came over in an instant. Hernandez ordered, and the man left as quickly as he'd arrived.

Hernandez turned back and looked at her for a moment before speaking. "This may be a bit awkward, but Jaime needs to... check you."

"Check me?"

"Yes. I dislike the word 'search'—it seems so unfriendly."

"All right."

"Excuse me, señorita," the bodyguard said. He stepped very close to her and ran his hands over her body, touching her everywhere, including her crotch, that she might have been able to hide a gun or a knife. He touched her impersonally, but still it embarrassed her, and she felt herself flush.

Then he opened her purse and stirred its few contents with a finger. When he found the two condoms, he glanced at her and smiled with his eyes if not with his mouth.

Smith had to force herself not to gasp when Jaime picked up the nail file. He slid about two inches of the file out of its case and peered at the flat metal as she prayed he wouldn't think to touch its sharp edge.

He didn't. He looked at her again, seemed to see nothing suspicious in her face, and then, after what seemed like the longest moment of her life, slid the file back and returned the case to her purse. He nodded to Hernandez just as he had after verifying her ID.

Smith kept her expression neutral, shifted on the stool, and picked up the drink that had appeared in front of her. After what had just happened she wanted to gulp it, but she took only a sip. Scotch. Good— she didn't care for scotch, so she wouldn't be tempted to drink too much of it.

"I apologize," Hernandez said, "but I am sure you understand."

"Yes, I know you have to be careful."

"And now that I have been, you and I can enjoy our evening." He spoke softly in Spanish to Jaime. She thought she heard the words for "tomorrow" and "see you later" but couldn't be sure.

The bodyguard seemed about to protest, but Hernandez cut him off with a quick gesture, and he shrugged his massive shoulders. "*Bueno.*" He turned to Smith and bowed slightly. "*Buenas noches, mi dama.*"

Pretty formal for someone who just felt me up, Smith thought. "*Buenas noches.*" She watched him head for the door, working his way through the crowded room and appearing light on his feet for such a big man.

She turned to Hernandez. "I don't think Jaime trusts me with you alone." She smiled, sincerely this time, relieved that the bodyguard had left.

"Ah, should he?" He touched her wrist and smiled back before picking up his drink.

She paused long enough for him to notice. "Maybe not. We'll see what the evening brings."

His eyes brightened. "Yes, we will. I am sure we will. Now I will get for us a table, and we can enjoy a good dinner. Afterward...."

"As I said, we'll see."

"Yes, that is the expression." He told her arm and led her toward the maître d'hôtel. "We will see."

CHAPTER TEN

Hernandez's condominium was on the top floor of its tall building in the Lomas del Mayab district and had a spectacular view of the city spread out below. The interior was spacious and well-furnished. Smith thought the décor and artwork were in surprisingly good taste for someone who'd worked his way up from manual labor. She wondered whether he'd done the decorating himself or hired a professional. Regardless, she made sure to compliment him on the place.

"Oh, this is just where I stay when I am in the city. My home is in the country, and I travel a lot for my work, so I am not here that often. But when I am here I like to be comfortable."

"Well, it certainly is that." She took the glass of cognac he handed her. She had slipped off her shoes and was sitting on the long sofa with her legs tucked under her. The lights were low, and soft, slow jazz came from hidden speakers. Hernandez had obviously played this scene many times.

"*Gracias.* I certainly enjoy the view." He looked at her and smiled, pausing so she'd be sure to get the double meaning. "From here one can easily believe that the city's name means 'hills of silver' rather than 'homes of the sharp stones,' which they say is another possibility."

"'Hills of silver'—how lovely. That's what they look like from here."

He put his glass on the coffee table and took off his suit coat, draping it carefully over the back of a chair. Then he sat next to her—close but not crowdingly so. "I am glad it pleases you."

"I liked the restaurant too. It's as good as you said. My paella was excellent."

"*Bueno.* I wanted to show you that even though this is a poor country, we do have some good things."

"You have many good things, which is why foreigners come here. And the people are not as poor as they once were."

"Yes, the unions have done that. We have forced the rich to give people jobs that pay better. Now we must force them to give other things—hospitals, schools."

He lifted his glass and clinked it against hers. "*Salud.*"

"*Salud.*" She wet her lips with the cognac as he drank.

"The rich will not give these things freely, but eventually they will give them. They will have no choice."

"What about democracy? Capitalism?"

His face, already rosy from the wine he'd had at dinner, turned a deeper shade of red. "Ah, yes. Those words Americanos love so much, especially when telling others what to do. We of the unions are socialists and proud to be so. What has capitalism ever done for the people in this country except to make them poor and keep them in the dirt?"

He paused as he put his glass back on the table. "But you do not want to hear a speech. And I thought that during dinner we agreed we would leave politics alone for the rest of the evening."

"Yes, we did." She put her glass beside his. "Then what do you want to talk about?"

"Perhaps we have talked enough. For a while." He looked into her eyes and then leaned over to kiss her. He tasted like cognac and, faintly, like the cigar he'd smoked as they'd lingered over dessert and coffee. She'd tasted worse.

He wasn't bad at kissing, and it was not as unpleasant as she'd feared. Still, she knew she would not enjoy it or any other part of what was coming. She told herself not to think of the past, not to let what had happened before interfere with what she had to do now.

He took his time, kissing her for several minutes before moving a hand to her breast. He had an experienced touch, gentle but sure, and she felt her nipples harden. She knew he felt it too.

He smiled at her as he eased a hand behind her back and slowly unzipped her dress. Just as slowly he pushed the dress off her shoulders.

Seeing the wispy lace of her bra and the rounded flesh it did little to conceal, he murmured, "Nice, very nice," and lowered his head to kiss the tops of her breasts.

Smith forced herself to keep from pulling back and pushing his head away. She saw the beginning of a bald spot in the crown of his thick, dark hair. She felt as though she were outside her body, watching this scene from the front row of a movie theater where she sat alone. She told herself to keep that perspective, that it might help when the time came.

And she knew that time would come soon.

He drew the bra cups off her breasts and licked and kissed and sucked her nipples. She felt heat building in her groin and wondered at how the body responds even when the mind does not. She was nervous and full of adrenaline the way she'd been before every race in high school. Or before running the obstacle course in boot camp.

She felt scared too—scared of doing what she had to do and scared of what he might do to her. She realized this was going to be harder than anything she'd ever done. Much harder than carrying out those three self-assigned missions.

As Hernandez slid a hand beneath her dress and up her thigh, she whispered, "Let's go into the bedroom—it'll be more comfortable."

He pulled back a few inches and smiled at her again. "An excellent idea. You must have read my mind."

"Oh? Can you read mine?"

"No. I do not think a man should ever pretend to know what is in a woman's mind."

"Good. Men and women are really not so different, but women want men to think we are."

He chuckled. "I will remember that. Now come with me."

Being sure to pick up her little purse, she followed him into what was obviously the master bedroom, a masculine-looking space with dark-green carpet and oak furniture. Above the king-size bed hung a large oil painting of a bull fighter standing triumphant over a prostrate bull. The picture was striking, done in a modernistic style with slashes of red and black.

As Hernandez turned the lights down, she looked quickly at the two bedside tables. The one holding a telephone, ashtray, and some books must be on the side of the bed he preferred. There was nothing but a matching lamp on the other. She went to that side and, keeping her back to Hernandez, softly put her purse on the table. Then she turned to face him.

When she saw that he was looking at her, she let her dress fall to the floor and stepped out of it. Her breasts were already uncovered, so she unhooked her bra and let it fall to the floor. She thought she heard him suck in his breath as she stood there in her black panties, garter belt, and stockings.

He loosened his tie as he came toward her. "I have never seen anything more beautiful."

"I know that's flattery, but it's sweet of you to say it."

"No, Maria, I speak only the truth." He gently took her head in his big, work-hardened hands and kissed her, probing her mouth with his tongue.

The kiss lasted a long time, and when he pulled back to catch his breath, she pulled off his tie and dropped it on the floor beside her. "Here, let me help you." She began unbuttoning his shirt.

He dropped his arms to his sides and watched her. She tugged off his shirt and ran her hands over his shoulders and chest. He had a muscular build—more evidence of the manual labor he'd done—and only a slight pot belly that he sucked in now as he stood in front of her.

He kissed her again but made no movement toward the bed. Smith knew what he wanted and what she would have to do to play her part correctly.

She unbuckled his belt and undid his trousers. She reached in and felt him, already hard, and then rubbed him up and down with her palm. Weaving slightly, he cocked his groin against her hand.

She lowered herself to her knees and pulled down his trousers. She wasn't surprised to see his tiny designer briefs. She pulled those down too and then put both hands on him.

Knowing she couldn't avoid it, she took him into her mouth. She didn't mind doing it with a guy she liked, but she'd never done it—except that one time, of course—for any other reason.

Hernandez put his hands on her head and made soft sounds of pleasure. She thought he probably wanted to come in her mouth, but she had to get him onto the bed, so after a couple of minutes she stood, cupping him in her hand. "Did you like that?"

"*Sí.* I mean, yes, yes, of course, but why do you stop?"

She looked into his eyes, now half-lidded and shining. "Because I want you inside me. I want you to fuck me—hard. Do you think you can do that?"

"Yes, I can. Better than anyone has done it before."

She tugged on him, her hand slick from the saliva she'd left. "Good. That's a promise, and I'll hold you to it. Now take your shoes and socks off and get into bed."

He seemed amused at being given orders but complied. When he was naked he padded to the far side of the bed, pulled down the covers, and reclined on the sheet, facing her.

She didn't want her clothes near the bed, so she threw his onto a chair several feet away and followed them with her dress and bra. As he watched, she unsnapped her stockings and took off the garter belt. She put a foot on the bed and slowly rolled down that stocking. Then she did the same with the other.

His gaze never left her. When at last she slid her panties down over her hips, she thought she heard him mutter something in Spanish. She didn't catch the words, but she thought she knew what he meant. She tossed the filmy underthings onto the chair.

Then she stood there a moment, letting him take in the sight of her nude body. She wasn't vain about her looks, but she worked hard to stay in shape, and now she wanted Hernandez so focused on having sex with her that he wouldn't think about anything else.

She forced herself to smile at him. Then she stepped to the bedside table and undid the clasps on her purse. She spread the opening and fished among the contents.

"Wait. I have...." She put her compact and the nail file on the table as though to uncover what she was looking for. Then she took out one of the condoms and held it up to him. "Here. I want you to wear this."

He frowned. "Are you worried about a baby? I thought all American women took pills to prevent such things."

"Many do, but I'm not one of them. I'm not in a relationship, so I usually don't have to think about not getting pregnant."

"I see. Well, I do not use those things. You will not become pregnant, and if you do, you know what you can do about it."

"Isn't abortion against your faith?"

His face turned dark, and he made an angry gesture. "Faith? My faith is in myself and my work. Why we are debating religion when we should be making love?"

"It's not just that. I don't want to risk getting a disease."

"A disease?" He shoved himself to her side of the bed and glared at her. "Do you think I go to whores and am diseased? I have not been with a whore since I was a boy."

"Still, I want you to—"

"You want? I am tired of hearing what you want. Now I will show you what I want."

He grabbed her wrist and pulled her onto the bed. She resisted, but he was too strong. He forced her onto her back and rolled on top of her. As she tried to buck him off, he used a knee to pry her legs open.

Holding her down with one hand, he jammed the other between her legs and rubbed her hard enough to be almost painful. What they'd done up till now had made her slightly wet, and from the expression on his face, she knew he could feel it. He slipped first one, then a second finger inside her, and the force of it made her gasp.

He smiled in a way that reminded her of the AD. "Oh, you like it rough, yes? Well, I can give you what you want."

"No, I—"

"Stop. Do not talk." He moved his fingers in and out, the motion becoming easier as, despite her revulsion, her body involuntarily responded.

"Wait. Wait a minute. Let's—"

"I told you to be silent." He withdrew his hand and slapped her face.

She'd been hit harder, but the force of the blow turned her head, and she began to cry, both from the pain and from the memory of the last time she'd been slapped. He ignored her tears, spread her legs farther apart, and forced himself into her.

He began moving his hips up and down, riding her. As he settled into a rhythm she opened her eyes and looked at the table. There was the black case, waiting. But the case was just out of reach, and even if she could reach it, he would see what she was doing and stop her.

No, she had to wait. Endure what was happening and find the right moment.

Hernandez looked down at her, and she closed her eyes so he wouldn't see what was in them. Earlier she'd wondered if she could do it when the time came—use the blade for its intended purpose. But now she knew she could. That slap had given her the resolve she needed.

He kept rocking in and out, moving faster now and going deeper. Perhaps because of the alcohol in him or because it was his first time with her, he didn't last long. After two or three minutes he came with a low groan that was a sound of pain as much as pleasure. She was no more aroused than she had been before he entered her, but she was glad it was over.

He lay still for a long moment, then rolled off her. He pulled the covers over both of them and turned to look at her. "That felt good. It is always good to be with a woman—to do what God meant for a man to do."

She didn't want to debate his opinion of the experience or his theology, but she knew he expected a reply. "Yes, it was good. I see why you are popular with women."

He laughed, pleased by the remark. "Who told you that?"

"I'm a journalist. I ask questions. That's my job."

"I think your real job should be making love to me. You are very talented at it."

"But that's not work, is it?"

He chuckled. "No, even though it can make you sweat like carrying bricks in the sun. But the result of one's labor is much more pleasant."

She thought fast. She needed to stay until he felt asleep and she could do what she had to. "I am always so sleepy... afterward. Do you mind if I stay for a while?"

"Of course you may stay. I want you to stay the night. We can make love again."

She wondered if he'd taken Viagra or something similar when he'd gone to the men's room at the restaurant. He must have if he thought that at his age there'd be a second round.

"All right. Now let's rest."

"*Sí*. Let us rest." He kissed her cheek, then lay on his back and closed his eyes. After a few minutes he was breathing deeply.

She lay motionless for what felt like an hour but was probably half that. He seemed to be sleeping soundly. She inched toward the edge of the bed and stretched out her hand for the nail file.

That slight movement woke him—or maybe he'd been feigning sleep to see what she'd do—and he began to raise himself on an elbow.

She snatched her hand back and turned to him. He moved toward her and kissed her, taking his time, sure of himself. To avoid arousing his suspicion, she responded, snaking her tongue inside his mouth and acting as though he were really her lover.

He obviously liked it, and he moved her hand down to show her he was getting hard. She didn't want to make love to him again, but she supposed she had no other choice.

But then he began rolling her onto her stomach. Instinctively, she knew what he wanted.

"No, I don't do that." She slid back toward the edge of the bed.

"You do what I say you do. I am sure it will not be your first time."

It wouldn't but only because of the desert. And she remembered the pain and how ashamed she'd felt, especially because she knew it was more about power than sex.

"I said no." She reached out and finally had the black case in her hand.

"And I said yes. You will take it and like it, you gringa whore." He slapped her again, much harder this time, and pinpoints of light wheeled in front of her.

She cried out from the pain, and everything seemed to turn red as a raw fury filled her. She shook the file free of the case and swallowed hard.

Hernandez sensed what was coming. His eyes widened and he threw out an arm to block hers but was too late.

She cut his throat backhanded. Remembering what Houston had taught her, she made sure to thrust the blade deep enough for a mortal wound and sliced from one side to the other.

Hernandez sucked in air, making a ghastly wet, bubbling sound. A hot, red curtain of blood gushed onto her, and she squeezed her eyes shut as tightly as she could. The sharp coppery smell filled her nose, and her stomach surged as the gory liquid splattered her face and chest. She fought a strong urge to vomit.

Still making that horrible bubbling sound, Hernandez managed to knock the file from her hand. Then he fell heavily on her and somehow got his fingers around her neck. He squeezed so hard she couldn't breathe, and she clawed at his hands and face, terrified that he might have enough life left to kill her.

But his grip grew weaker as the blood pumped out of him, dripping onto her face and hair. Just when she was about to lose consciousness she was able to loosen his fingers enough to draw breath, and her gasping was almost as ragged as his.

He tried to lock down his grip again, but she was able—barely—to hold back his hands, their entwined fingers now red and sticky, and she knew he was near the end.

He knew it too. For a few moments he muttered at her in Spanish, "*puta*" being the only word she caught. Then the only sounds were his labored breathing, gradually growing weaker, and her panting as she continued to catch her breath.

After another minute there was silence.

CHAPTER ELEVEN

She pushed him off her—his body seemed much heavier now than earlier—and rolled off the bed. She looked at him and then down at herself.

Both of them looked as though they'd crawled naked through a slaughterhouse. The line came to her without her willing it: "Yet who would have thought the old man to have had so much blood in him."

Her stomach roiled, and she dashed for the bathroom. She dropped to her knees in front of the toilet and heaved up her dinner. She put her hands on the rim to support herself, and when she thought she was finally finished retching, she saw the bloody handprints she'd left on the white porcelain, which made her retch again even though there was little left in her stomach.

Eventually she stood and looked at herself in the mirror. She was a complete mess—blood on her face and chest and even in her hair. She turned on the shower and stepped into the tub even before the water was warm.

She held her hands in the stream and watched as the water washed away the blood. Then she stepped into the stream and let the water, now warm, run over her body. She glanced down at herself and watched the pink rivulets run down her legs and rush toward the drain.

So much blood.

She wept then, her tears hotter than the water washing over her and mixing with the water as well as with what was left of the blood. Her stomach convulsed, but she was empty, drained, and had nothing left to give.

Still weeping, she fumbled for the soap and began to wash herself. She did it slowly, taking her time even though she knew she was in great danger now and needed to hurry. She also washed her hair, using shampoo from a bottle on the ledge with the soap.

By the time she finished she had stopped crying. As she rinsed her hands, she could not help thinking of another line from *Macbeth*—something the lady muttered to herself as she rubbed her own hands: "Hell is murky!"

Yes, it is, Smith thought. And right there in the next room. Where I have to go back for my clothes.

She dried herself and used the towel to wipe the steam from the mirror. The blood was gone. The only signs of what she'd been through were her red-rimmed eyes and the faint bruises around her throat. She had a scarf in her bag at the hotel. If she could get back to it... but that was a big if.

She used toilet paper to wipe her handprints from the toilet rim and flushed the bloody paper. The she steeled herself and walked back into the bedroom.

She forced herself to look at the bed, and the sight of the throat-cut corpse on the bloody sheets was bad but not as bad as she'd feared. She was getting over the shock now. Her brain was beginning to work again, to think about what she had to do to escape, to survive this mission.

Good. She'd need all her faculties—that plus a lot of luck.

She went to the chair where she'd left her clothes, the one she'd chosen because it was too far away to be sprayed with blood. She dressed quickly, fumbling a bit at first but then settling down and completing the task quickly.

When she was almost finished the bedside phone rang. The trilling wasn't loud, but it shattered the silence of the room, startling her.

It was probably the bodyguard calling to check on Hernandez. Maybe he wanted to see whether she'd left or was going to stay the night. Or maybe it was important news for Hernandez, something he needed to know about even though it was getting quite late.

In either case she couldn't remain there any longer. She zipped up her dress and went over by the bed. She forced herself to pluck the nail file from the floor and wipe off the blade with the towel. Then she wiped off the case, slid the file into it, and put the case in her little purse, which fortunately had escaped being splattered with blood.

She went down a mental checklist to make sure she had everything. When she was certain she did, she started for the door.

As she reached the doorway, something made her turn and look back at the bed. Hernandez... the fourth man she'd killed. The first three had led to this, and if she were lucky, if she escaped, there'd be more. She shuddered and put a hand to her eyes.

Suddenly she remembered from her mission briefing what Honduras meant in Spanish—the "depths." Well, she was in them now.

After a long moment she straightened her back and left the room.

At the front door she put her ear to the wood and listened intently but heard nothing. She eased the door open and looked up and down the hall. No one.

She stepped outside and quietly closed the door, hearing the lock click.

She found the fire stairs and walked down a flight before taking the elevator. She got off on the second floor and took the stairs to the ground level.

She cracked the door and peered into the lobby. There was no one there except the doorman, who was sitting at his little desk and reading a magazine. This man was not the same one who'd been on duty when she and Hernandez had arrived.

She started to step into the lobby but then froze. Jaime was coming through the front door. He spoke briefly to the doorman, who obviously knew him. Smith couldn't hear what Jaime said and probably wouldn't have understood him if she had, but from the doorman's shaking his head "no," she thought Jaime had asked the man a question.

Perhaps about her.

Then Jaime hurried across the floor toward the elevator. Once the doors had closed behind him and he was well on the way up, she left the stairwell and crossed the lobby, moving with purpose but not haste and keeping her face averted from the doorman.

But he glanced up as she passed. Something about her caught his attention—Jaime must have mentioned her dress—and he called to her.

When she didn't stop he half-rose from his chair, but then she was through the door and outside. Looking back, she saw him punching buttons on the phone, and she knew which condo he was dialing.

She had only a couple of minutes, if that, to get away. By now Jaime was probably standing in the bloody bedroom, a look of horror on his face. She imagined him drawing his gun and coming after her. If he caught her, the best she could hope for would be 20 years in a hellish prison. But it was just as likely, perhaps more so, that he'd simply shoot her and then use the union's clout to cover up the matter.

Fighting back the panic that threatened to engulf her, she looked up and down the street. By now it was nearly 2:00 a.m., and almost everything was closed even in this country where people stayed out very late.

Across the street a small dance club appeared to be open. She could go inside, but she'd be trapped if Jaime or another of Hernandez's men came in to look for her. Still there didn't seem to be any other option. Nothing else in the area was open, and no cabs were cruising the streets.

Then she got lucky. A cab came around the corner and stopped in front of the club. She immediately started for the car, the tapping of her heels sounding loud in the nearly deserted street.

When she got there two couples were piling out, and she heard their American accents. One of the men, the one not busy paying the driver, looked at her, smiled, said, "*Buenas noches.*" The woman with him tightened her grip on his arm and said nothing.

"*Buenas noches,*" Smith said, using her best Spanish accent and keeping her face blank. She waited for the other woman to finish exiting the cab, and then she quickly slid into the back seat and closed the door.

"*Vámonos—rápido.*" Her voice wasn't loud, but she put an edge of command into it.

The driver glanced at her in the mirror. "*¿Dónde a?*"

"I'll tell you on the way."

He shrugged and surged away from the curb.

"*Girar a la derecha.*"

At the intersection the driver followed her instruction to turn right. As the cab rounded the corner she looked back at the condo building. Jaime burst through the door, gun drawn, and looked up and down the street just as she had a minute earlier.

He saw the dance club and ran toward it, confirming her instinct not to go inside. But she knew he'd probably learn that she'd left in a cab, and he might even be able to get the cab's number.

She gave the driver the name of a hotel near hers, and he let her off in front. She went into the lobby, almost deserted at this hour, and pretended to look for someone. As soon as the cab left, she walked to her own hotel.

She retrieved her key and went to her room, thinking as fast as she could. Jaime might be able to trace her to the hotel where the cab had dropped her, and that might lead him to check the other two hotels in the area—one of which was hers.

She didn't have much time.

As soon as she walked through the door she began shedding her clothes. She opened her suitcase and took out hair dye, mousse, and a contact-lens container. Half an hour later she'd gone from being a brown-eyed dirty blonde to a slicked-back redhead with green eyes. She put on eyeglasses to help the disguise along and dressed in casual traveling clothes, knotting the scarf around her throat to hide the purple bruises that were now much more noticeable than they'd been at the condominium.

She stuffed the black dress, lingerie, and shoes in the hotel's plastic laundry bag and followed them with the blazer and skirt she'd worn at lunch. Next she threw in her reporter's notebook, fake ID, and Maria Tyler passport. She flattened the bag and hid it under a blanket on the closet shelf. She hesitated about the gun—taking it would be a comfort—but she knew she was now safer without it, so she left it where it was.

She grabbed her regular purse—making sure her other passport was in it—and her laptop bag. Then she wheeled her suitcase into the hall, closing the door quietly behind her.

Downstairs she checked out, accepting a copy of her bill from the sleepy clerk and murmuring a soft "*gracias*," which was as much for the fact that she'd never seen him before as for his service.

It was almost 4 a.m., and her flight was at 5:45.

She thought she might not be able to get another cab at this hour, and cold fingers of fear clutched at her. But her luck held. One—only one—sat in the area marked for taxis. She tapped on the window to wake up the driver and put her things in the back seat, sliding in after them.

"*A el aeropuerto, por favor.*"

"*Bien.*" He yawned and started the car.

A block away they neared the hotel she'd been in earlier. As they passed it, two police cars zoomed up—lights blazing but no sirens—and screeched to a stop. Four officers and Jaime tumbled out of the cars and strode into the lobby.

Smith was careful not to pay much attention. The driver slowed to look at the spectacle, and she had to clench her jaw to keep from screaming at him to drive—to get her out of there.

"*¿Excitante, no?*" he said.

"*Sí.*" She tried to sound uninterested and leaned her head back so that she wouldn't be as visible from the street.

After a few seconds that seemed to Smith to last forever the driver turned back to the empty street and picked up speed. They were at the airport in 20 minutes.

Inside the terminal every security guard and ticket agent seemed to be staring at her, but she fought down the panicky feeling and scanned the flight-status board to find her gate.

At the security checkpoint she assumed a neutral expression and forced herself to breathe slowly. A guard leafed through her passport while another searched her bags, and she wondered if they'd been alerted to be on the lookout for Maria Tyler.

The first guard peered at the passport photo of a redhead wearing glasses. "Justine McKinnon, that is your name?"

"Yes."

"And you are from Los Angeles?"

"Yes."

"I see. Why did you come to our country?"

To kill a man. "To scout movie locations." The AD had briefed them on how that ruse had worked years before to extract a few of the U.S. hostages in Iran. She had a few documents that would back up the story, but she hoped she wouldn't have to use them.

The guard seemed puzzled and glanced at his colleague, who held up a pair of thong panties and grinned at her before dropping them back in her suitcase.

"You know—places to make movies. Here in Tegucigalpa."

He nodded. "*Sí*. This city is very popular now. I hope you had a good visit."

She hesitated but only for a second. "It was very memorable."

"*Bueno*." He looked at the other guard, who shook his head and zipped up the suitcase.

He handed her passport back to her. "Have a good flight."

"*Gracias*."

She gathered her things and went to the gate, where she sat and pulled out a book. She kept reading the same paragraph over and over, glancing up every few seconds to see if any security guards—or maybe Jaime and his cop friends—were coming for her.

No one was. Yet. But right then her blood froze.

A large television screen was showing the early-morning news. The sound was turned so low she could barely hear it, and the anchor was speaking so rapidly she could have understood little even if she'd been able to hear it.

But she understood the file photo of Hernandez that came on the screen. And she understood the fuzzy photo of herself that followed it— a photo that Jaime must have taken of her press ID with his phone when he called to check on her.

And now, still without hearing it, she knew what the broadcaster was saying: be on the lookout for this American woman, who is wanted for questioning in connection with the murder of labor leader Juan Jesus Hernandez.

She suddenly realized she was holding her breath, and she forced herself to exhale and relax her vise-like grip on the paperback. She glanced around to see if any of the other few passengers in the area had noticed the news story's effect on her.

Apparently none of them had. But then she saw what had to be two plainclothes detectives walking through that wing of the terminal, their hard, cold eyes dissecting each person they passed.

She wanted to scream, to run, to do anything but what she knew she had to do—sit there and pretend to read her book. She managed, just barely, to do that, even turning a page to heighten the illusion.

So she sensed rather than saw when they stopped in front of her. She lowered the book slightly and saw their heavy leather shoes, the hems of dark trousers draped over them. She lowered the book further and looked up at the two men. One was holding what must be a copy of that fuzzy photo of her, and his eyes flicked from the paper to her face and back again.

"*Buenos días*. May we see your passport, please?" The other man's English was excellent—so good that she wondered if he'd studied in the United States.

Her mind raced as she thought of what an innocent person would say—someone who hadn't murdered one of this country's most important people a few hours ago. "Why? And who are you?"

"Routine check. We are police officers." The man briefly showed her his credentials while his partner continued to compare her face to the photo.

"All right." She dug in her purse and handed the passport to him.

"Justine McKinnon. *Americano*. Age thirty-three. You look young for your age."

That's because she wasn't 33. "Thanks. Shows what clean living will do for you."

He showed the passport to his partner, who looked closely at the picture and checked it against her face and then against the photo in his hand. The partner murmured something in Spanish, and the man nodded.

Smith tensed, getting ready to run if they tried to arrest her. She knew she had no chance of getting away, but she'd rather be shot dead here than go to prison.

But the man handed the passport back to her. "*Gracias*. Have a good flight."

Somehow she managed not to sigh in relief. She even managed a faint smile as she took the passport. "*De nada*."

After the two men walked away, still looking for a dirty blonde named Maria Tyler, Smith felt the shakes coming on. She forced herself to breathe slowly and deeply, and the feeling subsided after a few minutes. But she sat there, sick and cold with fear, until they called her flight.

She watched through the small window as the lush, green land fell away beneath her, and then she closed her eyes. She wept a few tears and was relieved no one was sitting beside her to see her wipe them away.

Finally she slept, fitfully, each lurch of the plane jolting her awake to see Hernandez staring down at her, blood dripping from his slashed throat and hate blazing from his dying eyes.

CHAPTER TWELVE

Three months later she was sitting with Lee in her apartment. He and Mori were in town to train with her for a mission the AD said would take the three of them to perform. They'd spent two long weeks at Andrews sharpening the skills they'd acquired as students together, and the AD was going to brief them on the mission in the morning.

Lee had invited her to dinner, and they'd gone to the Vietnamese restaurant where they'd been before. At her urging he'd also invited Mori, but Mori had politely declined in his accented English, saying he already had plans.

Lee didn't seem disappointed. "He's a little strange, don't you think?" Lee ate a bite of grilled chicken as she waited for her answer.

"Maybe. Nice guy but very quiet. I wouldn't have figured him for this line of work."

"No, me either. But he kicks ass at martial arts."

"Yes." She smiled. "Literally and figuratively."

Lee sipped his beer, studying her for a moment. "So, how did your... trip go?"

"Okay, I guess. I mean, I'm back, and, well, mission accomplished. But I won't say it was fun."

"No, I'm sure it wasn't. Mine wasn't either."

"I'd like to hear about it. Whatever you care to tell."

"Sure, we'll swap stories. Even if the AD wouldn't like it. But not here—too public."

She paused before replying, and the silence stretched out so long that she drank some wine to cover it. Then she said, "We can go to my place after dinner. Have coffee or a drink. You can tell me then."

He looked closely at her in the candlelight. "That sounds good. If you're sure."

She laughed. "I'm rarely sure of anything. But I feel comfortable with you."

"Thanks. Must be my strong back and weak mind."

Now she kept herself from laughing. "Exactly."

After dinner she drove them to her apartment in Arlington. Lee asked for a bourbon and water, and she had another glass of wine. She slipped her shoes off and curled on the couch, facing him.

He told her about his mission. He'd been sent to a part of the former Soviet Union that was largely Muslim and had attracted a senior al

Qaeda recruiter.

"The CIA couldn't drone him?"

"No, the guy was too smart for that. He never carried a phone. Plus, like Saddam, he never stayed in the same place more than one night."

"So why us—you—instead of a SEAL team?"

"I don't think we even had a good picture of him. And this guy wasn't considered important enough to send in a team. So—"

"So I guess we know where we rank."

"Exactly."

"How did you find him?"

"With great difficulty."

Lee smiled, and she thought, what a nice smile he has, warm and friendly. Natural, not like he's forcing it. She felt a tingling low in her abdomen that she hadn't felt in a long time.

"Seriously, that was the hardest part of the mission. Fortunately, we had someone on the inside who's more loyal to money than to Allah, and he identified the target. After that it wasn't too hard."

"Sniper?"

"Yeah. Fairly easy shot."

"How far?"

Lee had some of his drink. "Not that far."

"Come on, Marine, talk to me. How far?"

"Uh, about 800 yards. Maybe a little more."

"Good shooting, Lee!"

"Well, I got lucky."

She nodded. "Yes, I'm sure it was all luck." She could see he liked her teasing him, and she was enjoying the playful mood, something she needed after the recent past. But then he said something that seemed to dim the already low light in the room.

"Will you tell me about yours?"

She brought the glass to her lips and noted with surprise and some trepidation that her hand was trembling slightly. She didn't want Lee to notice, so she swallowed some wine and put the glass down.

"Not much to tell. I killed a man in South America. A labor leader, a Communist. I suppose he'd have been dangerous for us eventually." She paused, remembering. "Maybe."

"Well, we don't get to decide, do we? About the targets, I mean."

"No, we don't."

Lee looked at her over the rim of his glass. "Is that all?"

"All what?"

"All you care to tell me."

His question was reasonable under the circumstances, but somehow it made her angry. "What more do you want to know? How I cut his throat? How he died with his bloody hands around my neck, choking me? How I feel about it?"

She heard her voice rising. She paused, took a breath, then another, and added quietly, "How I dream about it—dark, red dreams—and wake up scared? Is that what you want to know?"

He put down the glass and took her hands. His were warm on hers, and she didn't mind the roughness, the hardness of them. "I want to know only what you want to tell me. Sounds like it was a tough job."

"Tough?" She remembered what she'd had to do, undressing Hernandez, taking him into her mouth, lying beneath him, listening to him grunt with effort. And later, when he'd tried to force her to... then that quick, backhand stroke with the blade.

"It wasn't tough, not that hard. But it was horrible."

"It must've been hard to get close enough to him to... do it that way."

She knew what he was thinking, and part of her thought he deserved to know. After all, here he was, at her invitation, sitting close to her, the two of them sharing a drink and this intimate moment. She could see her bedroom door from the couch—both of them could.

So why didn't she tell him? Another part of her thought she should keep that memory to herself. Or at least wait until she and Lee had shared more together.

But she knew the real reason was that if she told him, he might not want her anymore, and now she wanted him. She wanted him to make love to her—to comfort her, yes, but also to weaken the hold the memory of Hernandez had on her. She didn't want the last man she'd been with to be—again—a man she'd killed.

She weighed the options and then decided, pulling her hands away from his. "I went to bed with him, Lee. I didn't want to, but I had to do it to accomplish the mission and get out alive. It was the only way."

She paused, afraid to look into his eyes but then making herself look. She couldn't tell what he was thinking, and for a moment she wished she hadn't told him.

But then he said, "You did what you had to do. Just like I did, like any of us would. We have to carry out the mission. But I'm glad you told me."

"Really? That's something you want to know?"

He nodded. "I want to know all about you that I can." Then he leaned toward her.

Their first kiss was as nice as she'd thought it would be and not awkward at all. He must have liked it too—he spent a long time kissing her, doing it as though he had all the time there was.

When he finally put his hands on her, on her shoulders, arms, and breasts, they didn't feel rough at all. His touch was gentle but sure, and she felt as if she were melting in the summer sun.

After a while, a very pleasurable while, they got up by unspoken mutual consent and headed for her bedroom, shedding clothes along the way. Lee's body was as lean and muscular as she'd imagined, and she could tell he liked the way she looked as she stood there naked in front of him.

He cupped her head in his hands and kissed her again, drawing her to him. The tingling sensation was very strong now, and she felt her knees grow weak. She leaned against Lee, and he picked her up easily and put her on the bed.

She pulled the covers back while looking at him, all of him, as he got into bed with her. Then he kissed her again, slowly brushing fingertips down her body to where the tingling was centered, and she let herself float out onto a warm, welcoming sea.

□   □   □

Afterward, with the covers kicked, she lay in his arms while the lazy ceiling fan dried the sweat on both of them.

"That was incredible," Lee said.

"Yes, it was. I guess some of those clichés are true."

"I guess so. I'm glad you liked it."

"Lee, to say I 'liked it' is an understatement. I didn't know I could feel this way after... well, I didn't know I could feel like this."

"Like how?"

"Safe. Comfortable. Happy."

He kissed her temple. "Good. I'm glad you feel that way."

She hesitated, then said, "And you?"

"Me? What?"

"You know. How do you feel?"

"The same. Plus exhausted. I didn't know you were quite so... athletic in bed."

She smiled and hugged him. "Well, anything worth doing.... There's another cliché for you."

"Yes, and I'm glad you believe in that one."

"Oh, I think you do too."

He chuckled and lightly slapped her rump. "I try. Sometimes I succeed."

"Score one for the Corps." She was silent for a while, her ear against his chest, listening to his heartbeat. She wondered if he could feel her own pulse. Then she said, "Lee, what's going to happen?"

"What do you mean?"

"I mean what's going to happen to us. How many missions before we're free or...."

"Dead?"

"Yes."

"I don't know. Several, probably. They'll want to get their money out of us."

She remembered the Director's comment about saving a few dollars. "You're probably right. I guess we're in this thing for a while."

"Unless...." He didn't finish the thought.

"What?"

He squeezed her tight. "Unless we run."

She liked that "we." "Are you thinking of doing that?"

"Thinking about it? Sure. Planning on doing it? No. Remember Wright?"

She did, very well. The tall, cheerful Australian. She still wondered what he'd done to end up with the Enterprise and exactly how he'd died. She hoped they'd killed him quickly and as painlessly as possible.

Then she thought briefly of her own death. She'd always hoped to live a long, productive life, maybe marry and have children. But now that didn't seem possible. She'd probably be lucky to be alive in six months.

"Yes, I remember him. And I know that's what they'd do to any of us if we tried to run. I don't think we'd get very far."

"Us against the Enterprise? No, I don't think we would either."

She shut her eyes and tried to make her mind a blank slate, to think of nothing but being there with Lee, feeling the warmth of his skin next to hers. Then she blinked and looked at Lee. "You know, this is a pretty depressing conversation, considering our present circumstances."

"You mean—"

She put a finger on his lips. "I mean we can probably find something better to do than talk about death."

He smiled and put his hand on hers. "Yes, I think we can too."

So they did.

❑   ❑   ❑

It was better the second time, slower, more relaxed, their bodies fitting together as though intended to, which, she thought, was right—women and men were made to fit together. But sometimes the fit was awkward or even rough and felt wrong. This felt as right to her as anything ever had—no, more than anything ever had. She silently offered up a little prayer of thanks that she was able to share this oasis with her friend.

She looked over at him, sound asleep but—and thank God for this too—not snoring. With his face relaxed and his hair as mussed as its short length would allow, she could see something of what he must have looked like as a little boy. The thought made her smile.

Then she thought about what was coming in the morning, and her smile vanished. The AD was going to brief them on this special mission that required the three of them—Lee, Mori, and Smith. If whatever they had to do took three people to do it, the mission wasn't going to be easy. Probably just the opposite.

She wondered if any of them would live through it.

Then she looked at Lee again and wondered if this would be the last time—the only time—they would sleep together. She hoped not. But that was out of her hands just as was almost everything else about this insane existence she was living. Except for this interlude with Lee, it was mostly a bad dream from which she couldn't awake.

She thought briefly that it might have been better if Hernandez had killed her. He'd come close. Then she'd feel nothing, not this numbing dread that never entirely left her, not even lying there next to Lee.

She sighed and looked at the clock on her bedside table. Two in the morning. Later than she'd thought. And they had to be at the briefing early. She set the alarm for five-thirty, remembering how she'd sworn during boot camp that she'd never get up that early again.

But now she was doing lots of things she didn't want to do. And apparently would have to keep on doing them.

CHAPTER THIRTEEN

Smith and Lee were sitting in the briefing room when Mori arrived. He greeted them quietly and took a chair on the opposite side of the table.

Lee glanced at Smith, then turned to Mori. "Say, do you know what this is about?"

Mori met his gaze for only a second or two. "Yes."

"Well?"

"You know I cannot say. That is for the Assistant Director."

"Look, we're going to know soon. Just give us a preview—what are we in for?"

"Sorry, I cannot say."

Lee looked at Smith and shrugged. He checked his watch. "Two minutes. And you know he'll walk through that door right on time."

But five minutes later the AD still wasn't there.

"That's strange," Smith said. "He's always so punctual. Cold, arrogant, and a ruthless prick but punctual."

"Shh," Lee said. "You know they're probably listening."

"I don't care." Smith smiled a rueful little smile. "What are they going to do to us? Make us trained assassins and send us out to risk our lives for some secret organization?"

"Well," Lee said, "there's always that possibility."

Mori heard their interchange but said nothing. Afterward he shifted in his seat as though trying to get comfortable. As the silence stretched out, he looked over at his two teammates and started to speak, but at that moment the AD came striding through the door, followed closely by the Sergeant.

Lee stood at attention and the others followed his lead. The AD's expression didn't change much, but Smith could tell he was pleased by their sign of respect.

"Take your seats—you know we're not very military around here." He waited while they resumed their places. "I'm a bit late because the Director asked to see me. He had some unwelcome news."

He paused again, perhaps for dramatic effect, and looked intently at them. "Our president," he began, his tone making clear what he thought of the man, "has decided to replace the head of the CIA with someone more... sympathetic to the president's views. Apparently he now thinks that keeping the appointee from the previous administration was a bad idea, so he's making a change."

The AD seemed to want questions, so Smith gave him one. "Will this have any impact on us?"

He smiled frostily. "It might. I don't think the president knows about our little organization. The current CIA chief never felt it necessary to tell him. But the new man, once he's in place, will brief the president about us, and we might not be in business after that."

"What are we going to do? Put everything on hold?"

Smith was surprised, almost shocked, to hear meek little Mori ask a question. And he seemed to want the AD to say, yes, no more missions for now. Come to think of it, she wouldn't mind hearing him say that. She glanced at Lee and could tell he was thinking the same thing.

She liked the feeling that she could already tell what Lee was thinking sometimes. She wondered if he could read her mind too. Perhaps. She'd have to test that sometime. Right now she focused on what the AD was saying.

"No, we can't predict what's going to happen, so we'll just do our jobs. We'll proceed with this mission."

He clicked the remote in his hand, and a map of Japan came up on the screen behind him. "This is where you're going." He pointed to a small town on the coast. "Near there anyway. To a compound occupied by a group of eco-terrorists."

"Eco-terrorists?" That was Lee.

"Yes, extremists who don't want Japan—or anyone, for that matter—to use nuclear power. All they've done up to now is coordinate protests—marches and so forth—although some of their events have gotten violent. But now they're planning on attacking a nuclear plant, putting it out of commission."

"Why do we care?" Smith knew she shouldn't ask, but something made her do it. "I mean, how is that a threat to the United States?"

"Smith." The AD stepped next to her and stood there, towering over her. "You ask such interesting questions."

"You mean impertinent, don't you?" She noticed Lee shaking his head at that.

"Yes, I suppose I do. I was trying to be ironic. Do you know what that means?"

"I think I read it in a book once. And, no, it wasn't a comic book."

The AD looked at her for a long time, and the room grew absolutely silent. No one moved. She held the AD's gaze, wondering if she'd gone too far this time.

"Smith, one day you and I will have to come to an understanding." His tone, never warm, was as cold as she'd ever heard it. "A very clear mutual understanding of how our little organization works and your role in it. We'll have to find a suitable time and place so we won't be disturbed. Then I'll explain things to you in a way you'll understand—and never forget."

"Any time. Sir."

He looked at her a moment longer before walking back toward the screen. "We care because Japan is a close ally and trading partner, and these bastards will disrupt the Japanese infrastructure and economy. In addition, what they do in Japan could spread to the United States. They want a similar group to operate here, and we're going to use that fact against them."

Smith didn't quite follow the last point, but she figured she'd said enough for the time being.

The AD clicked the remote, and a satellite photo came on the screen. "This is what the compound looks like."

It was about the size and shape of a football field. There was a large building in the center with two smaller buildings nearby, all of them surrounded by some sort of fence. Three vehicles were parked in front of the large building.

"It's a former elementary school. In fact, this area was the playground. They use it for martial-arts training now. The group is well-funded by Japanese liberals, some of them the equivalent of our Hollywood left, and even protected to some extent by the liberal Japanese political party."

He clicked the remote again, and they were looking at a floor diagram of the main building. "These rooms at the front they use for conferences and training. This is a library with computers and printers for research. Kitchen and dining room here. Bedrooms here, here, and here. Latrines as marked."

"We seem to have a lot of intel about the layout."

Smith caught Lee's use of "we." Had he drunk the Kool-Aid?

"Yes, we do. For that you can thank your colleague. Mori infiltrated the group and spent six days living in the compound."

Smith and Lee looked at Mori, who seemed embarrassed by the compliment.

"He posed as a Japanese-American entrepreneur who's gotten rich in Silicon Valley and now wants to use his money for worthy causes—one of them being promoting green energy."

Smith thought about how hard that must have been, playing a role convincingly for six days straight, under close observation almost all the time. She had a newfound respect for him.

"Good job, Mori." She flashed him a smile, but he simply nodded.

"Yes, it was a good job, excellent in fact. Mori even planted some listening devices so that we've been able to keep tabs on the group since he left. They're having a conference soon to finish planning their attack on the nuclear plant. Of course, they never discussed the attack in front of Mori—they told him they were nonviolent and would use his money to buy anti-nuke ads, raise public awareness, things like that."

Another click and several faces with names below them appeared on the screen. "This man, Himura Iwao, is their leader, and this one, Tanaka Tadao, is his chief deputy. Last name first, first name last, of course."

The men looked young but smart and determined. Not people to be underestimated, Smith thought.

"Wakahisa Chikako is number three in the organization. It's unusual for a Japanese woman to have that senior a position."

Smith bristled but then realized what the AD said was, unfortunately, probably true. She studied the picture. This Wakahisa, the only woman depicted on the screen, looked as smart and determined as the men. She was also strikingly pretty, and Smith glanced at Mori, who was staring at the picture, his lips slightly parted.

Looks like he did more than talk to her about green energy, Smith thought. Fine, just as long as it doesn't compromise the mission.

"The others make up the rest of the organization although there are a few members for whom we don't have pictures. But that doesn't matter—you may assume that anyone you find in the compound is a member and therefore a target of your mission."

"And what is the mission, sir?"

Smith admired Marine Corps discipline, but she hated to hear Lee address the AD as "sir" without even a hint of, yes, irony. She needed to have a long talk with the boy—maybe when he was tired but relaxed after some pleasant exercise.

The AD looked at Lee, but his gaze wasn't as hostile as when he'd looked at Smith earlier. "That should be obvious. You go in and—"

"Kill everyone. 'Cause that's what we do, isn't it?" Smith paused before adding, "Sir."

The AD's face grew dark, and Smith could tell he was having trouble controlling himself. But he was a man of iron discipline, and he managed to do it. "Yes, Smith, that's what we do. I'm glad to see you understand that much at least."

She was beginning to understand a lot more about this shadowy Enterprise, but she didn't say so. She figured she'd pissed off the AD enough for one day. Probably more than she should have. She noticed the Sergeant staring at her, a look of annoyance on his normally impassive face.

"But often we do something more," the AD said, "something we need to do this time. After you've neutralized the place, collect all the intelligence you can. Hard drives, mobile phones—and photograph everything. You know the drill."

Yes, they did. They'd spent an entire week on it during their training. As she mentally reviewed the key steps for intelligence collection, Smith couldn't help thinking about the AD's use of "neutralize" to refer to killing the eco-terrorists. Well, maybe it was easier to think of the mission that way. Or maybe, after you'd worked in the slaughterhouse long enough, that's really how you thought. Otherwise, you couldn't keep pulling the trigger.

The AD's voice interrupted her thoughts. "For this mission, collecting intel will be almost as important as hitting the targets. Any questions?"

He paused, but no one had anything to ask about that aspect. "Okay. Mori will get you in. He'll claim you're friends of his, other rich Americans, who want to contribute to the cause. In fact, we chose you two to work with Mori because you all trained together and therefore should be able to play the part of having some shared history."

Lee—focused on the mission, not on tweaking his boss—asked the practical question. "What will we use for weapons, sir? I assume these guys will check us before they let us into their compound."

"Yes, I'm sure they will. But you'll be unarmed, so that won't be a problem."

"It'll be a problem if we have to take out six or eight people with no weapons."

Smith noticed that Lee spoke sharply and didn't add his usual "sir."

"Probably more like ten or twelve. As I said, you'll go in when they're holding a big meeting to get ready for the nuclear plant."

"They won't let us in," Smith said. "They won't want us around while they're doing that."

"We think you'll be able to get in. First, they know Mori and trust him—a fellow Japanese."

Smith glanced at Mori, who wouldn't meet her gaze. He shifted in his seat again.

"Second, they need money, and you'll have some with you. Enough to tempt them to use you to get more. And third, well, if they don't let you in, you'll have to find a way in. But you will carry out this mission."

"With no weapons?" Lee again.

"Remember your training. We taught you how to use knives, scissors, even pencils as weapons. Use your hands if necessary. You know how to kill a man with those."

"But against ten to twelve of them?"

"I didn't say it would be easy. In fact, that's why we're sending you as a team. But I certainly think each of you is as good as three or four relatively untrained opponents."

"Relatively untrained?"

"Yes, Smith, that's what I said. Mori tells us they've been doing some internal training, teaching themselves, but it hasn't been highly effective. So they know some things but probably not even as much as you knew when you came to us."

When you kidnapped me, Smith thought, giving me no choice in the matter.

"One more thing." The AD looked at each of them in turn, Smith last. "Once you're in and they're all there, move quickly. You don't know how long they'll be together, and the longer you wait, the more time they'll have to question you and perhaps learn who you are—or at least who you're not."

"No further questions?" He paused so briefly it would have been difficult to get a question in. "Good." He made a slight gesture. "Sergeant."

The Sergeant gave each of them a thick manila envelope. Someone had handwritten "Smith" on hers.

"You can open them later—they contain your passports for this mission, money, both U.S. and Japanese, and throw-away phones. There are no directions to the compound because with your cover story you wouldn't have them. Mori knows how to get there. And on the way he'll fill you in on the details of your cover."

He looked at each of them again. "It's a tough mission, but I'm sure you'll do fine. Now the Director wants to have a word with you." He nodded at the Sergeant, who then left the room.

No one spoke while they waited. The AD clicked the screen blank and put down the remote. Lee slid his envelope onto the table, and the paper crackled. Mori seemed lost in thought.

Smith was wondering what their chances were. Not good, no matter what the AD said about their being able to handle odds of three or four to one. It was fine for him to talk like that—he wasn't going to have to penetrate that remote compound in a foreign country with a foreign language and then try to kill everyone inside with no weapons except what they found there.

What was it he'd said? Use pencils if necessary. Yeah, right. That would do the trick.

The Director came in, causing her to break off that train of thought, and the three of them stood again. The Director looked tired and even a bit older than the last time she'd seen him—at their graduation only a few months ago.

He looked at them and smiled. "I am very proud of you, of what you have accomplished on your first missions. Each of you carried out his—or her—orders and came back safely. No small feat in each case."

He gestured toward the screen. "May I please have the overhead of the compound?"

The AD retrieved the remote and clicked it until the photo appeared.

"Thank you. And this is where you're going next. Mr. Mori made this mission possible, and we appreciate his skill and daring in doing so."

Smith glanced at Mori, whose face had gone crimson.

"But we know it is a tough job. All your missions are, which is why only you can carry them out, but this one will be harder than most." He paused, looking at them one by one. "I hope all of you make it back."

But he doesn't think we will, Smith thought. Then she forced herself to add what she didn't want to admit, even to herself. He's probably right.

CHAPTER FOURTEEN

They left the Washington area on separate flights from separate airports—Reagan National, Dulles, and BWI—and traveled nonstop to Los Angeles to catch a plane for Tokyo. The Director had said that for security reasons he really didn't want them to travel to Japan together but that, given their cover story, they'd naturally be on the same plane.

"Good luck," he'd said in his kindly way, shaking hands with each of them just as he'd done at their graduation. "I look forward to welcoming you upon your return."

And I hope you get to do that, Smith thought. For all of us.

She and Mori got to LAX before Lee and arrived at the Tokyo gate at about the same time. Mori, off by himself in a corner, pretended he didn't see her, but Smith went over and sat next to him.

"Hi." She gave him what she hoped was a reassuring smile.

"Uh, hi." He spoke softly in his lightly accented English. "I don't think we should sit together."

"You're probably right. But then we do lots of things we probably shouldn't do, don't we?"

He sighed and seemed to release some of his nervousness along with his breath. "Yes, that's true."

"So, Mori, what's the deal with you? I can't figure out why you're in this. You don't seem like the type to have done something bad enough to sell your soul to the Enterprise."

"That's a very personal question. And the AD says we're not supposed to talk about our backgrounds."

"Screw the AD." She gestured toward the area around them. "Is he here? No. We work for him—for the Director, really—but he doesn't own us. If I'm going to risk my life with someone, I want to know something about that person. So I want to know about you."

Mori said nothing. He clasped his hands in his lap and sat staring at them.

"Look, I'll go first. I killed three people. Three men I'd worked with. I shot each of them, two from a distance, one close up." She looked at Mori to gauge his reaction. He glanced at her, surprise showing in his expression, and then looked at his hands again. "They'd... done something to me, something bad, and I thought they deserved to die. Looking back, I guess I shouldn't have killed them, but I did and here I am. End of story. Now you."

Mori still said nothing. She saw him shake his head slightly. She knew he wouldn't talk in front of Lee, and Lee would be here any minute.

"Come on. I'm serious, Mori. I've got to be able to count on you."

"You can count on me." He lifted his chin. "The Enterprise recruited me, and I finished the training just like you did. That's all you need to know."

She took a deep breath. "Listen, when we're in that compound and the shit starts to fly, we've got to be able to count on each other. You'll need to be able to trust me, won't you?"

After a moment Mori nodded, clearly reluctant to do even that.

"Okay, go."

Mori hesitated again, longer this time. Then he began, speaking in a low voice she had to strain to hear. "I was born in Japan, and my family came here when I was eleven. The Japanese economy was bad then, and my father thought he could make more money here, buy a bigger house, that sort of thing."

He paused, and she touched his wrist to encourage him to continue.

"My father had been an electrician, but his English was so poor he had to take a job as a janitor. And my mother had to work—she got a job in a Japanese restaurant. Still, it was not a bad life for my sister and me."

He paused again and looked at her. She smiled and nodded. "Good. Go on."

"Well, I worked my way through college, majoring in political science and Japanese. The CIA recruited me during my senior year, and I went to work there right after I graduated. I wanted to be an analyst, have a desk job at Langley, but because I could pass as a Japanese citizen, they wanted me to work in the field. So they sent me to a place in Southeastern Virginia they call the Farm."

"I've heard of it. Isn't that where they teach tradecraft—spy stuff?"

"Right. Plus they taught me a lot more about martial arts than I'd learned to that point."

"They sure taught you enough to kick my butt. So what happened then?"

"I worked in Asia, China mostly, posing as a Japanese businessman looking for good export values. What I really did was pay a lot of money for the right sort of economic information."

"Which went to the CIA, not to the Japanese."

"Yes." Mori looked at his hands again. "It was hard. I mean, I was always scared I'd be caught and thrown into a Chinese prison. And I always felt that I was betraying my homeland—Japan, I mean. My cover required me to go there often, and whenever I was in Japan I felt like a complete fraud."

"Is that what caused you to get mixed up with the Yakuza?"

"What?" He sounded surprised.

She gently touched the stub of his finger. "This."

He smiled, one of the few times she'd seen him do it. "No, that happened when I was a teenager. I was working on my bike, spinning the pedals with my other hand, and that finger got caught between the chain and the sprockets. If we'd gone to a better doctor, not the GP for our neighborhood, I might still have the finger."

"So how did you end up in this shitty business? It sounds like you had a pretty good life even if doing covert ops for the CIA wasn't your dream job."

"My father. He felt ashamed that he hadn't made more money for his family, given us a better life, so he started gambling when I was in college. Cards, mostly. Maybe he thought he could make the money that way or maybe it was just a distraction from what he saw as his failure."

He paused, and she could see him remembering.

"Anyway, although he won sometimes, he lost more than he won, and over a period of several years he went deeply into debt. He borrowed all he could from the bank, then friends, and finally...."

"The Mob."

"Yes. And of course he couldn't pay the interest, the, uh—"

"The vig. Vigorish."

"Right. He couldn't pay, so they did what they do in such cases. First they broke his thumbs. He could still work, so that wasn't too bad. But the next time they put him in the hospital. And the last time they killed him. Two men beat him to death."

She couldn't think of anything else to say, so she simply said, "I'm sorry."

"Thanks. I was overseas when it happened. I took a month's leave and came home. After the funeral I helped my mother settle his affairs—there wasn't much left to settle—and I made sure my sister went back to college."

"I'm guessing you paid a big chunk of her tuition."

"Well, she had scholarships, but, yes, I paid some."

"You're too good to be one of us, Mori. Something bad must have happened."

"It did. I used what was left of my leave to find those two men. With what the Company had taught me, it wasn't that hard."

He paused again, so long that she prompted him. "And?"

"I killed them."

She wanted to ask him how, but then she realized it didn't matter. Just as it didn't matter how she'd killed her three. Mori's victims were just as dead as hers, and that was the only salient fact.

"Were you caught?"

"No, I was careful about the time and place. But I knew the people they'd worked for could figure out who'd done it—who had a motive to do it. So I thought they might come after me, and perhaps that would have happened, but the Enterprise found me first."

"I've wondered if the AD has contacts in the Mob."

Mori set his lips in a straight line. "You don't have to wonder. He phoned me three days later and suggested that if I wanted to avoid murder or prison, I should meet with him. And so here I am."

"Wow. That's some story." She thought about what he'd told her. "I guess he fixed things up with the CIA."

"Just like your right hand clapping your left. They're really just two sides of the same coin, you know—the Company and the Enterprise. The white and the black."

"Or both are shades of gray. Just like us."

"Yes, I suppose we are all gray."

"And we're shades. In the classical sense."

"What?"

"In Greek mythology 'shades' were the dead lingering among the living. That's us."

He thought about that for a moment. Then he looked at her. "You're right. That's us."

❑   ❑   ❑

Lee showed up a few minutes later. He looked hot and tired, so Smith suggested the three of them go to the bar for a drink. Initially Mori demurred, which made her wonder if he thought they were lovers and wanted to be alone, but she insisted and he finally agreed.

The bar was the usual airport overpriced tackiness, but the waiter was efficient and the drinks were cold. Smith smiled at her comrades and raised her glass. "To our success."

"Yes," Lee said, clinking her glass with his. "To our success."

Mori hesitated a moment, then joined in. "To success. At least I hope we're successful."

"Come on," Lee said, "that's no way to talk. Confidence is half the battle."

"What's the other half?"

Lee looked at her. "Kicking the other guy's ass. Hard."

"Then that's what we'll do."

She looked at Mori until he nodded, but he didn't say anything. He took a sip of his soda and then just sat there, staring into the glass. She glanced at Lee, saw him frowning at Mori, and shook her head to keep Lee from saying anything else.

After they finished their drinks they went back to the boarding area and eventually got on the plane. The three of them had widely separated seats—she was sure the AD had seen to that—and she politely discouraged the mild flirtation begun by the businessman sitting next to her.

The flight was long and Smith was tired, so she slept most of the way instead of reading as she'd planned. She passed Lee once on the way to the latrine—he was sleeping too—and she remembered their flight from the training base to Andrews.

That seemed like a long time ago.

They landed in Tokyo in mid-afternoon, tired and dehydrated. They'd traveled light—one bag each, small enough to fit easily into the overhead bin—so they went straight to the rental counter to get the car reserved for them. Mori asked for and got a road map, his Japanese earning him a bright smile from the attractive woman behind the counter.

Smith thought of the pretty woman, Wakahisa Chikako, who would be at the compound and how Mori had stared at her picture. She hadn't asked Mori about her just as she didn't want Mori to ask her any questions about Lee.

So many secrets, she thought. I begin to see why the AD is the way he is. The less he says, the less he reveals. Except when he reveals things in other ways—like the way he looks at me sometimes.

The AD had told them they'd find a briefcase full of money in the trunk, and they did: $50,000 in Japanese bills. Enough, the AD had said, to prove their cover story and whet the terrorists' appetite for more.

"But not so much that they'll be tempted to consider it enough and kill you to eliminate witnesses."

The AD had smiled then, but Smith didn't see any humor in his remark. She thought there was a very good chance the terrorists would kill the three of them—or at least Lee and herself. Maybe they'd spare

Mori, a fellow Japanese, but that wouldn't do her or Lee any good. No, she didn't see anything to smile about. But then, the AD wasn't going on the mission.

In the car they opened their envelopes, memorized their cover names, and put away their documents and pocket money. It was getting easier, Smith thought. Assuming a new identity, pretending to be someone you're not. Sort of like a snake shedding its skin.

She didn't like the snake analogy even though she knew it applied—especially if the snake were poisonous. She sighed and told herself to think of something else.

Mori drove. Lee had asked Smith if she wanted shotgun, but she told him to take it. She sat in the back and watched Japan go by—mile after mile of office buildings that finally gave way to miles of suburbs that all looked alike. She thought of the irony of doing all this traveling for the Enterprise but never really seeing anything of the places she visited.

Then she wondered if this would be the last place she'd see. She hoped not.

While they were still in traffic, Mori said nothing, concentrating on driving. But when they were finally in the countryside—farm land divided into small, neat parcels with indistinguishable figures moving in the fields—he briefed them on their cover.

"You work with me at a software company I founded a year ago. These people like the fact that I started the company and you work for me."

"We, the round-eyed people with big noses."

Mori glanced at her in the mirror and smiled, making her glad she'd forced him to open up at the airport. "Yes, that's exactly what they say. In Japanese, of course, so you don't understand."

"No reason they should be less prejudiced than anyone else. Us included."

"Anyway, we just made a lot of money selling an app to Microsoft."

"Can't they check that?"

She couldn't see Lee's face, but she knew from his tone that he was frowning.

"No, the deal was secret, and the app hasn't gone live yet. I've already told them that. I also told them that we have another killer app in the works that's going to make us a lot more money."

"You didn't really say 'killer app,' did you?"

Mori glanced at her again. "Uh, yes, I think I did. Over the top?"

"No, I've heard the term, but I can't picture your saying it. What if these people start asking me technical questions? I don't know shit about programming."

"That's okay—neither of you is supposed to be a programmer. You're the head of sales and Lee is our CFO."

"Lee, remember: that's 'CFO,' not 'UFO.'"

He laughed dryly and turned to look at her. "Don't worry. If they ask me anything, I'll say what they really should hear is your secret for making sales."

"How can I tell them if it's a secret?"

"Good point."

Mori cleared his throat. "The safest thing is just to say that we don't talk about what we have under development. I told these guys a lot about the company—in a general way, of course—so I don't think they'll have many questions other than how much more money we can give them and when."

"I assume that you're going to say 'a lot' and 'soon.' At least I hope so."

"Yes, Smith. That's the answer. The only answer."

CHAPTER FIFTEEN

By seven in the evening they were near the compound, but they had decided to wait until morning to make their appearance. Mori knew of a *ryokan*, a traditional guesthouse, nearby, and they went there.

They were lucky—the elderly innkeeper had two rooms available. Mori translated and then waited while Smith and Lee looked at each other.

Mori knows, she thought. Or at least he suspects.

After a moment Lee said, "We should let Smith have her own room," and Mori nodded.

Mori handled the arrangements, exchanging polite bows with the old man and speaking to him in Japanese. Smith could see that, despite the black cloud of the mission hanging over them, Mori liked being back in Japan.

And why shouldn't he? Smith thought. It's his homeland. She wondered whether that fact would affect his performance on the mission—whether it would slow him down, make him reluctant to act when the time came.

She hoped not. To have any hope of surviving this mission—walking unarmed into what amounted to an enemy fort—all three of them were going to have to be at their best.

They put their bags in their rooms and then relaxed together, drinking green tea from delicate porcelain cups, while the innkeeper and a young woman who worked for him prepared dinner.

They ate Japanese style, sitting at a low table on a mat made of rice straw—a *tatami*, Mori said—and using chopsticks to pick up the grilled fish, steamed vegetables, and, of course, white rice. Mori handled the sticks expertly, Lee awkwardly, and Smith somewhere in between. They were jetlagged, and none of them said much over the meal.

After they finished, the young woman came in to collect the dishes. Mori spoke to her, and Smith caught *arigatou*, "thanks," the only Japanese word she knew. The innkeeper returned and spoke to Mori, gesturing toward the garden Smith could see through a window.

"He says we are free to enjoy the, well, patio would be our word for it. He says that the spring flowers are fragrant in the evening air and that there is a good view of the moon tonight. Also, there is a *yoku-jou*, a hot tub, in case we want to—his words—'soak away our cares.'"

Smith had thought she was ready for bed, but the thought of soaking in warm water under the stars was enticing. She looked at Lee, who seemed to have the same idea.

"That sounds good," Lee said. "But I don't think I brought—"

"You just need a robe and a towel," Mori said. "They're in our rooms."

"Okay," Smith said, getting to her feet a bit more stiffly than she'd anticipated. "See you there."

In her room, which was small and simply furnished but had a certain charm, she undressed, hanging her clothes in the tall wooden cabinet that served as a closet. She was surprised at all the features of the Japanese toilet, which had a warmed seat and push buttons to spray water, activate a dryer, and even play music. After she used it and brushed her teeth, she slipped into the cotton robe with a long belt that she found hanging on the back of the bathroom door, picked up a towel, and padded out toward the garden.

The evening air was a bit chilly, but the scent of the flowers was as lovely as the innkeeper had promised, and the sight of the moon—a silver crescent against a black-velvet sky studded with stars—was almost breathtaking. The hot tub, wooden-walled and looking large enough to hold four people comfortably, sat in the middle of an area paved with flagstones.

She saw that Mori and Lee were already soaking in the tub, their robes and towels on a wooden rack next to it. For an instant she remembered the last time she'd seen a hot tub, the twitchy, foreshortened way it had looked in the crosshairs of her rifle's telescopic sight. And she remembered how her target had looked as he slid, dead, down into the water, rapidly turning it from blue to pink to red.

She closed her eyes and shook her head. Thinking about that wasn't going to help her accomplish this mission. She'd need all her wits and a lot of luck just to stay alive.

Her comrades' low voices hushed as she walked over to the tub. "Hey, guys, don't let me interrupt your conversation."

"We're just speculating about tomorrow," Lee said.

"Oh, God, don't talk about it. Please, anything but that."

"Okay," Mori said, "we'll talk about something else."

"Or maybe we don't have to talk," Smith said as she hung her towel on the rack. "Maybe we can just enjoy the view and the water and—"

"And what?" Lee said.

Smith didn't answer. She'd noticed Mori staring at her, a strange expression on his face. "What?"

"Nothing."

"No, something, I think."

"It's just that... your robe."

"What about it?"

"I should have told you."

Smith flushed, irritated. "Told me what?"

"In Japan you're supposed to tuck the right side of the robe—the *yukata*—under the left."

"What difference does it make?"

"The only people who have the left side tucked under the right are the dead—corpses."

Her hot feeling vanished as quickly as it had come. "Oh. Yeah, you should have told me."

"Sorry."

She unbelted the robe, took it off, and draped it over the rack. When she turned around she saw Lee looking at her, obviously admiring her body. Mori was studying the moon, pretending that she wasn't standing there naked.

"Forget it. What I was going to say was that we should just enjoy this time together." Smith left unsaid the obvious point that this might be their last night alive.

"Good idea," Lee said. "Come on in—the water's fine."

"To coin a phrase." She climbed carefully up the three steps and eased over the side to stand in the tub. "It's okay, Mori. You can look if you want. I'm sure you're way more embarrassed than I am."

Now he did turn to look at her, and she was certain that if the light were better, she'd see him blushing. She smiled at him as she slid down into the warm water, which felt wonderful on her body, tired from their trip and bruised from their intensive training. "There—that's one less secret I have for you."

"Yes," Mori said. Then he added abruptly, "You are very beautiful. I hope you do not mind me saying that."

"My friend, no woman ever minds being told she's beautiful. Even if, like me, she doesn't believe it."

"You should believe it," Lee said.

"You two are going to spoil me. If I get back, I'll have to spend some quality time with the AD to make up for it."

Lee looked at her. "Don't say 'if'—say 'when.'"

She stuck her tongue out at him. "When. And I hope saying it makes it come true."

He kept looking at her as though to memorize her face. "So do I."

They were silent then, each thinking his or her own thoughts. Smith had a question but wondered if this were a good time to ask it. Then she decided there would never be a better time.

"Mori, what about the woman—Wakahisa Chikako?"

There was a long pause before he said, "Uh, what about her?"

"What's she like?"

"Well, she's very smart. She actually makes a lot of the group's decisions, but she lets the men, especially Himura, the leader, take the credit."

"I know how that works," Smith said dryly. "What else?"

"She's very dedicated to this cause. Her great-grandfather and his wife died at Hiroshima, so Chikako hates—I mean really hates—nuclear weapons and even nuclear power. That's why she's part of this group."

Smith noted his easy use of the woman's first name. "Well, I can understand her position even if I don't agree with it."

"Yes, me too. And...."

"What?"

"Nothing."

"Come on, Mori. We're walking in there tomorrow with nothing but big smiles and a wad of cash. We have to know what we're up against."

"Well, she's very nice."

Smith glanced at Lee, whose expression told her that he was thinking the same thing she was.

"'Nice'? What does that mean?"

"Just what I said. Nice. Easy to talk to. She was very good to me—she made me feel welcome, not like...."

"Not like what?"

"A banana."

"What?"

"A banana," Lee said. "Yellow on the outside, white on the inside."

"Yes," Mori said, clearly embarrassed by the subject. "The men tended to treat me like any other American who speaks Japanese. Not like this is my homeland."

"Mori." Lee spoke quietly but there was an edge in his voice.

"Yes?"

"Are you sure where your loyalties lie in this thing? I mean, are you prepared to do what we came here to do?"

He hesitated briefly before he said, "Yes."

Despite the warmth of the water, Smith felt a chill down her spine. "Mori, please don't think this question is intrusive, but we really have to know—are you and Chikako lovers?"

"That's none of your business!"

She sighed, pretty sure she already knew the answer. "Yes, it is. Because if you are—well, that's a major problem for this mission. So we have to know."

This time Mori hesitated for so long that she could hear crickets chirping and the night wind rustling the leaves of the trees. She wondered if this garden was the last beautiful thing she'd ever see.

Then Mori spoke, so softly that she had to strain to hear it. "Yes, we made love. Only once. Iwao found us in bed together and was furious."

"Iwao? Oh, Himura, the leader."

"Yes. They used to be together, and he was very jealous. Plus he thought it was undisciplined of her."

Well, it was, Smith thought, but then love always is. Maybe that's part of the reason we love to be in love.

"What did he do to her?" Lee asked the question before she could.

"He dragged her into the hall and hit her—several times. She had bruises later. I wanted to stop him, but another of them pulled a gun on me. And because of my cover story, I couldn't do anything to take it away from him. After that Chikako avoided speaking to me, and Iwao made sure that she and I were never alone together."

"Well, soon you'll get a chance to pay him back."

"Yes. Please leave him to me."

"If we can," Lee said. "We don't know how things will play out."

"Of course." Mori was silent for a few moments. "I don't like that memory, but I think it will help me. To do what I have to, I mean." He looked at Smith and Lee. "Well, I'm going to bed. See you in the morning."

He climbed gracefully out of the tub, and Smith admired his sleek, smoothly muscled body as he put on his robe. He hesitated a moment, then pointedly tucked the left side under the right. "This is no time to be superstitious. Whatever happens tomorrow, we'll deal with it. Good night." He gave them a little wave and walked away.

Smith glanced at Lee, who was watching her, a slight smile on his face. "What?"

"Nothing."

"No—what?"

"You like to look, I see."

"Don't be silly. I... I was just curious, that's all."

"Sure. And he was just curious when he looked at you earlier."

She slid over to him. "Maybe. But when you looked it wasn't from curiosity, was it? Because you've seen me naked before."

"Yes, and I don't mind saying I enjoyed it—both times."

She found him with her hand and stroked him gently, feeling him swell against her fingers. "And how about this, Marine? Do you enjoy this too?"

"You know I do, but let's not get carried away. That old man or the girl could come out here any time."

"But what if you... come first?"

"No, seriously, we need to talk about something."

"All right." She took her hand away. "What is it?"

"This Chikako. How did the AD miss that? I mean, what happened between Mori and her?"

"I don't know. Maybe he's just not interested in romance—or sex—and doesn't factor those things in when planning a mission."

"Well, she's going to be a problem."

Smith sighed. "Yes, I know. It doesn't sound like Mori's in love with her, but I'm not sure he'd kill her. So you or I will have to, no matter where we are or what position we're in."

"I'll do it."

Smith looked at him. "Why? You think I can't kill a woman?"

"No, I'm sure you can do whatever has to be done. But let me do it. That way it'll be easier for you—afterward."

"Afterward? Do you... do you have dreams about it?"

"The last mission?"

"Yes."

"Not every night but often enough. Bad dreams. I remember you told me that you do too."

"Yeah. Nightmares. I wake up sweating and crying, alone in the dark."

He kissed her cheek and hugged her. "Don't worry. They'll stop."

"You sure?"

He paused. "No. But I hope so. For both of us."

"I hope so too. All right—I know it won't do any good to argue with you. You take the woman."

"Good. Now we should get some rest. We'll need it tomorrow."

They got out of the tub and into their robes and walked inside. At the doorway to her room she pulled his face down to hers and kissed him long and deeply. Then she took his hand and led him inside, closing the door softly behind them.

She'd been afraid that he, with his constant focus on the mission, might say no, that both of them needed to sleep. But she couldn't bear the thought of not making love to him on what might well be their final night together.

She slid off her robe and stood there before him, proud of her toned body and glad of the way the sight of it aroused him. She kissed him again, and it was even better this time.

She untied his robe and slipped it off his broad shoulders as she kissed his neck and chest. After a moment he pulled his arms from the sleeves and let the robe drop to the tatami. He put his arms around her, and she leaned into him, feeling warm and secure in his embrace.

"There's only one good thing about this whole shitty mess I've gotten myself into," he said.

"What's that?" Before he had time to answer she kissed him again, wishing that the two of them could stay forever just as they were at that moment.

He pulled his head back just far enough to look at her. "You."

She smiled and reached down to cup him in her hand. "Hmm, I can tell that you mean what you say. At least this part of you does."

"The part that does my thinking."

She laughed. "Some of it anyway. But that can be a good thing from time to time. But aren't we wasting time talking?"

"I thought women liked to talk when... well, now."

"You don't know much about women, do you?"

"No, I guess I don't."

"Then it's my job to teach you."

He started to speak, but she put a finger on his lips. "No, no more talking for a while. Not until later. I'll show you that actions really do speak louder than words."

And she did. She took him to bed, and they made love in a long, slow rhythm that was like ocean waves rolling into shore.

At first they used their lips and fingers, gently for a while and then more and more urgently. She felt her insides growing warm as her breathing quickened and she opened herself to him as a dew-wet flower opens to the morning sun.

Then they came together like two different but interlocking parts of a whole—which of course they were—and when he entered her it was as though she were a girl again, experiencing love for the first time.

They moved together, each conscious of the other's pace, and once she opened her eyes to see him above her, his eyes closed, the taut muscles of his face showing he was focused solely on the moment, solely on what was happening between them.

She felt herself melting in the heat of that moment, and then, simultaneously rising to meet him and pulling him down and deeper into her, she felt something like an electric current run through her body. She caught her breath, bit her lip, tasting blood, and then sobbed out his name.

He made one final thrust, drilling down to the core of her being, and spent himself in one long stream, groaning as he arched his back and clutched her arms so hard that she bit her lip again.

Then they lay still, each of them panting lightly, each of them conscious of the cool night air moving over their naked, sweating bodies. After a minute Lee moved off her and lay on his back, pulling her to lie on her side, facing him. He kissed her on the forehead.

"I hope that's not the last time, but if it is, I'm satisfied."

"Me too. It's...."

"What?"

"It's never been that like before with me."

"Like what? I know you've had an orgasm before. At least I—"

"No. I mean, yes, I did. I wouldn't try to fool you about that. It's just never been so... strong, so powerful. Oh, I don't know how to describe it."

"Must be my superior technique." He grinned to show he was teasing.

She slapped his chest lightly. "Your technique is okay—just fine, in fact. Maybe it's that we're getting comfortable with each other... this way. Or maybe it's...." She didn't finish the sentence.

"Maybe it's the thought of tomorrow." He whispered the words.

"Yes, and you know I don't want to think about that now."

"Nor do I. So think about this: I love you."

She raised up to look him in the eye. "You do? You're sure."

"Yes, and I'm sure."

"Even knowing that I've killed people?"

"Yes. It's not like I haven't."

She thought about that for a moment, then nodded. "I know. I love you too even though...."

"What?"

"I'm not sure I deserve love."

"Why? Why don't you deserve it as much as anyone?"

"Because I don't think I'm a good person."

"Well, I think you are. Having this job doesn't make you bad. It's not like you had a choice."

She moved closer to him and kissed his cheek. "Yes, I did. We all did. We didn't have to take the job, and we certainly didn't have to do what we did to be offered the job."

He frowned. "I don't know. I'm not sure life gave us much choice."

"So you believe in fate?"

He thought about that for a moment. "I don't know. I believe in me— and in you. And I believe we should do what we have to do to stay alive. Every day."

"Including tomorrow."

"Yes. Definitely tomorrow."

"I guess we should get some sleep then."

"Yes." He began to get up.

"No, don't go. Stay here tonight."

He rolled out of bed and stood, looking down at her.

"You know that if I do we won't sleep much."

"But we'll be together. Maybe for the—"

"Hush." He put a finger to her lips. "Don't say it. Don't make it come true."

She wanted to protest, to talk him into staying with her, but she knew he was correct that they needed sleep and would get more of it in separate beds. "Okay. I guess you're right. I'll see you in the morning."

He leaned down to kiss her. "Good night. Sleep well."

"You too."

He took a step and then turned to look back at her. "And no dreams."

She smiled. "No dreams. Good night."

He picked up his robe and towel and left, closing the door softly behind him.

She lay in the strange bed in the strange house and thought she would have trouble falling asleep. But she was so tired from the flight and the long day that sleep came quickly.

And she slept soundly enough to keep the dreams away.

CHAPTER SIXTEEN

They were close enough to the compound that they didn't need to leave early in the morning. Smith got up a little after eight and felt better than she'd expected, given their long trip and the stress they were under. After she showered and dressed, she found Mori having a simple breakfast at a table in the garden.

"Mind if I join you?"

He stood and gestured at another place setting. "Please do. I hope you slept well."

"Pretty well, considering."

He knew what she meant, so he said nothing while she poured herself some tea and put fruit and steamed vegetables on her plate.

Lee came out while they were still eating. He was clearly on edge, thinking about what they were going to do that day. He got a cup of tea and drank it while he roamed around the garden.

When he came over to refill his cup, Smith said, "Why don't you sit down? Eat something?"

"Too keyed up. Too much adrenaline."

"Already?"

"Sure. I was always like this—right before a football game, right before a field exercise in the Corps. And now...."

"I know." She looked at him, trying to memorize his face so she'd never forget it. She didn't let herself think about why she was doing that. "I know."

She put down her own cup and looked at Mori. "Guess we better go soon, huh?"

He glanced at his watch. "Yes. I'll pay the innkeeper and meet you at the car." He took a last bite of breakfast, then stood and walked back inside.

Smith stood too and looked around the garden, feeling grateful to have experienced something so simple and lovely. So peaceful. Even if peace was something she didn't know much about.

"Ready?"

Lee nodded and put his cup on the table. "As ready as I'll ever be. I hate to tell you this, but I have a bad feeling about the mission. Going into that compound, outnumbered...."

"Yes, but much better trained. And knowing what's going to happen."

"Knowing what we want to do, but not what we'll be able to do.

That's partly up to them, how they react to us."

"Sure. That's always the case in a mission like this, one where you have to get close."

"Like your last one?"

She shook her head, not wanting to think about it. "Not like that, I hope, but close. A lot closer than I'd like to be."

He stepped next to her and put his hand on her cheek. "But not as close as we were last night."

She put her hand on his. "No, there's nothing as close as that." She gave him a quick smile and then turned to go inside. He followed her without speaking.

As she carried her bag from her room she saw Mori counting bills into the old man's palm. When he finished they bowed to each another. The old man spoke quietly to Mori, who responded. Then the old man came over to her and bowed.

She didn't know what else to do, so she bowed back. That seemed to please the old man, and he said something to her in Japanese.

She looked at Mori, who said, "He thanks you for honoring his humble house and hopes that you will take his blessing and God's with you as you leave."

"Please thank him for his hospitality and tell him that I enjoyed our stay here—most of all I enjoyed his peaceful garden."

Mori translated, and the old man smiled. He bowed again, and she bowed back. Then she and Mori walked out to the car, where Lee was waiting, staring off at the distant mountains.

"Game time, Lee."

He turned to look at her. "That's right—and some game."

They put their bags in the trunk and got into the car, Mori behind the wheel. Then they drove out of the courtyard and headed for the compound, each of them wondering whether it would be a one-way trip.

An hour later they pulled up in front of the compound. A sliding metal gate barred the entrance. Someone had reinforced the gate by welding steel bars onto it, and the structure looked very solid.

"This is new." Mori waved toward the gate. "I mean, they had a gate before but not this strong. Just the original school gate."

"Maybe they know they're beginning to attract attention," Lee said.

"Maybe. I guess that won't make our job any easier."

"No." Smith glanced at Mori, then back at Lee. "It won't."

Mori got out of the car and walked to one side of the entrance. He pressed a button that was on the wall just below a speaker grille.

Smith put her window down. After a few seconds she heard a tinny voice speak in Japanese. Mori answered in the same language, and he and the tinny voice talked to each other for a while. As the conversation went on, Mori became animated, raising his voice and making gestures. Finally he heard something that caused him to stop talking and return to the car.

"You have to get out. They want to see you."

"Why? Don't they trust you?" Smith kept her voice low so that the microphone at the entrance wouldn't pick it up.

"Yes, I think so, but only up to a point." Mori spoke as softly as she had. "I'm sure they think my timing is bad—returning while they're planning their big operation. Plus I never said anything about bringing other people, so they're surprised you're here. But come on—let's not take too long discussing it."

Smith and Lee looked at each other. She asked a question with her eyes, and he shrugged. Then they emerged, moving slowly, from opposite sides of the car.

Keeping his back to the gate, Mori made a slight gesture. "Come with me."

The three of them went wordlessly up to the gate. Mori spoke briefly, and the voice answered with what sounded like a single word.

After several seconds Smith said, "Are they going to come out?"

"No, they can see us." Mori nodded toward the cameras mounted on each side of the gate.

Smith spotted more cameras inside the compound. And there must be some we can't see, she thought. There'll probably be lots of surprises on both sides before this is over.

Mori spoke in Japanese but got no answer. After a few seconds he spoke again, more insistently. This time the voice answered. Even though she didn't understand the words, Smith thought the voice sounded annoyed.

"All right," Mori said, "they're going to let us inside. They're not happy that I've brought you with me, but they said they'll give me—us—a chance to explain. And I mentioned that we brought them some money."

Shit! Smith thought. Should've saved that in case we need the leverage. But it's too late now.

Mori glanced at the cameras again, then looked back at Smith and Lee. "Okay, let's get in the car."

As they walked back to the car and slid into their seats, the gate began to open. By the time Mori drove forward, there was enough room for them to get through.

Smith turned her head and saw the gate begin to close as soon as they had passed through it. "Well, we're in. Now let's see if we can get out. I'm not sure the car can crash through that gate."

"Let's hope we don't have to try." Lee's voice was tight. "We'll find the control. Let's look around for it as we go in."

"All right, but let's not be too obvious about it," Smith said. "Remember we're supposed to be normal young Americans—rich and not too bright."

Mori went slowly down the driveway until he came to where several other vehicles were parked in front of the main building. He pulled in next to a light van and turned off the engine. They sat silently for a minute, but no one emerged from any of the buildings.

"Now what?" Smith heard the hint of nervousness in her voice and silently cursed herself. She hoped Lee and Mori hadn't noticed how she sounded.

"I guess we knock on the door," Mori said. "That's the main entrance over there." He pointed to double doors fronted by a flag pole. There was no flag on the pole.

"Let's go." Lee opened his door and got out. Smith followed and Mori came last, locking the car and putting the key in his pocket. Watching him, Smith wondered if the Japanese group would let him keep the key.

Well, it wouldn't matter. If the three of them were successful, they'd get the key back. And if they weren't successful.... She forced herself to finish the thought: then they wouldn't need the key.

Mori led the way to the double doors. There was no bell or knocker, so he rapped on the glass with his knuckles. There was a loud click, and a man who'd apparently been standing to one side of the doors reached out to swing a door inward.

They walked inside, and the man shut the door behind them. The lock clicked again as loudly as before. Smith saw a man standing about 10 feet in front of them. He was unarmed, but the two men behind and to either side of them cradled small machine guns—Uzis, Smith thought.

She recognized the face of the man in front of them and, glancing at the man who'd opened the door, recognized him too. She didn't see the woman.

The man in front of them looked angry, but nevertheless he bowed slightly before speaking in Japanese. Mori returned the bow and the greeting.

"This is Himura Iwao," Mori said. "He welcomes us to his... well, I guess 'headquarters' is the right word. And this is Tanaka Tadao, his deputy." The man by the door, whose face was expressionless, also bowed and greeted them.

Smith didn't know what else to say, so she simply said, "Hello." Lee just nodded. Neither of them bowed.

Mori spoke at some length in Japanese, and Smith caught the use of her cover name and Lee's. When he finished, Himura was silent, studying them. Then he said, in heavily accented but correct English, "We are encouraged by your wish to help us. However, your appearance here is highly unusual and does not come at the best possible time. Still, let us discuss how you and we may be able to work together."

Tanaka added something in Japanese. Mori nodded and turned to Smith and Lee. "First they are going to search us," he murmured. "It's standard procedure with visitors—not that they let many people in here. Take everything out of your pockets and put it on that table."

The three of them emptied their pockets and made separate piles on a low table near the doors. Tanaka went through their goods, handing their passports to Himura, who took a long look at each one. While he was doing that, Tanaka patted them down. He did it effectively but, Smith was relieved to note, impersonally, not taking advantage of the procedure to touch her more than he needed to.

When he was finished he spoke a single word in Japanese and Himura nodded as he handed the passports to Tanaka. "To ensure that there is no possible basis for... misunderstanding, we are going to verify your passports."

Smith wondered how they were going to do that, but then she remembered the AD's saying this group had contacts within the Japanese government. The check itself didn't worry her—she knew it would show that the passports were legitimate and that the three Americans were who they said they were. But she could tell that Himura was no fool and might question their cover story.

He looked at each of them closely, letting his gaze linger on Smith, who looked into his eyes with what she hoped was a neutral expression on her face. After a few seconds he smiled slightly and made a gesture. "Please collect your belongings and follow me."

They stuffed their wallets and other things back in their pockets. Smith made sure to retrieve the lucky quarter she'd had since finding it at the end of an exhausting run in boot camp. She wasn't superstitious, and having the coin hadn't kept bad things from happening to her. Some very bad. Still, touching the coin reminded her that she had inner reserves of strength she could draw on when necessary.

Like now, she thought.

Himura led them to a conference room that obviously had formerly been a classroom. The whiteboard still hung on the wall, and a low line of cubbyholes showed where the students had stored their books and backpacks. The room reminded Smith of her several elementary schools, and although she was only 26, those days seemed a lifetime ago.

"Please sit down." Himura pointed toward the chairs around the rectangular table.

The three of them chose places—none facing away from the door—and sat. As soon as they did a woman rolled in a cart holding tea and rice cakes. Smith looked at the woman closely. She was young and pretty, but she wasn't Wakahisa Chikako.

"I hope you will have some refreshment." Himura stood just inside the doorway, not obviously blocking the exit but blocking it just the same. "Our food is simple but nutritious. We try to be health-conscious in all things."

Smith noticed that the woman served Lee first, then Mori, and her last. Smith took the cup offered her and said one of the few Japanese words she knew: "*Arigatou.*"

"*Douitashimashite.*"

Smith assumed that meant "you're welcome," and she smiled at the woman, but the woman kept her face impassive.

Himura turned to Smith. "Do you speak Japanese?"

"No, unfortunately not. I know only a few words. But your English is excellent. Did you study in the United States?"

"Yes, I was at Stanford for three years. I earned a master's degree in economics."

"Impressive." Smith really was impressed. She regretted her lack of formal education and envied people with college degrees. Her schooling had been of an entirely different sort.

"It was his study of economics that led Himura-san to believe that the world's present path is unsustainable," Mori said. "We cannot go on poisoning the earth forever. Eventually it will die, and we will die along with it."

"I see you have thought about the lessons you have learned when you were here before." Himura seemed pleased.

"Yes, and I have taught them to my colleagues. That is why they are here. And why we brought money to donate to the cause."

At the mention of money Himura's eyes brightened. "Yes, you said that. Excellent! You have it with you?"

"In the car."

Smith could tell that Himura wanted to ask how much they'd brought but was too polite to do so. "Fifty thousand dollars," she said. "We all contributed."

"Most impressive." Himura bowed. "You have our thanks."

"You are welcome," Mori said. "We want to do what we can to help you—all of you." He paused. "By the way, where is Chikako?"

Now Himura's smile was cold. Exactly like the AD's, Smith thought.

She suddenly realized that Himura and the AD might have a lot in common. If they did, she might be able to needle Himura, which could give her an advantage against him. And it would piss off the AD when she told him.

If she lived to tell him, she reminded herself, and that was a big if.

"She and three of our colleagues should be returning soon," Himura said. "I know she will be glad to see you." Again that cold smile.

"And I will be happy to see her again. She was my best teacher about the importance of your cause."

Smith couldn't tell whether Mori meant that ironically, but it seemed unlikely. Mori wasn't given to irony.

"I am sure she was."

But Smith felt certain that Himura was being ironic. Yes, just like the AD. She almost nodded before she saw Himura glance at her and caught herself.

"And Wakahisa Chikako will be pleased to meet you, Ms. Smith. I know she sometimes misses the company of other women."

"But you have at least one other woman here—the woman who served us." Smith wanted to find out exactly how many people they would have to deal with.

"Yes, but she is only a servant. She is not part of our organization."

Then perhaps we can spare her, Smith thought. But, no, the woman was now a witness, so she couldn't be left alive.

Tanaka entered the room, followed by the two men with machine guns. He went to Himura and whispered in his ear. Himura listened intently, frowned at what he heard, and looked at each of them in turn.

"Tadao is having difficulty verifying that you are who you say you are."

"What?" Mori sounded surprised, and Smith also heard a worried tone.

"Just what I said. He cannot find enough information to confirm your passports."

Smith thought about arguing that their passports were valid—and they were, in the sense that the U.S. government had issued them—but she knew that a real Margaret E. Jenkins wouldn't have made that argument. "Check our company's website—there's a bio for each of us."

"Yes." Himura gazed at her, his face impassive. "We have done that— we have read your company biographies. However, we cannot find anything else on the internet about you."

"We like to maintain our privacy. At least as much as one can do so these days." Lee sounded calm and sincere, and Smith nodded as if to confirm what he'd said.

"That is the point—no one can do it so well in this world of computers and networks."

"Computer experts can," Smith said, hoping no one would ask her about her nonexistent expertise in computers.

"Perhaps. But some of our friends in the Japanese government have warned us that occasionally young, fit Americans appear in unusual places around the world, and afterward people are found dead. People whose interests differ markedly from those of your government."

"That's crazy," Mori said. "It sounds like something out of a spy movie."

"Yes, it does. But that does not mean it cannot be true." Himura stared at Mori, his expression harder than before. "I have reason to regret that we were not more careful when you were with us previously. However, we will certainly make up for that now." He turned to Tanaka. "Lock them up separately, and we will question them."

Once again he looked at each of them in turn. "If you are who you say you are, you have nothing to fear. But if you are not... well, we shall see."

CHAPTER SEVENTEEN

Two hours later Smith was still sitting alone in the small, window-less room where they had left her, locking the door behind them. The chair she sat on was the only thing in the room, which looked as though it had been an office when the school was in operation.

The Enterprise had taught her how to pick locks like the one in the doorknob, but she had nothing to use as a pick. The door looked too solid to break down, either by kicking it or hitting it with the chair. Moreover, she didn't think that breaking down the door was the right tactical move even if she could do it.

She assumed that Himura and his team were questioning Mori and Lee separately and would eventually get to her to compare their three stories. She hoped that no matter how tough the questioning got, Mori and Lee would stick to the cover story. She was pretty sure Lee would, but she wasn't so sure about Mori. Especially if Wakahisa questioned him. But maybe she was wrong. She hoped she was.

Finally she heard footsteps and then a key sliding into the lock. She stood so that they wouldn't be able to come in and stand over her.

A tall, slim woman entered, and Smith recognized her as Wakahisa from her photograph. With her long black hair, high cheekbones, and bright-dark eyes she was even more striking in person than she'd been in the picture.

Smith was surprised to see her—she'd expected Himura himself or maybe Tanaka. But maybe they thought a woman could get more in-formation from her. Smith resolved not to let that happen.

A large, muscular man Smith hadn't seen before followed Wakahisa. She must have brought him and others back with her, Smith thought.

The man carried a folding chair. He opened it and put it a few feet from Smith's chair. Then he went back to the door, closed it, and leaned against it. He didn't touch the pistol, a Glock, that hung from his belt, but he kept his hand near it.

Smith noted that the door was now unlocked, but she tried to put the thought out of her mind so that her face wouldn't betray what she was thinking.

Wakahisa bowed politely. "Ms. Jenkins, I am Chikako Wakahisa."

Smith noticed that the woman said her name in the Western order. She returned the bow, hoping it would buy her some goodwill.

"I understand that you were searched but not strip-searched. Is that right?"

Smith decided that Maggie Jenkins would be offended by the question. "Of course! I didn't appreciate being searched at all, and I certainly wouldn't agree to get naked for it."

Wakahisa paused. "I regret the necessity, but now you must do exactly that."

Smith acted stunned. "Why? Why on earth would I?"

"Because I am asking you to. And if you do not agree, I—we—will force you." She said a few words in Japanese, and the man pushed off the door and stepped next to Wakahisa.

"What is the need?" Smith wasn't carrying anything in her body, so she wasn't afraid of being searched, but she knew that her cover character would be terrified simply because of the humiliation.

"We have reason to believe that you and your companions are not who you say you are. That you are not really here to help us."

"But why else would we be here?" Smith put a plaintive note in her voice.

"I do not know. To spy on us perhaps. You tell me."

"We're here because we believe in your cause and want to support you! We believe in a green world just as much as you do."

Wakahisa arched one of her delicate eyebrows. "Really? Then how do you explain this?" She pulled something from her pocket and held it in her palm.

Smith looked down and had to force herself not to react. Wakahisa was holding a small surveillance microphone, probably one that Mori had planted.

"What's that?"

"I think you know."

"No, I don't."

"It is a listening device put here to intercept our conversations. We think your friend Joe did it." She was referring to Mori's cover name, Joe Yamaguchi.

"I can't believe that."

"Well, I can. We found it two days ago, and we are glad to have this unforeseen chance to ask him about it in person."

The timing could explain why the AD hadn't told them the Japanese had found the mic. Of course, he might not have told them anyway. Although the mission was already compromised when they began, she knew that wouldn't necessarily have stopped the AD from sending them on it. Not if he thought that despite the increased risk they could still find some way of carrying it out. They were all expendable in his eyes, and she knew that too.

"I'm sure Joe told you he didn't do it."

Wakahisa smiled slightly. "Yes, he denied everything. Despite our... encouragement that he tell the truth."

Smith drew in her breath. "What did you do to him?"

"Nothing permanent—yet."

"How could you? I mean, the two of you—"

"What?" Wakahisa leaned toward Smith, anger in her eyes. "What about the two of us?"

Smith chose her words carefully. "I thought that perhaps you cared about him."

"Perhaps I do. Or did until we discovered that he is a spy. But I care about our cause more." She paused. "I am sure you understand. The one who calls himself Bill Roberts keeps asking about you, asking whether we have done anything to hurt you. I think he is more than just your colleague, yes?"

Smith knew she meant Lee. "He is a good friend."

"I am sure he is. So good that you must know about the tattoo on his arm."

Shit! Lee was supposed to have that removed. Enterprise operatives weren't supposed to have any identifying marks.

"What about it?"

"You seem to have many questions but little information. His bull-dog tattoo means that Roberts was in the U.S. Marine Corps at some point."

"So?"

"So it seems unlikely that such a man, a soldier, would be who he tells us he is."

"Nevertheless it is true."

"Well, we will see. Now take your clothes off."

Smith hesitated, as she knew Jenkins would. Then slowly she began getting undressed. Wakahisa and the man watched her—the woman clinically and the man with more personal interest. Soon her clothes were piled on the chair and she stood before them in the nude.

Wakahisa walked around her, looking her up and down. "You are very fit. Not fat like most Americans. You must work hard at staying in shape."

"I like to work out. You look like you do too."

"Yes, I believe in a sound mind in a sound body. And one never knows when one will be called on for strength or endurance. Is that not so?"

Smith turned to look into the woman's eyes, trying without success to read them. "Yes, very true."

Wakahisa finished her circuit and stood in front of Smith again. "Now squat and cough."

"What?" Smith knew the drill from having been a guard in an Army prison overseas, but she figured Jenkins wouldn't know it.

"You heard me. Squat and cough. I want to see if you are hiding anything."

Much more than you know, Smith thought. She did as the woman directed, but nothing fell from her body. Despite her training and her determination not to, Smith felt herself blush. But she knew that Jenkins would have the same reaction, only enhanced, so it didn't matter.

Smith stood without being told and began putting her clothes back on. Wakahisa watched her, saying nothing.

When Smith was dressed, Wakahisa said, "Come with me."

The man opened the door and stood back while Wakahisa led the way out of the room and back to the conference room where they'd been earlier. When Smith saw what was in the room, she gasped.

Mori and Lee were gagged and bound to chairs. The cuts and bruises on their faces showed that the Japanese had beaten them. Apparently Mori had taken the worst of it—his head was lolling and blood dripped from his nose. He opened his eyes when he heard them enter the room. He looked at Smith and shook his head very slightly. For a moment there was fire in his eyes, but then it went out, and he closed them again.

Lee appeared more defiant. He held his head up and, despite his obvious pain, tried to grin at Smith. The gag kept most of his grin from getting through, but Smith was glad to see that he was still in the fight.

Five of the Japanese group were already in the room: Himura, Tanaka, the two armed men Smith had seen before, and a new man. Smith thought he must have been with Wakahisa when she returned to the compound.

She wondered if there were any more of the group around. She didn't want the odds to get any worse than they already were. As she glanced around the room she noticed the banded bundles of Japanese bills piled on the table next to the empty case. They must have done that while they were questioning Mori and Lee, she thought. It doesn't look like the money is going to buy us much after all.

Himura stepped toward Smith, anger darkening his face. "We trusted

Joe, and he has betrayed us. We now know that he hid that microphone and that he has come back to spy on us, bringing you as his accomplices."

Smith looked him in the eye. "Did he tell you that?"

"No, neither of them will say anything except to repeat what must be your cover story. But there is no other possible explanation. We can find nothing to verify who you are, and neither can our friends in the Japanese government."

"What about the money we brought you?" She gestured toward the stacks on the table. "That should prove something."

"It proves only that you are well financed, as you would be if you are what I think you are."

"Then what about our passports? They're certainly legitimate."

"Ah, yes, your passports. They do not appear to be counterfeits, but then they would not have to be if your government sent you here." He paused. "And speaking of passports, let me show you something." He snapped his fingers, and Tanaka handed him a small blue booklet.

"Here is your passport." Himura opened the booklet to the page that displayed her photograph and showed it to her.

"Now look at this." He turned to a laptop computer that sat on the table. He tapped a few keys and waited a moment while an image appeared on the screen. "Here is an enlargement of the passport photo an American woman used when she visited Honduras a few months ago." He stepped aside so she could see it.

The Justine McKinnon passport. Smith thought her blood would freeze in her body.

She forced herself to draw a breath, and then she glanced at Lee, who was watching the scene intently. When she turned back she saw that Wakahisa had noticed the look that had passed between the two of them. She also saw the ghost of a smile on the woman's face.

"Japanese intelligence got the picture from the Hondurans," Himura said. "They flagged Justine McKinnon, who also used the name Maria Tyler, as a probable U.S. government agent suspected of assassinating a labor leader there. When I sent my friend in intelligence your passport photo today, he sent me the other passport picture and this comparison."

Himura tapped a key and another image appeared. It was the McKinnon photo with her current passport picture superimposed on it. The hair styles and colors were different, and the mouth was blurred because of the different expressions in the original pictures, but the eyes, nose, and cheekbones matched.

"How do you explain this?" The sarcasm in his voice made Smith think of the AD, and she felt a surge of anger that he'd sent them on this hopeless mission. He must have known they wouldn't get out alive, but he was concerned only with how many of the Japanese eco-terrorists they could take with them.

"I can't explain it." Smith looked Himura in the eye. "I don't know anything about the McKinnon woman or how this comparison was produced. I do know that photos can be manipulated now so that they'll show almost anything."

"So you're not McKinnon or Maria Tyler? Not an American agent sent here to spy on us and perhaps kill us?"

"No, and I would think that the money we brought would be enough evidence of our good faith."

"We are glad to have the money, but the amount you brought would be a tiny investment for your government to make in moving against us."

"Then I guess nothing I say will convince you."

"I am already convinced that you are lying, all three of you." He turned to look at Mori and Lee. "But at least one of you will tell me the truth before we are done today."

Wakahisa spoke to him in Japanese. Whatever she said made Mori open her eyes again and look at Smith, then at Lee. Smith saw terror in Mori's eyes, and she felt a drop of cold sweat run down her back.

"Yes," Himura said, speaking almost to himself. "That would work." He looked at Tanaka and said something in Japanese.

Tanaka nodded and left the room. No one spoke during the short time he was gone. When he returned he was carrying a big kitchen knife. The blade glinted in the light and looked very sharp.

Himura looked at the knife and then looked at Smith. "You may not know this, but we have a tradition in Japan of marking in a permanent way those who make mistakes. I am sure your friend Joe understands—you must have noticed his finger."

"Yes, but that was not done by the Yakuza, and surely you are not comparing yourselves to criminals. I thought you were fighting for a better world."

"We are, but sometimes evil must be purified with blood. And we will use any means that may gain us victory."

"Victory will be worthless if you exchange your souls for it." Even as she spoke Smith realized the hypocrisy of her saying that. She also realized that it was the truth, and she wanted to scream at the position they were in. Maybe prison would have been preferable after all.

But not preferable to death, and it looked as though that's where they were headed.

"Enough of this talk. We want the truth, and you are going to give it to us." Himura looked at the two armed men and barked out what sounded like a command.

One of the men went to Lee and clamped his hands over one of Lee's, leaving Lee's fingers uncovered. Lee looked at Smith, his eyes wide and his gaze darting from his hand to her.

Smith took a step toward Himura. "Wait—"

The other man came to Smith, pulled a hand on her shoulder, and pulled out his pistol, another Glock, which seemed to be the group's standard firearm.

"No. We have waited long enough. Chikako is right—you care for this man and will talk rather than see him mutilated." He glanced at Tanaka and made a gesture.

Tanaka walked over to Lee. The deputy had a grim expression on his face as he held the knife above Lee's fingers. He looked at Himura, who turned back to Smith.

"Well?" He didn't raise his voice, but it seemed loud in the room, which had been silent except for the sound of Lee's rapid breathing.

"We've told you—"

Himura nodded and Tanaka moved the knife in a slicing motion. The little finger of Lee's left hand fell to the floor, and blood spurted from the wound. The gag muffled most of Lee's scream, but some of it got through.

Smith gasped and tried to go to Lee, but the armed man stopped her. Lee was slumped in the chair, staring at his hand, his blood covering the arm of the chair and dripping onto the floor.

"Now are you ready to talk?"

She glanced at Lee, who looked up at her, his eyes dull now, and shook his head.

"I have been talking, but you won't believe me—"

Himura made the gesture again, and again Tanaka used the knife. He cut off most of Lee's ring finger, and more blood spurted. Lee's muffled voice was now a howl of pain, and Smith knew that he might go into shock soon.

She made her decision. "Okay. Yes, we're government agents sent here to spy on you."

For a moment there was complete silence in the room. Then Himura looked into her eyes. "Just spy?"

Smith looked right back at him. "Yes, just spy. We have no weapons—what else could we do?"

Her answer seemed to satisfy Himura. He visibly relaxed, and the other Japanese did too, all except Wakahisa, who stepped toward Mori with anger in her eyes.

Himura turned toward Wakahisa and spoke in Japanese. His movement put his back to Smith, and she knew this moment was the only opportunity she might get. Moving faster than she knew she could, she snatched the pistol from the belt of the man next to her, threw her arm around Himura's neck, and put the muzzle against his head.

CHAPTER EIGHTEEN

Her sudden move froze the Japanese, and when she cocked the pistol the sound seemed loud in the room. By this time the other armed man was reacting. He raised his pistol and pointed it toward her, which meant he was really pointing it toward Himura.

"Drop it!" Smith squeezed her arm tighter, pulling Himura's head up and cutting off his wind even more. "Drop it right now or your boss is a dead man!"

Himura gurgled some words in Japanese. Smith thought he was probably telling the man to shoot anyway, but Tanaka stepped forward and said, "Do as she says."

The armed man spoke sharply in Japanese, and Tanaka answered in English, looking at Smith with a grim expression. "Do not worry. None of them will leave here—alive."

The man dropped his pistol, an angry look on his face.

Smith swung her gun toward Tanaka. "We'll see. Cut them loose." When Tanaka didn't move, she said, "Now! Or I'll shoot you."

Tanaka seemed to be calculating the odds of whether she would actually use the gun. He must have decided they were not in his favor. He moved slowly behind Lee and cut the ropes with a few swipes of the knife.

Lee stood and threw the remnants of the rope off him. He pulled a handkerchief from his pocket and wrapped it around the bloody stumps of his fingers. The white cloth quickly turned red, but at least he had slowed the bleeding.

Lee scooped up the dropped pistol as Tanaka finished cutting Mori's ropes. He pointed it toward Tanaka. "Drop the knife and get away from him."

Tanaka complied, and Lee pulled Mori from the chair. Mori moved sluggishly as though most of the life had gone out of him. Certainly most of the fight had.

"You are not going to make it." Tanaka looked at Lee, then at Smith. "There are too many of us, and others have guns. You may kill some of us, but you will be killed. Drop the weapons and we will let you go."

Smith didn't believe him, but the offer was tempting. Right now she'd settle for getting out alive even if that meant abandoning the mission. She glanced at Lee, who shook his head.

"That's bullshit, Tanaka." Lee let go of Mori, who managed to keep standing although he was swaying a little. "After what you've done and said to us, you can't afford to leave us alive."

"That's right," Wakahisa said. "So we won't."

She sprang catlike toward Mori, making a sound that was somewhere between a growl and a sob. She launched a high sweeping kick to Mori's head, and Smith thought she heard the snap of his neck breaking.

As Mori slumped to the floor Wakahisa spun toward Lee, who seemed frozen by what had happened to their friend. Smith quickly pushed Himura away and then aimed and fired at Wakahisa.

The bullet caught her in the shoulder and slowed her a bit, but she kept coming toward Lee. Smith shot her again, this time in the chest, and she fell toward Lee, her arms reaching for him. Lee finally moved, stepping out of the way as Wakahisa hit the floor and lay still.

When Himura gasped and moved toward Wakahisa, Lee shot him in the head, and he collapsed almost on top of her body, covering the blood that was beginning to pool under her.

Running footsteps made Smith turn, and she fired at Tanaka as he raced for the open door. She missed him, but she got two of the others and Lee got the remaining one as they followed Tanaka.

Smith ran to the door, kicked a body out of the way, and slammed the door shut. She stood to one side of the door with her back against the wall while Lee checked Mori for a pulse. Lee looked at Smith and shook his head.

"Goddamn it," Smith muttered. Well, at least his death had been quick and painless. Wakahisa had seen to that.

She checked the other three bodies, finding an extra magazine on the second one. She shoved the magazine in her pocket and checked the third man, the one who hadn't been armed.

He was still breathing. She dropped to her knees and took his head in her hands. His eyelids fluttered briefly and then closed. Smith jerked his head to one side and the breathing stopped.

She stood and looked at Lee. "That's five down. How many more do you think are out there?"

Lee tightened the handkerchief over the stumps of his fingers. The cloth was now brick-red but had stopped dripping blood. At least for the moment. "Maybe another five or six. They're probably all armed now."

"And we don't have much ammunition even with the extra mag."

"No, but we can't just sit here with our thumbs up our asses, waiting for them to get organized."

"No, and you still losing blood."

"Don't worry about me." He had a strange look on his face she'd never seen before. "I owe these bastards for chopping off my fingers. So I figure to get some payback. The main thing is to get you out of here."

"To get us out. And that laptop—must be tons of intel on it. Can you carry it?"

He closed the lid, tucked the computer under his left arm, and clamped down on it. "Yes," he said through gritted teeth. "At least until the shooting starts. Not sure after that."

She wished she had something to give him for the pain, but she didn't. Faint hope was all she had left. That and the gun.

"Maybe there won't have to be any shooting." She cracked the door open, being careful not to show herself in the opening. She saw that the Japanese had turned off most of the lights, giving themselves an edge in a building they knew and the Americans didn't.

"Tanaka! Can you hear me?"

Silence. She called again. "Tanaka! Talk to me!"

After a few seconds they heard his voice, sounding scared and angry at the same time. "What is there to talk about?"

"About no more killing. You killed Joe and cut off Bill's fingers. We got five of your people in return. Let's call it even. You let us leave, and we won't kill anyone else."

He laughed bitterly. "That is not even. And you will never get past us."

"Maybe not, but more of your team will die. I can guarantee you that."

There was another pause, and Smith thought she heard whispering. The faint sound reminded her of the rats she'd heard in the walls of the junk houses she'd lived in as a child. She remembered her father's killing some of them, most with traps but two or three with a shovel. He'd made her bury one with the same shovel, rat blood still on it.

After a minute she heard Tanaka again. "Okay. Throw out the guns, and we will let you leave."

"No, they're our insurance. You throw yours out."

More whispering sounds. She looked at Lee. His face looked as white but also as hard as marble. She thought of a tombstone and shuddered.

He must have noticed her slight movement. "Stay frosty, soldier. We'll get out of this."

She tried to grin but knew it was a sickly effort. Her mouth felt parched as though she'd gone on a long march without a canteen.

Never again, she thought. If she got out of this mess—and she didn't think she would—it was the last time. She didn't care what the AD would say or what they'd do to her. It was the last time.

Finally Tanaka said, "All right," and metal clattered on the tile floor of the hallway.

Smith peered down the hall to where it intersected with another corridor. She saw two pistols near the intersection. In the dim light the guns were completely black against the light-brown tile.

She worked her tongue to produce some saliva. "Two," she whispered to Lee.

"That can't be all they have. Not this bunch."

"No, but it's two less than they did have and maybe more ammunition for us."

"If we can get there."

"Yes, if. You ready?"

"Yeah. If we're going, we better go now."

She knew what he meant. He didn't think he could hold on much longer. And waiting would just give Tanaka time to get his people better organized.

"Right. I'll go first. You cover me and watch the rear."

"But—"

"Don't argue, Lee. You're already hurt, and we don't have time."

He looked at her a long moment and then nodded.

"Good. You can be chivalrous when we get home."

He managed a slight smile. "If we get back, that's not all I'll be for you."

"Hold that thought." She stuck the pistol in her waistband and wiped both sweaty palms on her pants. Then she seized the gun again and took a deep breath. "Okay, here we go."

She yanked the door all the way open, sprinted across the hall, and crouched to present the smallest possible target. She held the pistol in front of her as prescribed by the tactical manual, but no one fired at her and no target presented itself.

"Come," she said softly.

Lee scuttled across the hall, crouched behind her, and turned to look toward the opposite end of the hallway. "Nothing."

"Let's move."

She dashed forward about 15 feet and crouched again. Lee moved up behind her.

"They may be waiting for us to pick up those pistols," Lee whispered.

"Yes, or get into that open area where they can bring a crossfire."

"But we have to get the guns."

"Yep. No options left." Except surrender, she thought, and that would be the same as committing suicide.

She ran forward again and crouched where she could reach the pistols. Just ahead the hallway intersection formed a square. She knew that Tanaka and at least some of his people must be just out of sight.

She took another deep breath and stretched her arm toward the nearest pistol. Just before her fingers touched it, a man on the same side of the hallway as she was leaned into the intersection, aimed, and fired. The muzzle of his gun flashed like lightning in the darkness.

The bullet plowed into the tile a few inches from her hand. She snapped off a return shot, missing but getting close enough to force the man back behind the wall.

She snatched the pistol from the floor as Lee ran up and crouched behind her.

"Who's that?" he whispered. "Tanaka?"

"No, someone else." She stuck the pistol in her waistband. "A new face. And a good shooter."

"Shit! Reinforcements."

"The AD said they'd all be here."

"I wish he'd been wrong for once."

"So do I. Well, here goes." Smith moved forward, still in a crouch, until she was almost close enough to reach the other pistol. Again the man leaned out and fired. Again he missed although the bullet came close enough to drive slivers of tile chips into her hand.

But this time she didn't miss. Her shot caught the man in the shoulder, and he fell into the open, where she shot him again, now in the chest, and he flopped onto the floor and lay still.

Someone—it might have been Tanaka—shouted in Japanese, and a man with a shotgun leaned into the intersection from the other side. He swung the gun toward them and fired. The *blam!* sounded like an explosion in the confined space.

The man wasn't a good shot, but from that close and using a shotgun, he didn't need to be. Several pellets slashed into Smith's side and leg, stinging like a thousand hornets and making her gasp from the pain.

She raised her pistol and was about to shoot when Lee fired, hitting the man in the stomach. The man dropped the shotgun, clutched his belly with both hands, and staggered back out of sight.

"That's two more down," Lee whispered. "Maybe only three or four left. Are you hit?"

"Yes," Smith said through gritted teeth. "I can still move but maybe not for long."

She edged forward to pick up the pistol on the floor. She turned and tucked it behind Lee's belt.

She looked into his eyes, knowing it might be for the last time. "Okay. I say we charge. Neither of us is in any shape to wait them out."

"We could try going back down this hall."

Smith glanced that way, then looked back at the intersection. "They're between us and the main exit. And they know this building—we don't. Sometimes the boldest way is the safest way."

"True. Well, it looks like they're on both sides. Which one do you want?"

Smith wanted to give Lee the easier route, but she didn't know where that was, so she chose the side where the shotgunner had gone. "I'll take the right."

"Got it. See you at the front door."

She reached back to touch his knee, letting her fingers linger for a moment. Then she drew and cocked the other pistol so that she had a ready gun in each hand.

"Now." She stood, trying to ignore the stabbing pain in her side and leg and the blood reddening her clothes. Telling herself to act, not think, she ran toward the intersection. The pain was so bad that she couldn't jump over the dead man on the floor and had to go around him. She heard Lee running right behind her and breaking toward the other corner.

She expected someone to pop out and shoot at them before they got there, but no one did. She reached the intersection and flattened against the wall. She peeked around the corner and saw someone mostly hidden behind an overturned table halfway down the corridor.

Whoever the person was saw her too and snapped off a shot. It went wide, and her return fire forced the shooter to duck.

"Looks like two this way... down at the end," Lee said, and she heard the ragged breath in his throat. She knew that with the loss of blood, he was nearing the end of his strength. They had to end this thing soon or it would end them.

"One over here, behind cover. Want to swap?"

"No, I'll take them."

She risked a glance his way. "Semper Fi, Marine."

Lee managed a grin. "Semper Fi."

He fired twice to force the Japanese back. Then he began running toward the end of the corridor, moving awkwardly because of the laptop under his arm.

Smith knew that their best bet was to attack in both directions at once, so she took off right after Lee did, keeping low to present a smaller target. She hadn't gone more than 10 feet when she heard shooting behind her.

Resisting the temptation to turn and look, she focused on whoever was behind the table. The person popped up, and she saw Tanaka's face, twisted with rage.

He fired, and what felt like a hot poker ripped through the flesh of her upper left arm. Without willing it, she screamed. The high-pitched sound, a cry of pain, anger, and fear all at once, reverberated off the bare walls.

Her scream froze Tanaka just as he was preparing to fire again. She used her good arm to swing one of her pistols higher and shoot him in the chest. Tanaka sagged against the wall, and she took advantage of the moment to put a round through his forehead.

She was already moving before he collapsed to the floor. She turned and scanned the corridor behind her. She saw a man down and sucked in her breath but then realized it wasn't Lee.

She heard two shots fired from somewhere around the corner where Lee must have disappeared. Holding a pistol in front of her, she limped down the hall, her leg stiffening from the shotgun blast. Pain stabbed her with every step.

As she approached the far intersection she heard another shot, and then there was only silence.

At the corner she flattened herself against the wall again and edged her head out into the intersection. Down the near hallway there was nothing but rows of blue metal lockers on both sides. But down the far hallway she saw three figures on the floor, blood on all of them. One was Lee.

She checked the two Japanese first. Both were dead. Lee was unconscious but alive. A bullet had caught him in the shoulder, and she knew he would die unless she could stop this fresh bleeding.

The school was now deathly silent, and the air stank of cordite. Underneath that odor she could smell her own fear, and she shivered. Apparently they'd killed all the Japanese—mission complete—but Mori was dead, and Lee was badly wounded. Her wounds weren't as serious, but they needed attention.

And they were a long way from home. A very long way. Maybe too far to get back. She closed her eyes for a moment and shook her head.

Then she began looking for a first-aid kit.

CHAPTER NINETEEN

An hour later Smith had bandaged Lee and herself as well as she could from the school's—no, make that the terrorists'—surprisingly large medical kit. She'd given Lee a light sedative for his pain, and he was sleeping on a sofa in one of the offices. She wanted to take something for her own pain, but she was afraid she'd go to sleep too and not wake up until someone found them.

She'd used her phone to photograph all of the wall boards, equipment, and weapons that she thought might have some intelligence value. While photographing the room in which Mori and Lee had been tortured, she'd seen Lee's severed fingers lying on the floor. She'd taken a plastic bag from the kitchen and sealed his fingers in it. She didn't know whether they could be reattached, but she hoped they could. Remembering the feeling of Lee's hands on her, she wept for a moment before telling herself she had to keep moving if either of them was going to stay alive.

She'd heard two or three phones ringing on the dead Japanese. She'd quickly searched the bodies, taking all the mobiles and a few scraps of paper that looked as though they might be important.

Although she couldn't read the Japanese messages popping up on the phones, she knew that at least some must be from other members of the terrorist group and that however few of them were left, they'd eventually come to investigate why they couldn't get in touch with anyone at the school. She and Lee didn't have much time. If they were going to avoid capture, they had to move.

She checked on Lee again—no change. Then she called the AD and gave him a quick summary of what had happened.

"Good work, Smith. You accomplished a tough mission."

That was high praise from him, but she couldn't enjoy the moment. She'd already told him once, but now she repeated it. "Mori's dead."

"Yes, I know. Those things happen."

Smith wanted to scream, curse, throw the phone at something, but she needed the AD's help to get away, so she forced herself to breathe deeply and calm down.

"With Mori dead, how do we get out of here? Lee's hurt pretty bad, I'm not much better, and we don't speak Japanese."

"Wait a minute."

For what seemed a long time Smith heard only the whisper of the airwaves. She glanced at Lee, who stirred and moaned a little. That was a good sign. Although he'd still be in pain, she'd soon need him awake and capable of walking to their car.

Finally the AD came back on the line. "There's a village on the seacoast about two hours west of you." He spelled the name, and she repeated the letters back, closing her eyes as she memorized them. "Be there when it gets dark. Walk down to the beach, and keep your phone on so that we can find you by GPS. Someone will come to pick you up."

"All right. We'll try."

"You can do it, Smith. You've come this far—don't quit now."

"There's no quit in me!"

He paused. "I know."

He sounded almost tender, and she was surprised to hear that tone in his voice. She was curious about the reason, but she didn't have time to think about it now.

"We'll do our best."

"You'll make it. Just keep cool and remember your training."

For a moment she flashed back to their tense standoff in the barber shop, and she almost said something about that, but then she thought better of it. She didn't want to risk losing his full cooperation in their extraction.

"I will. We'll get going now."

"All right. I'll be available if you need to call again. Good luck."

We're going to need it, Smith thought grimly before signing off. We're going to need every bit of it.

She dropped the phone into her pocket and shook Lee awake. She had to shake him more roughly than she would've liked, but finally she got him to open his eyes and sit up.

"We're leaving, Lee."

He shook his head, perhaps because he was still groggy. "No place to go. Mori's dead. And both of us should be in the hospital. That's where they'll put us if they find us—and then prison."

"They won't find us. The AD has a plan to extract us."

"How? Where?"

She pulled him to his feet, grunting with the effort. "I'll tell you on the way to the car. Can you make it?"

He tried to give her a grin, and she saw a ghost of the old Lee behind his mask of pain. "Sure. And then some."

"Good. Lean on me."

She'd found a canvas bag to hold the laptop, the phones, and three of the pistols, not counting the one she kept in her waistband. She strapped the heavy bag over her shoulder and put her other arm around Lee to support him as they shuffled toward the front door.

With every step she took Smith felt dull knives stab her in the leg and side. She thought she might pass out from the pain, but she kept going. She glanced at Lee and could tell he was on the verge of collapse himself. She wondered if they'd be able to make the drive to the town the AD had mentioned. It didn't seem likely, but they had to try.

As they neared the door she knew she'd forgotten something, maybe more than one thing, but she was so tired she could barely think. She closed her eyes and slowly went through a mental checklist of what she had to do in the next few minutes. Then she remembered.

"We have to open the gate."

"That's right—that damn tank barrier. I didn't see the control. Did you?"

"No. Or their video monitor and audio hookup, but they're probably all together. Just not out in the open. Wait here."

She eased Lee onto the floor and looked around. Off to one side was a small, empty office with a glass door and three glass walls. The fourth wall was wooden with a door set in the middle. She'd seen the office coming in but hadn't focused on it. Now she did.

Smith suddenly realized what she was looking at. The office must have belonged to the school receptionist. She went through the glass door, crossed the room, and opened the wooden door.

The office beyond was large and carpeted with a picture window that looked out on the school playground. On what had probably been the principal's desk—a big one in the middle of the room—sat two computers, several video monitors, and a microphone.

Bingo! She limped to the desk as quickly as she could. The computers were on, and the monitors showed split images of the compound, including outside and inside views of the front gate. A sound like a bird squawking came softly from a computer speaker. She looked toward the sound, and in one of the images on that computer she saw a crow sitting on the wall of the compound.

Some of the images had writing in the lower right corner, but she couldn't read the Japanese. She wondered whether she'd ever be able to figure out how to open the gate—at least in the time they had left, which was running out fast.

Then she saw that in the inside image of the gate there were two circular icons—one red and one green, the red icon glowing more brightly than the green one. She took a deep breath, dredged up a prayer from her short childhood, and clicked the green icon.

Nothing happened for a moment. Then she saw the gate begin to swing open. The curse she'd been forming came out as whispered thanks to God. Assuming He was still willing to listen, she thought, which was doubtful.

She wanted to remove the hard drives from the computers, but she knew she was already running on borrowed time. Whatever was on the laptop would have to do.

She went back to Lee and helped him up off the floor. "Success to crime, partner."

"You got it?"

"Yep. Let's get the hell out of here."

They emerged from the darkened building and blinked in the late-afternoon sun. It was like coming out of a movie theater in the daytime—only she never wanted to see this movie again.

But she knew she would... in her dreams. In dreams that would come night after night for a long time.

The distance to the car seemed endless, but they finally got there, both of them panting from the exertion. Smith put down the bag and fumbled for the keys she'd taken from Mori's pocket—no, she mentally corrected, forcing herself to do it, the keys she'd taken from his dead body.

She unlocked the car and swung open the passenger door. She was helping Lee slide into the seat when she caught movement from the corner of her eye.

Without thinking she shoved Lee into the car, whipped out her pistol, and turned toward what she'd seen. Over by a wall, partly shaded by the corner of the building, was the young woman who'd served them tea and rice cakes—the woman she hadn't seen again during the shootout with the Japanese.

That was the other thing she'd forgotten.

And now the woman was pointing a pistol at her, holding it straight out with both hands as though she didn't want to touch it. The woman was crying but had a look of grim determination on her tear-streaked face.

She must've hidden, Smith thought. Waited until the shooting stopped and then crept outside. Set up this ambush. But where did she get that gun? Well, it didn't matter now. She was probably a lousy shot, but anyone could get lucky and hit something.

Smith agonized but only for a moment. The woman had made her decision when she picked up that gun, and now Smith made hers. She aimed and fired at almost the same instant the woman fired at her.

The woman's shot went wide. Smith's didn't. Her bullet hit the woman square in the chest. The woman dropped her pistol, made a half-turn, and collapsed like a broken doll. On the ground she lay very still.

"What the fuck's going on?" Lee had drawn his own pistol and was trying to pull himself out of the car.

"I forgot about one of them—that other woman. She was waiting for us."

"Is she—?"

"Yes."

He paused only for a moment. "Then like you said—let's get the hell out of here." He slumped back on the seat, groaning as he did so.

"Right." Smith put the bag at his feet, closed his door, and walked around to get into the driver's seat.

As she started the engine Lee looked over at her. "Where are we going?"

"Some town on the west coast. The AD said they could pick us up."

"Do you believe that?"

"What? That he can do it or that he will?"

"Either. Both."

She glanced at him and then looked over her shoulder as she backed into the driveway. "Let's say both. I don't think we have much choice."

He didn't answer until she'd swung the car around and was headed for the gate. "No, I guess we don't."

The gate was still open when they came to it, and she said another little prayer of gratitude. As they rolled through the gate she couldn't help glancing at the compound in the rear-view mirror. It looked peaceful from here—no sign of the carnage inside or the woman she'd left dead outside. She wondered how long it would take the police to hear about what had happened and investigate.

When they did, they'd find surveillance video showing Mori, Lee, and her and their car, video she hadn't had time to locate and erase. She could have burned the school, but that definitely would have brought the police.

So she just had to hope that someone from the Enterprise would find them before the police did.

She remembered how to get back to the main highway. As they approached the intersection she found the roadmap and handed it to Lee.

She was very glad that Mori had had the foresight to bring one printed in English as well as Japanese.

"We need to find that town on the coast." She spelled the name the AD had given her. "See it?"

Lee brought the small-scale map closer to his face and squinted at it. He moved his forefinger up the coastline and then stopped.

"Yes. This highway will get us pretty close, and then there's a smaller road that leads to the town. How's our gas?"

She glanced at the gauge. "I think we can make it. No need to risk buying more unless we absolutely have to."

Lee nodded and sank back in his seat, clearly exhausted.

"Get some sleep. You need it."

"Like you don't." He laid his pistol on his lap, keeping his hand on it. With his other hand he used the map to cover the gun.

She noticed the movements. "We won't get stopped."

"Let's hope not. But if we do, I'm not giving myself up."

"No, I know you won't. I won't either."

"I didn't think you would. That's settled then."

She didn't answer for a moment as the events of the last few months flashed through her mind, almost deadening the pain throbbing in her body. She tightened her hands on the wheel until they were bone white. "I think the Enterprise settled it for us."

Lee didn't reply. He looked out the window at the Japanese countryside flashing by, and she wondered if he felt the way she did.

Probably. But it didn't matter—there was nothing they could do but run and hope that they got away.

She drove.

CHAPTER TWENTY

They reached the village in twilight. The little fishing town sat on a hill that led down to the sea and ended in wooden docks with dozens of boats bobbing among the piers. The air coming through the open windows smelled of saltwater and fish, and birds wheeled overhead, their cries echoing off the shops close to the water and, more faintly, the houses farther back.

It was dinnertime and few people were outside. The houses glowed softly with yellow lights that looked warm and inviting in the cool evening. Smith thought the scene would have made a beautiful painting, a mix of earth tones and the slate-gray sea with the yellow lights for contrast.

No red, she thought. Not like the compound. That was all red now. She wondered if anyone could ever get all the blood off the floor. Including hers. And Lee's. Mori's.

She glanced at the gas gauge—something she'd been doing anxiously for the last half hour—and saw that the needle was almost pegged to the red line on the left. They were running on fumes or soon would be, and then they'd be stuck wherever the car stopped. They had to get to a suitable pick-up point before that happened.

Holding her breath most of the time and keeping her foot as light as possible on the accelerator, she drove the two or three miles to where the town petered out and the road continued parallel to a rocky beach that was almost black in the fading light. She found a flat place and turned off the road. As the car rolled onto the sand, the engine began knocking.

She braked to a stop and switched off the engine before it died. In the ensuing quiet she could hear the birds more clearly and now the ticking of the engine as it cooled. She exhaled, relieved but also frightened at how close they'd cut it.

She looked over at Lee, who'd been silent for most of the trip, saving his strength. "Well, we made it this far. Barely."

"We'll make it all the way."

"Maybe—with a little luck." She didn't share his optimism, but she hoped he was right. She checked her phone to make sure they had reception outside town. The signal was weak but there.

Lee watched her. "Now we wait?"

"Now we wait. The AD said they'd send someone for us."

"By sea?"

"I guess. He didn't say."

"Maybe he didn't know at the time."

"Maybe. If so, he better have it figured out now. We can't go anywhere on our own."

The truth of her statement was so obvious that Lee didn't reply. He closed his eyes, his lips pale and set in a thin line. She knew he must be nearing the limit of his endurance. And she knew she wasn't far behind him.

She gazed out at the ocean, the sky so dark now that it and the ocean and the beach were almost indistinguishable from one another. Out here the world was only black and gray, and the gray was vanishing with the last dregs of daylight.

Suddenly there was a white light behind her. She looked in the mirror and saw the headlights of a car moving slowly toward them. As she watched, colored lights began flashing from the roof of the car, and she knew it was the police.

"Shit! There's probably only one police car in this podunk town, and it has to come out here to investigate."

"Maybe someone saw two strange anglos driving through town and called the cops." Lee brought up his pistol and flipped the safety. "Anyway, this is what they'll find."

"No, Lee."

"What?"

"No more killing. I'm sick of it. Let's try another way."

He snorted. "What way? Are you going to charm them into leaving us alone?"

"Maybe. And maybe there's only one cop."

"By the time you know, it'll be too late."

"Let's see." She looked in the mirror again. The police car had stopped about 20 feet behind them. Despite the glare from its lights, she could see the outline of the driver. But she couldn't tell whether there was another person in the car. She didn't think so, but she wasn't certain.

She decided to take a chance. They'd been lucky so far—maybe their luck would hold.

She opened her door and slid out. She stood next to the car, her arms at her sides, trying to look as small and nonthreatening as she could.

The driver leaned out the window and said something to her. A male voice, rather high-pitched. He was probably telling her to get back in the car.

"I'm sorry. I don't speak Japanese."

The driver spoke again, sounding more insistent this time, and she repeated what she'd just said. She sensed Lee shifting in his seat and hoped he wasn't getting ready to shoot.

Then she began walking slowly toward the car, being careful to keep her hands open and out where the driver could see them. When she was about halfway to the car the driver got out.

He was young and of medium height. Trim and handsome in his dark uniform. He had a flashlight and other things clipped to his belt, but she didn't see a gun. Maybe Japanese police officers didn't carry them, at least not in a little town like this.

She bowed to him, and the unexpected sight of a white woman making that gesture froze him for a moment. Then he bowed slightly and stepped toward her.

She heard a car door open and knew it must be Lee, covering her. She forced herself not to turn to look. Instead she watched the young man's face and noticed his eyes widen as he saw the bandaged and bloody Lee draw down on him.

The officer fumbled for his radio microphone, and Smith jumped between him and Lee. "No!" she said, speaking to both of them.

She whirled and kicked the officer in the face, causing him to stagger back and fall onto the hood of his car. She leaped forward and punched him, hard, in the stomach. As he covered up to protect himself, she grabbed his head and banged it once, twice, three times against the hood. Then she stepped back, letting him slump to the ground.

She bent to look inside the police car. There was no one in it. She slumped a little herself, realizing what would have happened if she'd been wrong about that.

Lee walked up next to her. "Is he out?"

"Yes. Let's gag him and tie him up."

"He's got handcuffs on his belt—use those."

"Good idea."

She tore a strip from the officer's shirt and shoved it in his mouth. Then she twisted his arms behind him and snapped the cuffs on his wrists.

Lee helped her pick him up and slide him in the back seat of the cruiser. She switched off its lights, cracked the windows slightly, and locked the doors.

She shoved the car keys into her pocket. "That should hold him for a while."

"Yes, but now he's a witness. He wouldn't have been if you'd let me kill him."

She jerked her head around to face him. "I told you—I'm sick of killing! There's been enough death."

"We're just doing our job, the one they make us do."

"Yes, and I hate it. So would you if you had any conscience." She regretted the second remark as soon as she made it, especially when she saw his expression. "Wait, Lee, I didn't mean that the way it sounded."

He didn't reply for a long moment. Finally he said, "Maybe I do. Hate it, I mean. But I want to say alive."

"At any price?"

"Maybe. At least for what I've paid so far."

"The price will get higher."

"Then I'll deal with that if I have to!" He paused again, looking at her. "When I have to. Right now I just want to get off this beach and go somewhere safe."

"So do I, amigo." She checked her phone. No messages. She sighed.

They got back in their car and sat there silently. Our first fight, Smith thought. And maybe our last. She wondered if their friendship—she hated the word "relationship"—would survive this mission. Assuming that they survived it, which was highly in doubt at the moment.

She glanced at Lee. He lay sprawled in the seat, eyes closed again. She knew he was at the end of even his tremendous strength.

Then the phone vibrated. Her heartbeat quickening, she answered. "Yes?"

"This is Dietzler."

She hadn't heard his name in a long time, and she hadn't seen him for even longer. Images from their basic training flashed in front of her—that pale face with its penetrating stare and his wiry body. The way he'd looked cursing her when she bought them an extra mile by being late for a run.

Dietzler. She'd heard that he'd carried out a couple of missions, using a car bomb in the first and going high-tech in the other with a poisoned pen—literally. Maybe for that second mission the AD had allowed an exception to the "no James Bond" rule. If so, why? Or maybe in both cases Dietzler had just been afraid to shoot someone up close. But somehow she didn't think he was.

What she knew was that having a guy like Dietzler assigned to pick them up was consistent with the shitty luck they'd had on this mission. Well, it was better than having no one come for them.

"Hi. We're on the beach."

"I know that, idiot. I can track your phone."

She swallowed the sharp retort she would have given a lot to make. There might be time later to deal with this asshole. Right now she had to think about getting herself and Lee to safety.

"Okay, what's the plan?"

"I'm off shore in a rubber boat. I'll come in to pick you up. Wade as far out as you can so we won't be spotted on the beach."

"Lee's hurt pretty bad, and I'm not much better."

"Tough. You'll have to wade out. It's too risky otherwise."

"I'm not sure Lee can make it."

"Then leave him!"

She didn't even consider it. "No. He comes or I don't."

Dietzler snorted. "Very touching—the bonding of comrades. Well, make up your mind. I'm leaving in three minutes, with or without you."

She knew he meant what he said. "Okay, we'll wade out."

Without hanging up she shoved the phone into a pocket and leaned over to wake Lee. "Come on, Marine. Time to go."

He stirred and opened his eyes. "What? What is it?"

"Dietzler's here. In a rubber boat. We have to wade out."

"Have him come in. He can beach the boat."

"No, he won't do it. He's afraid of being seen."

"He's afraid? We're the ones who've been shot!"

"I know, but that's just how it is. We have to go. Unfortunately, I can't carry you."

Lee opened the door, groaning a little, and began to swing his legs outside. By the time he was easing himself out of the car, Smith was there to help him.

He leaned on her, looking down into her eyes. "Thanks. I'll try to repay the favor sometime."

"Please don't if it means I'll be as banged up as you are."

"Good point." He chuckled and then sucked in his breath from the pain it caused him.

She shouldered the bag, silently cursing its heaviness. Then they limped toward the water, Lee moving slowly and Smith supporting him as much as she could. The beach was dark and, as far as they could tell, deserted.

Smith looked for a light off shore but didn't see anything. She pulled the phone out of her pocket and spoke softly into it. "Dietzler?"

"I'm here. About a hundred yards out."

She wanted to yell, but she still kept her voice low. "We can't go out that far! That'd be swimming, not wading, and we're in no condition to do it."

He made an impatient sound. "Of course. I'll close in when you've gone as far as you can."

Smith thought he was making things unnecessarily difficult for them, but they didn't have any choice. Staying on the beach wasn't an option. Someone—another cop maybe—could come along anytime. With the first cop unable to radio in, they were already pressing their luck.

"Okay." She looked at Lee, who was panting from the exertion of the long shuffle through the sand. He was beginning to have that thousand-yard stare she'd seen a few times in the desert—usually right before someone became careless and got killed. Well, Lee wasn't going to die if she could help it. They were too close to safety.

She put her hand on his arm. "Hey, I'm sorry, but we have to take a little ocean dip."

He didn't reply, but he let her lead him down to the water. The gradient was steep, and the waves, driven by the brisk wind in their faces, slapped hard against the sand, throwing spray over them. The water was cold, and she knew it would feel even colder once they were wading in it.

It did. Icy cold after they'd taken only a few steps, and the shock was almost painful. She wanted to scream into the phone, to tell Dietzler to get his ass to the beach and pick them up. But she knew he wouldn't do it. He'd make them come out as far as they could. Smart, sure, but smart wasn't what she wanted right now.

At least the water numbed her pain. She glanced at Lee but couldn't tell whether it was having the same effect on him. Maybe he was too far gone to feel anything.

"Hold on, Lee. Just hold on and we'll be okay."

He turned his head slowly toward her and nodded. She squeezed his hand and felt his fingers move in return.

Lights flared up behind them, and she ducked, pulling Lee down with her so that only their heads were above the water. She turned to look and saw a car's headlights illuminating the police car. What if she'd been wrong in thinking that the village might have only one cruiser? Then first the cop—or cops—in this one would check on the handcuffed officer and search their empty car, but after that it wouldn't take long to find their footprints leading to the water's edge.

"Shit. Now we really have to move." Supporting Lee, which was easier now that they were in the water, she began walking forward as quickly as she could while still keeping low. She fumbled with the phone, terrified that she might drop it, and hissed at Dietzler.

"Can you see us?" She knew he must have night-vision equipment.

"Yes. I'm a little to your left. I'll move toward you. Keep going."

"You see what's on the beach?"

"Of course. Very careless of you."

She clamped her jaws so that she wouldn't, couldn't, damn him as she desperately wanted to. Now wasn't the time to cut their only lifeline. She could deal with Dietzler later. Maybe. If they lived.

"Let's hope they don't have a searchlight," Dietzler said.

She hadn't thought of that. She didn't remember seeing one on the other car, but that didn't mean this car didn't have one.

She began to move faster, dragging Lee along with her. He was trying hard to keep up but was barely conscious, and the icy water didn't help. Now it was up to her chest. And she still didn't see Dietzler.

When it was up to her neck she heard excited voices behind them. It sounded like two men at the water's edge. She glanced back and saw a flashlight beam stabbing the darkness. Fortunately the beam was too small and weak to illuminate them this far out in the black water. But if she hadn't waded out as quickly as she could, the light would have found them.

She looked to the front again, and now she saw Dietzler, his pale face smoky in the starlight. He was dressed in black and sitting in a dark boat of some kind, so the rest of him blended into the night.

She knew better than to call out, and so did he. She pushed forward, having to tilt her head back to breathe. She swallowed some seawater and coughed, trying to be as quiet as possible.

The boat was about 20 yards ahead now. She ditched her gun and the guns in the bag and slipped out of her shoes. Then, still carrying the captured laptop and phone, she began to swim for it, dragging Lee along behind her. Her clothing made stroking difficult, and the bag weighed her down. But she swam with desperation, kicking as hard as she could and slicing the cold water with her free hand.

She swallowed some more water and coughed again, not worrying about the noise this time. Just as she thought she wouldn't be able to make it, Dietzler threw out a line with a flotation ring on the end. The ring landed a few feet away, and she frantically splashed to it. She hooked her free arm into the ring and let the ring support them as she tried to catch her breath. Dietzler pulled on the line, drawing them up to the boat.

"Here, take Lee." She pushed his inert body in front of her, and Dietzler reached out to haul him over the gunwale.

After Lee was onboard she rose high enough to see two dark figures behind Dietzler. They wore black wetsuits and had swim masks pushed up on their foreheads.

SEALs, she thought. That explains how Dietzler got here. And Dietzler's being in charge of the rescue explained why the SEALs hadn't swum out to get them—he wanted to make Smith and Lee do things the hard way just to show he was in command.

"Now take this." She slid the bag off her shoulder and handed the strap to Dietzler. As he put the bag down, she used the last of her strength to roll into the boat. She collapsed next to Lee and lay there, gasping.

Dietzler's ghostly face loomed above them. Over her labored breathing she heard him say, "Okay, let's go."

One of the dark figures turned aft and did something that caused a low humming sound. The boat began to move.

Electric motor, she thought. No noise, no wake.

That was her last thought before she sank into darkness—darkness that closed over her like a big wave from the black ocean that lay all around them.

CHAPTER TWENTY-ONE

After being home for only three weeks Smith received orders to report to the Enterprise's office near Washington, D.C. She'd slept much of the way back, first on the Navy sub Dietzler and the SEALs had taken them to and then on the plane from the Navy's Diego Garcia base in the Indian Ocean. Lee had slept even more, drugged to dampen his pain.

Then both of them had had surgery, hers relatively minor and Lee's more serious. The doctors had tried but hadn't been able to reattach his fingers. They'd talked to him about the possibility of prosthetics once the stumps had healed.

The Director came to see them while they were in the hospital. He visited Lee's room first and then hers. At first she was embarrassed about his seeing her lying in bed wearing a hospital gown and numerous bandages, but he treated her in a fatherly way, and soon she relaxed.

He'd brought her a small bouquet and spent the first couple of minutes finding a glass, half-filling it with water, and placing the flowers in it. Then he put the flowers by her bed so that she could see and smell them.

"Thank you—that's very kind. I love flowers, but I'm not sure Lee does."

The Director smiled. "I'm not either, so I brought him some beef jerky. You know how Marines like that. He might have preferred some whiskey, but I didn't want to bend the rules quite that far."

"No, we can't bend any rules—not in our business." She said it lightly, but when she saw the look that flashed across his tired, lined face, she knew she'd hurt him. "Sorry—bad joke. I didn't mean it the way it sounded."

He started to speak, then waited a few seconds before continuing. "I've spent my whole life trying to protect our country from its enemies. And we have a lot of enemies—people who are jealous of our material wealth, our power, our influence. People who hate us because of the freedom we represent. We're essentially at war with those people, a long, dark, vicious war that I may never see the end of. *You* may never see the end of it."

She looked at him but said nothing. He had never spoken this way to her before.

"To win this war, we have to use every weapon we can. One of those weapons is assassination. Is it illegal? Yes, now—although it wasn't always. Am I proud that we do it? No. But do I think we have to do it? Absolutely. Those people you dealt with in Japan might have killed thousands, tens of thousands. Who knows how many? So it's good that they're dead."

He paused again, giving her a chance to reply, but still she said nothing.

"By the way, the Japanese government has already thanked us. Quietly and informally of course. Still, they've thanked us."

"But the terrorists have—had friends in the government."

"A few, perhaps, but almost all Japanese officials feared them as much as we did. They were too violent, too unpredictable. That's why they were so dangerous."

"Well, not anymore."

"No, and I thank you for that—you and Lee. But most of all Mori, who gave his life for this mission."

He looked away, rubbing his face. "Forgive me. I didn't mean to go on. But war is a dirty business—any war but especially this kind of war. We can't help getting some of the dirt on ourselves."

"And in our souls," Smith said. "Not just on our hands—the dirt along with the blood."

"In our souls? Yes, I suppose that's true." The priest's words came back to him then, and he was silent for a moment. "But I must be tiring you, and you need your rest."

She knew he was busy and needed to go. "Thanks again for coming to see us. It means a lot."

"And you mean a lot to me—to us, that is." He cleared his throat. "To the Enterprise. Well, please let me know if we can bring you anything."

"I will. But with these flowers I think I have everything I need." She smiled and held out a hand to him.

He took her small hand in his big one and held it for a moment. She thought he was about to say something, but he held back whatever it was. He lowered her hand to the covers, laid it there, and patted it gently.

"Get some rest now."

She nodded, and he went to the door. As he was closing it behind him, he turned toward her, a faraway look in his eyes.

He whispered something she couldn't quite make out. It sounded like "goodbye" and a woman's name. Elizabeth? She couldn't tell.

Then she was alone again. She lay awake for a long before finally drifting into a troubled sleep.

Later the AD came to see her. She thought he might have questions about the mission, but he said he'd save them for the formal debriefing. He didn't bring her a gift, but he did ask if she needed anything. She badly wanted something to read, but she didn't want to ask him for any favors, so she just shook her head.

He came close to the bed and looked down at her. "Well, if you think of anything, let me know. You're a valuable member of the Enterprise, and we want to take good care of you."

"Thanks." She was terse, wishing he would leave.

Then, without asking permission, he lifted the sheet covering her and looked at her bandaged wounds. She was wearing a hospital gown, but it was quite short, and she wasn't wearing anything underneath it. She reddened with a hot mix of embarrassment and anger.

Snatching the sheet out of his hand, she said, "Don't do that—I'm not some piece of property for your inspection."

He raised an eyebrow. "No? I think you are. Not property perhaps, but a very useful tool, one we want to keep sharp and ready for use."

"Fuck you." She couldn't believe she'd said that to a man who could kill her or have her killed and probably never face any consequences for it. But she didn't apologize or try to take the words back.

The AD didn't seem offended. In fact, he seemed pleased that he'd struck fire from her. "Smith, such language." He shook his head slightly. "I'm surprised at you. But if you really mean it...."

She didn't understand at first. Then she did, and her anger flared even more. She wanted to say something—she couldn't think of what—but he had turned to go, not saying goodbye, just heading for the door. And then he was gone.

She spent a lot of time with Lee in the hospital and went back to visit him after she was discharged. He was depressed over the mutilation of his hand, and she tried hard to cheer him up but didn't have much success.

After both of them were out of the hospital, the AD and three CIA analysts debriefed them at length, first Smith, then Lee, and finally the two of them together. The AD sat at the conference room table without a scrap of paper in front of him, but the spooks—two men who looked at her a lot and a woman who didn't—busily took notes. Smith didn't see a camera or microphone, but she was sure they were recording the whole session.

Smith described the compound, the Japanese who'd been there, and what had happened to them and to Lee and herself. Listening intently, the AD said nothing, but the CIA analysts peppered her with questions, occasionally referring to something they'd found on the laptop or phones she'd brought back. The questions came so fast that she often had to stop and backtrack.

Finally the AD held up his hand. "Wait. Keep quiet and let her talk. Save your questions for the end—she'll remember more that way."

And she did remember more. As she told the story, her voice rose, her breathing became ragged, and she dug her nails into her palms. The shooting, the bodies, all that blood. What they'd done to Lee. And to Mori, who didn't come back.

When they brought Lee in and sat him next to her, she looked at him and tried to smile, but she knew it was a feeble effort. He didn't even make the attempt, looking at her as though he didn't recognize her and then staring at the bandaged stumps of his fingers. The psychiatrist treating her had said it would take some time for Lee to adjust, and she could see that he was right.

So she touched Lee on the arm and gave him a slight nod to tell him that she understood. The old Lee was in there somewhere, and she'd wait for him to reappear.

Neither of them had much to add to what they'd said separately, and the analysts' questions focused on resolving minor discrepancies in their stories. After another hour of the long process Smith was so tired that she could barely keep her eyes open.

The AD noticed and gestured for the spooks to wrap things up. Smith was surprised—he certainly wasn't known for his solicitude. But she was grateful and said so after the CIA representatives had gathered their things and left the room.

The AD smiled his almost-smile. "No, thank you for a successful mission. I know it was a difficult one."

Smith looked at the stubs of Lee's fingers. Her eyes grew hot, and she closed them. When she did, she saw Mori lying on the floor, his head twisted at an unnatural angle. She wiped her closed eyes, and her fingers came away wet.

"Yes."

"What? I couldn't hear you."

She opened her eyes and looked at him. "I said, 'yes.' Yes, it was."

"Well, you'll have some time now to rest and complete your recovery. It won't be as long as I'd like—only ten days—but there's another mission coming up, and I need you for it."

"What? You must be kidding."

"I wish I were. No, there's something big in the works, and I'll need you for it."

"I almost died over there, you know. Don't you remember—I was shot."

A cloud came over the AD's face. "I am well aware of the details of your mission, Smith—that's my job. It's also my job to select your next mission, and I have done so. You must be ready for it in ten days' time."

"What about Lee?"

At the mention of his name Lee looked at her, then at the AD, but didn't say anything.

"I have some good news for Lee—he's retiring. Young and with a comfortable income, courtesy of the Enterprise."

"And with this." Lee's voice was rusty as he held up his bandaged hand. "Also courtesy of the Enterprise."

Good for you, Smith thought. Give it to him. Maybe Lee hadn't drunk the Kool-Aid after all.

"Rules of the game, Lee. You knew the risks."

"Not that I had much choice about accepting them—the rules or the risks."

"You had a choice. You could be in prison right now. Instead you're free and will have enough money to live on the rest of your life. You can do anything you want—as long as you keep your promise not to discuss the Enterprise with anyone."

"That won't be hard. I just want to forget all about it. And all about you."

The AD flushed, and his jaw tightened. Smith waited for the explosion. But after a long moment the AD said, "I don't blame you, son. I'd want to forget all about me too."

He looked at his watch. "All right, that's enough for today. I don't want to see either of you for a week. Then, Smith, you come back for a mission briefing. You too, Lee, for a different kind of briefing."

He rose. Looking down at them, he said, "Lee, you can live anywhere you want to now. Just let us know where you are."

He waited until Lee said "Yessir." Then the AD said, "Well, I guess that's all then," and left the room.

Smith didn't move until the door had closed behind him. Then she stood and put her hand on Lee's bandaged one. "All right, Lee. Let's go."

That evening the early-summer weather cooled enough for her to open the windows in the apartment, and the night air was fresh in her nose and delightful on her bare skin as she lay naked in bed with Lee.

She'd suggested they go out for dinner, but Lee had said he wanted to stay home. So she fixed something simple—once again wishing she were a better cook—and they ate sitting on the balcony, watching the sun go down and the stars come out.

Lee had a couple of beers, and the alcohol plus his medication made him sleepy. He offered to help clean up, but she insisted that he go to bed, and he let her persuade him.

When she finished in the kitchen, she took her glass of wine and tiptoed into the darkened bedroom. She slipped off her clothes and got into bed, feeling Lee's naked body warm next to hers.

She'd thought Lee was asleep, but when she lay down next to him, he turned on his side and spooned into her, putting his uninjured hand on her shoulder. She wanted to make love, but she assumed he was too tired, and she had to admit that she was probably too tired herself.

She pulled the covers up to her chin and sought for sleep, hoping that no bad dreams would come. As she was beginning to float into unconsciousness, Lee said, "Thanks," his warm breath tickling her ear.

She was pleased that he wanted to talk. He'd been unusually quiet for so long that she was worried about him.

"For what?"

"For everything. Starting with saving my life."

"You'd do the same for me."

"Yes, but I didn't have to. You were the one who made the mission work."

"I don't think it worked very well. Mori's dead, you were cut up and shot, and I'm not in much better shape."

"We got the bad guys, and two of us made it home. I'll bet the AD didn't think any of us would come back."

"No, probably not." She reached up to touch his hand, intertwining her slim fingers with his thicker, rougher ones. "But were they really bad guys?"

He shifted his weight, then came to rest against her again. "What? Of course they were. They were terrorists. They killed people."

"Then what are we? We kill people too."

"But only when we're told to—ordered to."

"So that makes it all right?"

He gently pulled his hand away from hers and let it rest on her hip.

"Well, it keeps us alive. And out of prison. I think that's a pretty good justification."

She wasn't convinced, but she didn't want to argue. Certainly not at a time like this. She pulled the covers up a bit higher and let herself relax in their bodies' commingled warmth.

"Will you tell me something?"

Something about his question put her on guard, but she tried to answer in a normal tone. "What?"

"Your name."

"Don't be silly. You've been calling me by name for months."

"Don't you be silly. You know I mean your real name."

She did know what he meant, but she didn't know what to say. The Director and the AD had drilled into her that she should never tell anyone her real name. And more important, at least to her, was that her name belonged to someone else—to the person she'd been before becoming whatever she was now. Spy? Assassin? Or just someone who killed to survive?

"My name is Smith."

"No, it's not."

"Yes, it really is. That's my name now—the name of who I am, this person you're in bed with. The person you work with and make love to. That's my only name now."

"Don't you want to know my real name?"

She thought about that. In a way she did, but then she realized that the same reasoning applied to him.

"I do know it. You're Lee. You're the man who chose that name and has done what he's done under that name. Your name is Lee."

He didn't reply, and she wondered whether he was angry. But she'd said what she meant, and she wasn't going to take it back. If he loved her, he loved her as she was, and she wasn't going to change for him any more than she was going to try to change him.

After a minute or two his breath tickled her ear again. "Okay, Smith, let Lee ask you something else. Who did you kill?"

"What? You know who we killed in Japan."

"Before that."

"My prior mission?"

"No. I mean, if you want to tell me about that sometime, I'd like to hear it. But I want to know what happened to make you an Enterprise recruit."

She closed her eyes, thinking of how each of the three had looked at the moment she'd pulled the trigger. And how they'd looked afterward.

"Smith? You said once that you'd tell me when you got comfortable enough—I mean, comfortable with me."

"I think I said maybe."

"It's the same thing. If you're not comfortable enough now, you're never going to be."

He had a point. If she couldn't tell Lee—her only friend, her lover, a man she'd been to hell and back with—she'd never be able to tell anyone. And maybe she needed to tell it. Maybe she'd kept it buried inside long enough.

CHAPTER TWENTY-TWO

She sighed and turned over so she could look at him. "All right. I killed three men. The men who raped me."

"Raped you? When? And where?"

"In Afghanistan. When I was in the Army. They raped me and my best friend, Laura." Saying Laura's name brought hot tears to her eyes, and she blinked them back. Laura....

"How did it happen?"

She paused, remembering. "We'd been on a long, tough logistics mission—three days out and back, bouncing in the trucks in the dust and heat. We'd found and disarmed some IEDs and exchanged fire with the bad guys, but they never came very close, so it was hard to tell how many of them we got."

She'd killed two herself, matching what any of the men had done and surprising all of them, but something kept her from telling Lee that. She told herself she didn't want to brag, but she knew it was really because she didn't want to admit to still more killing.

"A couple of our guys were hit, but none seriously. It was just the usual shitty job of doing what we were told and trying to stay alive. You know?"

"Yeah. This job's been reminding me. Then what happened?"

"We got back to the base late in the afternoon. Laura and I shared a room, so we cleaned up and talked about heading over the chow hall for dinner, but we were too tired to eat. She had some vodka squirreled away, and we started drinking. You know—just to unwind."

"Sure, I know about that too. You have to do something to bring yourself down."

"Right. So after an hour, maybe a little more, we were pretty high. We were lying on my bed and passing the bottle back and forth. I wish I could tell you it was ladylike drinking, but it wasn't. I think both of us wanted to get drunk."

"Sounds like you needed to after that mission."

"Maybe. Anyway, these three guys came to see us on their way back from chow. When they knocked on the door I didn't want to answer it—we were just in panties and t-shirts—but Laura hollered for them to come in, so they did. I didn't think too much about it—I mean, we'd served with them for months, and they were like our brothers at that point."

"That's what you thought."

"Pretty stupid, huh? In hindsight. Well, I pulled a blanket over my legs, but Laura just let them look. And she was a beautiful girl...."

Lee wisely didn't say anything, giving her a moment. After she wiped her eyes she continued. "The guys could tell we'd been drinking, and they said we should share. The bottle was about empty at that point, so I would have just let it go, but Laura jumped up and pulled the other bottle out of her locker. She said, 'Let's party,' and the guys started passing the bottle around while she turned on some music. They were hitting it pretty hard—I guess they felt about the same way we did—and it wasn't long before two of them were dancing with Laura, and the other guy was trying to get me to dance."

"And you said no."

"Exactly. I said no, and the guy didn't like it very much. He made some crack about Laura and me being lovers—after all, they'd found us in bed together, nearly naked and half drunk—so of course we must be lesbians. He said some more stuff, very crude and very personal, and I told him to shut the fuck up. Then he slapped me."

"A mistake."

"One of the biggest he ever made. I jumped on him and starting punching—I could tell he was surprised by how hard I could hit. The other two guys pulled me off, and the three of them started laughing, which just made me madder. I told them to clear out, and Laura backed me up even though I could tell she really didn't want them to go."

"I'm guessing they didn't leave."

"No, they didn't. They just laughed some more and said they'd go when they were good and ready—and they wouldn't be ready as long as there was vodka left. One of them tried to get Laura to dance some more, but I could tell the whole thing was beginning to make her nervous, so she wouldn't do it. Then the guy said something like, 'Hey, loosen up,' and he started kissing her."

"Didn't you think of calling the MPs—yelling, screaming, anything?"

"I guess I still couldn't believe what was happening. Like I said, these guys were our friends—we thought."

"I'm sure they were. But by that point they weren't thinking, not rationally anyway."

She tensed, and he could almost feel the temperature drop. "Hey, you're not defending those assholes, are you?"

"Of course not. But I'm a guy, so I know how guys are. I'll bet I could draw a picture of what happened next."

After a long moment she said, "Yeah, you probably could. Well, it didn't take long. The guy with Laura got real physical, rubbing his hands over her, pulling up her shirt. She tried to stop him, but you could tell he just didn't care. And when I tried to go over to them, the two guys held me down. And then they started doing to me what the other guy was doing to her."

"And you still didn't scream?"

"By then I would have, but one had his hand over my mouth, so I couldn't. I bit him, and he hit me so hard I thought I'd pass out, but I didn't." She paused. "I wish I had. Then I wouldn't remember so much."

Lee caressed her, soothingly, his fingertips gently brushing her skin. She hugged him, warming herself with his body. "I'm glad you're here. I'm even glad to be telling you this, finally."

"You don't have to say any more. I can guess what happened."

"No, I want to tell it—then perhaps I won't think about it so much. Although I know I'll never forget...." She put her hand on his. "The three of them raped Laura, taking turns while one held me down. They hit me some more—I don't know how many times. They didn't have to hit Laura. She just sort of gave up, crying and keeping her eyes shut. Maybe the alcohol dulled her pain. I know it helped when they hit me."

He squeezed her shoulder, saying nothing else.

"Then it was my turn. One watched Laura—I think she was unconscious or nearly so—and one held me down while the other...." She swallowed hard. "Raped me. Then another one did. And another."

She let the words vanish into silence. It was a few seconds before she spoke again. "After the first one I tried to pretend I was somewhere else. Or even that I was someone else—that it wasn't happening to me. But of course it was."

"And after?"

She laughed bitterly. "The lead asshole—Jack Williams, a big farm boy from Iowa—said it was all in fun, that they knew we wanted it. And we better not say anything because it would be our word against theirs, and anyway we'd been drinking, a lot, before they showed up. Kolenko and Bugatti—that's Chris and Francis although he preferred "Frank"—didn't say much. Chris looked ashamed—I think he'd had a crush on Laura. Frank—no, fuck him, Francis—just looked mean, like the jerk he was, which is why no woman would want to have anything to do with him. But I could tell the guys were getting scared about what might happen to them, and they left pretty quickly."

"So what did you do?"

"I reported them, naturally. The very next day. Of course I should've done it the night before and had the medics check each of us with a rape kit, but I was too hurt and angry and drunk—just too everything. Stupid, I know."

"No, understandable."

"Well, anyway, I put Laura in bed and gave her two sleeping pills. She cried herself to sleep. I was too mad to sleep, so I just lay there in the dark and thought about what I'd like to do to those guys."

"And eventually you did it."

"Yes, but not just for myself. The real... the real reason...." She had to stop then and give herself a minute, at first wiping her eyes and then just letting the tears flow. "The real reason was that Laura killed herself. While the investigation was going on. She... cut her wrists. I found her in our room... her face as white as paper, blood all over her and the bed... it was awful."

"My God! That must've been terrible."

"It was." Her voice was flat now, calm, as though she was simply reading from the official report. "She left a note asking me to forgive her. She said she was sorry she wasn't strong enough to deal with it. But she knew I could. She asked me to make sure that justice was done. And I tried... I tried so hard. But with Laura dead and no physical evidence, it was even more my word against theirs, and the Army wouldn't prosecute."

"Wasn't the note evidence?"

"Not really, because Laura didn't say what had happened or who the men were. It was a very personal note, meant just for me. A good defense lawyer would have poked holes in it and trashed Laura's character along with mine. The prosecutor—a woman, by the way, a very no-sense lieutenant colonel—told me to let it go. She also said not to hang out with guys when I was drunk and nearly naked." Smith laughed bitterly again. "Good advice. I don't know why I never thought of it."

"That's when you decided to kill them."

She didn't reply. He said, "That's when you decided."

"Yes." She exhaled slowly. "That's when I decided."

"How long did you wait?"

"Quite a while. I knew I'd get caught if I did it over there, so I waited until I was out of the Army. I rotated back to the States two months after... it happened, so I didn't have to be around those guys much. I just ignored them—or tried to. Williams asked me to go on a 'date' with him—that's what he called it, but I knew what he had in mind. I told him in front of a bunch of people to fuck off, and he didn't ask again. Pretty soon I was home and out, back in Civland again."

"But then you had to track them down."

"Yes. It wasn't that hard. I knew their names, where they were from. And the internet's a great research tool."

"Were you afraid that they might still be in contact with each other? Especially after you did the—after the first one died?"

"Yes, but that was a chance I had to take. That's also why I held off until I knew I could get them quickly, one right after the other. But I didn't see any signs that the second or third guy had been warned. Two of them were out of the Army by then, and the other was in a stateside billet. They seemed to have gone their separate ways."

"Sounds like you really scoped things out."

"Yeah—great training for my present job." She paused a moment before continuing. "I chose my weapons and practiced with them. Then I watched and waited. When I thought the time was right, I moved."

"And took them off the board."

"It wasn't like chess—or any other kind of game. I planned everything and tried to be as careful as I could, but I knew what I was doing: killing three men. Committing three murders. There's no other way to put it."

"You were killing snakes. They deserved it."

"I thought so then. Now I'm not so sure."

He raised himself on an elbow. "Why?"

"This... thing we're in. This stupid Enterprise. All this killing. It's got to stop."

"I don't think the AD is big on stopping. Or on troops who quit."

She didn't say anything for a long moment. Then, pulling him down to her, she said, "No, he's not."

□   □   □

They didn't have to go back for a week. During that week they slept late, sweated through long workouts in the gym, cooked new dishes, watched several movies.

And made love every night.

They tried new restaurants, bought books they'd been wanting to read, spent a lot of time in bed reading or talking or just lying in each other's arms.

And making love.

Smith thought it was almost like being married. Something she'd never tried and had begun to think she never would. But with Lee... maybe. If he wanted to—she was pretty sure he did—and if the Enterprise would let them.

But she knew the AD would object, would find some reason the two of them couldn't be together. He'd tell her, and then he'd smile that cold smile of his, knowing there was really nothing she could do about it unless she wanted to go to prison for life.

And then she could never share her days—or nights—with Lee.

She thought about their situation all week. She didn't want to interfere with Lee's happiness or hers during that time, so she didn't bring up the subject despite the strong temptation to do so. Then at the end of the week, with her prospective mission, whatever it was, hanging over both of them, Lee brought it up.

"We've got to get you out of this."

"Out of what—the Enterprise? Can't be done. Not until they let me retire or...."

"You don't come back from a mission."

"Exactly."

"No, there must be a way. We can run, hide. Go someplace they'll never find us."

"There is no such place. You know that—it's the Enterprise. They'd find us in hell."

He frowned. "Well, maybe. The AD does sometimes have the look of the devil about him."

"What's this? I thought you were on the team. 'Yes, sir. No, sir.' All that."

He held up his mutilated hand. "Having your fingers chopped off changes your thinking some. At least it did mine. I did what I had to do on those missions, but now I'm a free man. Well, more free. So let's figure out a way to make you free too."

"I'll be focused on just staying alive."

"But you hate this life!"

She took his face into her hands and looked into his eyes. "Yes, but it's the only life I have now. And you make it bearable. Okay? So just be here for me and help me stay alive."

He put his good hand on one of hers. "I'll never be anywhere else. You can't get rid of me now."

She smiled. "Good." She kissed him, and he responded eagerly.

Soon they were headed for the bedroom, moving awkwardly because they were still kissing as they walked.

□   □   □

Afterward, as they were lying in bed together and she was thinking how lucky she was to have Lee in her life, even at this fucked-up point in her life, he said, "I need to tell you something."

She raised her head from his chest and looked into his eyes. "That's rarely a good start to a conversation."

"I know. But you've been very honest with me, told me private things I know were hard to tell. There's something like that I want to tell you."

"As long as it's not that you're married." She tried to say it lightly, but the effort fell flat.

"No, I'm not married, never have been. But I was involved with someone once, a long time ago."

Reassured, she said, "That's okay. Each of us has a past—it's what made us who we are. Just as long as you're not still in love with her."

The silence stretched out so long that she wanted to shake him to make him speak. "What? You are still in love with her?"

"Well, yes. I mean, naturally. You see—"

"See what? I don't see a goddamned thing. What are you trying to tell me?"

"It was Amy."

Now it was Smith's turn to be silent. When she could speak, she said in an unbelieving tone, "Your sister?"

"Yes. My sister. I... we...."

"What? You were *lovers?*"

"Yes. That's right." There was a sound of relief in his voice as though he were glad to be telling her, glad to be free of this secret he'd kept from her. "When we were teenagers. For about a year after our mother died."

"You... you seduced her?"

"Actually, Amy took the initiative. Came to my room one night. I knew it was wrong, but I didn't stop her. Didn't stop myself. And then it just seemed to go on for a while."

Smith didn't know what to say. She knew things like that happened—perhaps had happened in her own family—but she'd never thought she'd be in love with someone who'd... done that. She didn't know what to think.

"Amy broke it off too. She said that it was wrong and that we shouldn't do it anymore. I'm ashamed that I tried to get her to change her mind, but she'd grown up faster than I had, and she stuck by her decision. She was right, of course."

"Yes, of course." Smith thought her voice sounded faint and far away.

"Anyway, I wanted to tell you. I hope...." He trailed off.

"Hope what?"

"That you won't hold it against me. I was fifteen, for Christ's sake."

"But old enough to know better. I mean—my God, you knew it was wrong."

"Yes. Yes, I did. I was just weak, that's all. Both us were."

She reflected on that. And on things she'd done, three things in particular. Doing them, she'd thought she'd been strong, but maybe it had really been weakness. Not an act of courage but a yielding to temptation.

"It's all right. None of us is perfect. I'm sure not, God knows. But thanks for telling me."

She closed her eyes. After a few minutes Lee's slow, regular breathing told her that he was asleep. She tried for sleep herself, but she couldn't stop thinking about what Lee had told her. She was glad he'd shared the secret, but she wished he hadn't had that particular secret to share. She didn't want what he'd done so many years earlier to change the way she thought about him, but she couldn't help feeling that it might.

That was the last time they made love before they had to report to the AD.

CHAPTER TWENTY-THREE

They went back to the place where the AD had briefed them the last time, a nondescript office building in Northern Virginia. They took the elevator to the same floor he'd previously indicated and found the Sergeant waiting for them behind a bare metal desk. He folded the sports page, stood, and came over to them, a slight smile on his dark face.

"Well, here you are. Two of my students who've done some good work. I'm glad your training paid off."

Smith said nothing. Lee held up his bandaged hand. "Not entirely."

"That's not a big deal. You're still alive, aren't you? And the boss says you're retired now. Got lots of time to learn how to do things without those fingers."

Lee flushed and took a step toward the Sergeant, but Smith stopped him by putting a hand on his arm. "Come on, Lee. He didn't mean anything by it."

The Sergeant arched an eyebrow. "No, I didn't. You're lucky to be alive—that last mission was a tough one. And I've had a lot of students who didn't come back. Some on their very first mission."

"Wright never got to go on his first mission." The words were out before Smith could stop them, but she looked the Sergeant in the eye, daring him to rebuke her.

"No, he didn't," the Sergeant said, no heat in his voice. "And I regretted that. I liked him."

"So did I." Smith remembered Wright's dazzling smile and quick wit, the way nothing ever seemed to bother him. Maybe that had contributed to his death. Maybe if he'd taken things more seriously.... Then she shook her head. Maybes weren't good in this business. Maybes could get you killed. And she very much wanted to stay alive. For Lee, of course, but also for herself.

"That's the worst thing about this life." The Sergeant looked at the floor and scuffed it with his boot. "You lose too many friends." After a moment he looked up at them. "Okay, let's move. We don't want to keep the boss waiting."

The AD was sitting at the table when they walked into the briefing room. Dietzler was sitting next to him.

The AD rose and said, "Good morning." Dietzler continued to sit, stone-faced, and said nothing.

"Good morning." Smith nodded at the AD and looked at Dietzler, who held her gaze for a moment, then looked away.

"Hi," Lee said. He didn't offer to shake hands, and neither did the AD.

"Here, Lee, this is for you." The AD handed Lee a manila folder. "The Sergeant will take you to someone who can explain how things will be for you going forward."

Lee took the folder, pointedly using his bandaged hand. "Thanks. Will I need to see you again or should I just say goodbye?"

"It's possible that you'll see me again but unlikely. In fact, you don't want to see me again. If I have to visit one of our retired agents, that means he's revealed something about our work, and—"

"Yeah, I know. You're right—I don't want to see you again." He smiled faintly. "Not even in my dreams. Well, so long, AD. Dietzler." He gave them a little wave with his free hand.

Then he turned to Smith. He looked straight into her eyes but didn't say anything. After a few seconds he nodded slightly and walked out, followed by the Sergeant.

When the door had closed behind them the AD said, "Lee's a good man. Too bad about what happened to him on that last mission. At least he's still alive." The AD paused, waiting to see what she would say in response, but she didn't speak. "And I know the two of you are... involved."

Dietzler's head snapped toward her, and she saw the surprised expression on his face. There was something else too—a look of contempt. I'm sure he thinks it's very unprofessional to get involved with a coworker, she thought. Especially when your work is to kill people. Well, he's probably right, but when did love ever make sense?

"I'd tell you not to see him anymore, but I know you wouldn't follow that order. I don't give an order unless I know it will be obeyed." The AD paused, making sure he had her full attention. "But keep this in mind—I'll hold you personally responsible for any problems that your relationship causes."

The threat was veiled but still there, and she knew he meant what he said. "Okay," Smith said, wanting to change the subject, "what are my orders for this mission?"

The AD continued to look at her for a moment before gesturing to a chair on her side of the table. "Sit down, and I'll tell you."

He resumed his seat and slid a manila folder over to her. She didn't know what she expected to see when she opened it, but she didn't expect to see an official photo of the new head of the CIA. She recognized his face from having seen him on TV several times, including when he told Congress that the CIA had gotten out of control and needed to be reined in.

She looked at the AD. "This is Mr. Peters."

"Yes."

"What relationship does he have to the target?"

The AD shook his head slightly. "Smith, I thought you were smarter than that. Peters *is* the target."

Dietzler smirked but didn't say anything. He must already know, Smith thought, which means the AD told him before telling me. And that means the AD trusts him more. She decided not to turn her back on Dietzler—not that she ever had.

She looked at the AD. "We can't kill the director of the CIA."

"Yes, we can. And we will."

"But why? I thought we worked for them."

"We do—or did. But Peters wants to shut down our little operation, and we can't allow that."

"What? Of course we can. It's illegal—we shouldn't be doing this at all."

The AD stared at her, and she didn't like what she saw in his cold, gray eyes. "Smith, I've known since your training days that you'd be trouble. You're effective on missions, but you've never learned to submit to discipline. Your job isn't to question orders—it's to do as you're told without asking why."

"That's bullshit. I may have to work for the Enterprise, but I don't have to love it. Or believe whatever you say just because it's you saying it. Does the Director know about this mission? I can't believe he'd be a part of anything like this."

"You need not concern yourself with what the Director knows or doesn't know. Part of my job is to give him cover, plausible denial. So let me worry about that. You need to start worrying about surviving a hit on someone who's closely guarded by highly trained professionals."

The Director doesn't know about this, Smith thought. He couldn't. He'd never approve killing one of our own. But then she remembered what had happened to Wright, and something the Director had said came back to her. He'd said that if she tried to quit, he'd have her killed "just like that"—as quick as the snap of a finger. She knew he'd meant it, so maybe he did know about this plan to kill Peters.

"Okay, I'll listen. What's the plan?"

"That's better. You know where Camp Peary is?"

"Yes, that's the special training facility near Williamsburg."

"Correct. Peters will be there on Thursday—he's flying down in an Agency plane for a meeting that afternoon. The next morning he'll fly to Naval Air Station Oceana in Virginia Beach and then take a car or maybe a van to the Navy's Dam Neck base nearby. He's been invited to address the students at CID."

"Sid?"

"The Center for Information Dominance Unit Hampton Roads— what used to be NMITC. You know, the Navy Marine Corps Intelligence Training Center. Peters was in the Navy with the guy who's now the CO there."

"If you know all that, you must have Peters's daily schedule."

"Yes." The AD permitted himself one of his wintry smiles. "We have friends at Langley who understand, as we do, how dangerous Peters is to national security."

"If he's so dangerous, why did the president appoint him?"

"This president?" The AD made a dismissive gesture. "He's just as dangerous—more so, actually, because he has more power. I'd take him out if I thought we could do it without blowing our entire operation."

Smith's eyes widened. From anyone else that remark would just be big talk, but she knew the AD was serious. And the thought of killing the president... it was just insane.

She'd hated doing what the Enterprise had forced her to do, but at least she'd been able to tell herself it was in the service of her country. Now this—killing a senior U.S. official. There was no way this served the country. Or if it did, she didn't recognize the country anymore and didn't want to serve it.

She wanted to quit. She wanted to walk out right now, find Lee, and go home with him. Start a new life together. Try to forget what she'd been through in the past year, what she'd done.

What she'd become.

But she knew she couldn't. They wouldn't let her quit—or, more precisely, they wouldn't let her live if she did.

And somewhere in the back of her mind she knew that she'd taken an irrevocable step toward whatever she was now when she hunted down the first of the men who'd raped her, and then killed him. Then taken the second step. And the third.

So there was no going back from where she was—who she was. There was no way out.

She closed her eyes and put a hand to her face.

"Are you all right?"

The AD's tone of concern surprised her. She turned her head up and looked at him. "No, not really. But it doesn't matter. Not now. Let's get on with the mission."

"Good." The AD handed a folder to Dietzler and then opened his own. "Here's the timeline. You, Dietzler, and I will enter the Dam Neck base in two vehicles. You and Dietzler, being military age, will be in uniform and have military IDs. I'll be in civilian clothes with an ID that says I'm retired military."

Clever, she thought. He's really thought this through.

"None of us should have any trouble getting on base. Nevertheless, each of us will have enough weapons in the trunk to carry out the entire mission. That way if even two of us are stopped and searched by the gate guards, the third person should be able to do the job."

"How many security personnel will Peters have?"

"We think just two—they're going from one military base to another, and the drive is short, so the situation seems safe. Another break for us is that they'll be in a Navy vehicle, not one of the armored SUVs that the CIA uses around Washington. Both of the security people will be CIA—well armed and well trained—but we'll never have a better chance to get at Peters."

"What about the driver?"

"Most likely a Navy chief or junior officer. He—or she—could be armed but probably won't be. And Peters won't be armed—he doesn't like guns."

The AD sneered when he made the comment about Peters, and Smith felt her face flush with anger. "Anyone else with them?"

"Maybe. It depends on whether the CO of Oceana thinks he or his XO should accompany Peters. We're trying to find out, but our connections in the Navy aren't as good as those in the CIA."

"So there could be at least one more person, making five or maybe even six total."

"Yes. Could be a gaggle. The important thing will be to hit the security personnel first and then get Peters. We'll have to take out the rest too so that there won't be any witnesses."

That made sense, Smith thought. If they got Peters first, the security team would probably kill them. She hadn't worked with CIA security before, but she knew they must be superbly trained and equipped. She wondered if she and Dietzler and the AD would be able to handle them.

"Shouldn't we assign targets? Increase our chances?"

"That would be ideal, but because we don't know exactly who'll be there, we'll have to wait until we see them."

"Couldn't we plant someone at Oceana to tell us?"

The AD looked at her appraisingly. "That's a good idea, Smith. I should have thought of it. I guess I've gotten too used to keeping mission teams as small as possible."

"Lee could do it."

"Lee?"

"Sure. He wouldn't have to use a weapon, so his hand... I mean, he's fully capable of being a spotter. And this way you wouldn't have to bring in someone new, someone who hasn't worked with Dietzler and me before."

Smith wasn't quite sure why she'd suggested Lee. She was glad he could get out of the game, and she certainly didn't want to put him in danger. But being their spotter shouldn't be risky—all he had to do was watch and report. And things might go better if he were around. If there were no other reason, her instinct told her that Lee should be part of this mission, and she'd learned to trust her instinct.

She noticed the AD hadn't said anything. He was still looking at her, and she wondered what he was thinking.

He was trying to decide whether Smith had some ulterior motive for wanting to add Lee to the team. Maybe, but he couldn't think of one. He hadn't forbidden her to spend time with Lee, so she didn't need an excuse to see him. As to the merits of the suggestion, well, Lee had proved that he was solid and reliable. Having him along couldn't hurt, and it might help.

In fact, maybe Lee could plug the last hole in the plan... yes, that was an idea, especially with him in the spotter role. The AD thought about the reports he'd received a few days earlier, the follow-up background reports on Dietzler, Smith, and Lee. One had been particularly interesting—and potentially useful.

The more he thought about it, the more he liked Smith's suggestion. He'd have a private talk with Lee and make sure he that understood what might be required. And that he'd have no choice but to do it.

"Okay, Lee can be our spotter. Dietzler, go find him. He can get the muster-out briefing after this last mission."

Dietzler frowned. "You sure you want to have him along, knowing the two of them are fucking each other?"

Smith was very glad she was not the recipient of the look the AD gave

Dietzler.

"Dietzler, never question my orders. Never. If you don't want to participate in this mission, say so, and I'll find you a job shoveling shit somewhere cold and dark. Understand?"

Dietzler gave the AD the yard stare that Smith was sure he'd learned in prison, but he managed to keep his anger in check. After a tense moment he said, "Yes, sir," making it sound almost like an insult. Then he left the room.

The AD shook his head. "Dietzler's good with weapons and isn't afraid to use them, but he's just like a bomb that could go off at any moment, and you never know when that moment will come."

"Then why do you use him? I mean, why is he in the Enterprise?"

"Good question. As you may have noticed, there isn't a long line of people who have or can develop the skills we need, are willing to do what we ask people to do, and are good at doing it. Dietzler is all of those things. I'll grant you he's not the most pleasant fellow I ever came across, but not everyone can be charming, right?"

As he made the last remark he looked straight into her eyes. He knows what I think of him, she thought. It's like he can read my mind. Well, maybe I've just been too obvious.

"I suppose. Being charming has never been a goal of mine."

"Oh, don't sell yourself short, Smith. You're the sort of woman who gets a man's attention not just because of her looks but because she doesn't try too hard to get that attention."

His comment surprised her. He'd never paid her a personal compliment in the past, and it was strange to hear him doing it now. Of course, she'd seen the way he looked at her—he'd seen her naked after all. At least that one time, and she was pretty sure there'd been hidden cameras in their training barracks. She knew how a man looked when he was admiring her or, to be frank, when he was thinking about having sex with her, and she'd seen that look in the AD's eyes a few times. Most recently when he'd visited her at the hospital.

But the thought of sleeping with him repulsed her, and she'd tried to ignore that look of his whenever she'd seen it. She'd never brought the subject up with Lee. She didn't want Lee distracted by anything that might affect his judgment when he was dealing with the AD or carrying out a mission.

She glanced at the AD and saw that he was waiting for her to reply. Once again she didn't know quite what to say. "I'm just being myself."

"Yes, I know." He paused, studying her. "Lee's a good man, as I said earlier, but I don't think he's the right man for you."

"That's none of your business."

"Smith, everything that affects you is my business. In this line of work you shouldn't have any close personal relationships, but if you're going to be romantically involved, it should be with someone worthy of you."

"Then despite what you said, you must not think much of Lee."

"No, he's been a good operative, and I appreciate your suggestion about having him as our spotter. But you're worth five of him. You're one of the best we've ever had, and you deserve someone who really understands you, knows how to value you." He looked into her eyes. "How to treat you... in every way."

She forced herself not to shudder and look away from him, but her hands gripped the chair arms so tightly that her fingers hurt. She wanted to tell him to shut up and never speak this way to her again, but she knew what he could do—would do—to her if she made him angry enough.

Wait, she told herself. Wait. Your chance will come. He may make a mistake, go too far, and then you can do whatever you have to do. Maybe even what you did to those three after the desert....

Again he was waiting for her reply, so she said, "Well, I like the treatment I'm getting now, but I'll let you know if I find it lacking."

She wondered if the AD could read her mind now. If he could, he wouldn't like what she was thinking. She looked down at the folder in front of her, wishing they could just get on with the briefing.

She was afraid the AD would continue the conversation where he'd left it, but he didn't. Instead he glanced irritably toward the door and tapped a finger on the table as he waited for Dietzler to return with Lee.

They didn't have to wait long. In less than a minute the two men walked in, and Dietzler closed the door behind them.

The AD waved them toward seats. "Lee, I've decided we can use you on this mission, so you'll have to postpone your retirement for a while."

Lee looked at her, but knowing the AD was watching, Smith keep her face carefully neutral. "Fine," Lee said. "I'm not much on fishing or golf anyway. What's the mission?"

"We're going after Jeffrey Peters, the head of the CIA. He wants to disband the Enterprise, stop us from protecting the country. We can't have that."

"The head of the CIA?" Lee looked at Smith again, but still she kept her face blank. She wasn't going to give the AD and Dietzler the satisfaction. "Are you sure about this?"

"Yes."

"But how will we get away with it? Won't they come after us—CIA, DIA, NSA, all of them?"

Good question, Smith thought. The same one had occurred to her, but she was so resigned to her fate that she hadn't bothered to ask it.

"No," the AD said, "they'll go after the Muslim extremists who claim responsibility."

Lee looked skeptical. "And who might they be?"

"They don't exist. Well, not in reality, but CIA and NSA and the FBI will create evidence that they do. E-mails, telephone metadata and intercepts, money transfers. Just enough clues to deflect attention from us but not enough to lead anywhere. I'm afraid that these particular extremists will never be brought to justice, as the stock phrase goes."

"No one can keep something like that quiet forever," Smith said. "Someone will talk. The truth will come out."

"I don't think so." The AD made a church steeple with his long, slim fingers. "I know all of the people involved at the various agencies, have known them for years. It's a small, handpicked group. They're all very dedicated to our cause, to keeping the country safe. And as you might imagine, they know how to keep secrets—they've kept some as big as this one."

Smith thought about that. Maybe he was right. Maybe he could keep the thing hushed up. Smith was increasingly aware that she was living in a hall of mirrors, some convex, some concave, but all of them distorting the truth, whatever that might be. Or, she corrected, whatever the Enterprise said it was.

She looked at Lee and shrugged. He held her gaze for a moment and then turned to the AD. "Okay, how will we do it? And what's the way out afterward?"

His second question was another good one, Smith thought. Assuming any of us survives the hit, which seems unlikely.

"Look on with Smith, and I'll tell you." He waited as Lee edged his chair closer to Smith's. He glanced at Dietzler and then looked back at Smith and Lee, smiling his cold smile. "Ready? Then let's begin."

CHAPTER TWENTY-FOUR

Because they'd need two vehicles for the mission, they took separate cars to Virginia Beach. Smith was afraid the AD would insist on her riding with him, but he took Dietzler and let her ride with Lee. His hand was well enough now for him to drive, and his expression—calm and relaxed if not exactly happy about the prospect of their mission—showed he was glad to be alone with her again.

The AD's only requirement was that they meet him and Dietzler at the hotel by ten p.m., so they had time to take back roads through the Virginia countryside south of the Rappahannock River. The summer afternoon was sunny but not too hot, and the farm fields spread out fresh and green on both sides of the highway.

"Nice day for going to a ball game. Or maybe having a picnic."

Smith looked at Lee. "Nice day for anything except what we're doing—driving to set up an ambush for the director of the CIA. And that won't be any picnic."

"Don't think about it. Just think about this—us being together on such a nice day."

"I can't help thinking about the mission. In fact, it's all I can think about."

Lee sighed. "I know. I try to pretend I can compartmentalize well enough to focus on the moment, but it's hard."

"'Compartmentalize'? I didn't know Marines used such long words."

He glanced over at her and smiled. "There are a lot of things about me you don't know."

"I'm sure that's true. But I'd like to know them—I hope I have a chance to."

"You mean you hope we live long enough."

"Who said not to think about the mission? Yes, that's what I'm hoping. But in this business maybe it's better to give up hope."

"No, never. Hope can give you strength, help keep you alive. Don't ever lose that."

She put her hand on his thigh. "All right. I hope I never lose you."

He put his hand on hers. "You won't. No matter what."

"Good."

They stopped talking then, each lost in thought and the beauty of the countryside. Soon they crossed the York River and got onto the interstate that led through the Hampton Roads Bridge-Tunnel and out to the connecting highway that would take them to Virginia Beach.

As they approached their destination Lee made several attempts at conversation, but Smith was too tense for small talk, and they'd already said the important things to each other. She had a bad feeling about this mission, and she thought Lee probably did too but didn't want to admit it. At least not to her.

Lee knew a good seafood restaurant on the water and drove there for dinner. They got drinks, skimmed the menu, and ordered. Then they sat silently, gazing out at the big ocean, flat and empty, its blue darkening to black as the light faded in the west.

"Do you know how to sail?"

Smith looked at Lee. "Where did that come from?"

"Just wondering."

"No, I've been out on power boats—ski boats, that sort of thing—but never a sailboat."

"I think you'd like sailing. I learned how when I was stationed at Gitmo. Sailing is the closest thing humans can do to flying. Moving with the wind, I mean, not flying in a plane."

"What about a glider?"

"Yes, I guess that's similar. I've never been in one though. But I can tell you that being on a sailboat is like nothing else."

"Better than anything else?" She smiled at him.

He smiled back. "I can think of one thing better, with you at least, but sailing's great. I wish we were out there now, sailing away to some deserted island, just the two of us."

She heard the wistfulness in his voice. "That would be nice, wouldn't it? But here we are. And here we have to stay. For at least a while longer."

"Yes, at least for a while."

After dinner they went to the hotel and, as the AD had instructed, left their bags at the front desk. They killed a few minutes sitting in the lobby and skimming through the newspapers left there, neither of them really reading anything, each of them glancing at the other every several seconds.

At exactly ten o'clock they went to the AD's room.

Dietzler was there with him, and they had maps and diagrams spread out on the king-size bed. Smith and Lee had seen them all many times but knew the AD wanted to go over the mission once more.

The AD did it efficiently, checking off the key points one by one and stopping occasionally to make sure they understood. For the first time he told them how they'd escape—the one part of the plan he hadn't worked out earlier.

He had to have help with that, Smith thought. Just like when they pulled us out of Japan. But this sounds riskier.

Smith kept her doubts to herself. She asked a couple of questions, mostly to let him know she was following the briefing. Lee asked a question about his spotter job. Dietzler said nothing.

Dietzler is a scary guy, Smith thought. More than a little creepy too, but he must be as good as the AD said or he wouldn't be along on this particular mission.

For an instant she wondered if Dietzler and the AD were... involved. Stranger things had happened.

But it seemed unlikely. She remembered when the AD had told her where and how to get onto the Dam Neck base.

"Be careful to stay within the speed limit. They have a lot of students marching in formation to various schools, and they don't want anyone hit by a car. So if the sign says fifteen miles an hour, you don't go any faster. Got it?"

Lee had been out of the room then, and the AD had put his face very close to hers—so close that she'd pulled back a little. Was he trying to intimidate her? Surely he wasn't flirting. But if he were, it was a poor effort.

For the first time she wondered if he were married. If he were, she felt sorry for his wife. He didn't wear a ring, but that didn't mean much. A lot of married men didn't wear wedding rings, and she knew from experience that wearing one wouldn't necessarily stop a man from coming on to her.

It was hard to imagine the AD's being married—he was so cold, so austere—but he could be. She'd been surprised many times at the men some women chose, and perhaps her own choices had surprised some of her friends. She wondered what Laura would have thought of Lee. She probably would have liked him—they were alike in some ways—and she would have been glad that Lee made her happy.

After an hour or so the AD seemed satisfied, or at least as satisfied as he ever seemed, that they understood the plan and knew their jobs. "Okay, I guess that's it." He tossed the pen he'd been using as a pointer onto the bed and nodded at Dietzler, who began folding the maps.

"Here." He dug in his pocket and pulled out two card keys. "Smith and Lee." He handed each of them one. "I wrote the room number on each one. The hotel should have delivered your bags by now, so get some sleep—you'll need to be sharp tomorrow."

"You think it's going to be tough?" Lee glanced at the card and looked at the AD.

"Yes, I do. CIA security people are professionals and good at their job. Then we've got the base police to worry about. They're not CIA quality, but they're not idiots either. And there are SEALs on that base. Heavily armed, trained to move fast. They might decide to get involved." He paused, looking at Lee, then at Smith. "So this mission could be very... interesting."

Smith thought about the odds against them. "Well, as the Chinese say, 'May you live in interesting times'."

The AD gave her a sharp look. "That's actually a curse, isn't it?"

"Yes, I think so."

"Thanks, Smith. A curse on our mission is all we need."

"We're already cursed, sir, just from having to do it."

"I don't agree. It's an honor to serve one's country."

"Sure. If that's what we're doing."

The AD stared at her for several seconds, and she forced herself to keep looking at him. It wasn't easy.

"One more thing, Smith."

"What?"

"I want your mobile phone. Both for security reasons and to make sure you rest tonight. You too, Lee. You'll get them back tomorrow."

It sounded like a stupid order, but she'd heard plenty of stupid orders before and obeyed most of them. Tonight she didn't feel like arguing, especially in front of Dietzler and Lee. She pulled her phone from her hip pocket and handed it to the AD. Lee followed her example. She noticed that the AD didn't ask Dietzler for his phone, but maybe the AD already had it. Or maybe he thought that Dietzler simply had no one to call.

"All right. That's it." The AD opened the door for them. "You better get to bed."

Lee heard the commanding tone. He gave Smith a little wave, almost too slight to notice, and headed for the door. The AD leaned down and spoke softly to him. Smith caught only a snatch of it: "...alone tonight...." Lee stiffened but said nothing. He left without looking back.

The AD told Lee to stay in his room, she thought. She wondered briefly whether Lee would obey the order, but then she decided it didn't matter. If he didn't come to her, she'd simply go to him.

No, wait, she couldn't—she didn't know which room he was in. And he didn't know where her room was. Calling the front desk wouldn't help. The AD had registered all four rooms under some name she didn't know. And that business with the mobiles—he must have planned it this way. He was obviously determined to keep them apart the night before the mission.

And apparently his plan was going to work. She glared at the AD, sure he could see the hatred in her eyes.

Maybe he could. But if he did, he didn't react to it. He looked at her for a moment before checking his watch. Then he smiled his cold smile and said, "It's getting late. Good night, Smith. Sleep well."

She couldn't bring herself to make a civil reply, so she gave him only a curt nod and went out. She hoped to catch Lee in the hall, but the AD had delayed long enough for him to be gone.

She clenched her fists so tightly that the room key almost cut into her hand. That bastard—always trying to manipulate people, to keep them doing what he wanted them to do. And usually succeeding.

How had she ever gotten into this mess? She asked herself the question for the thousandth time, and for the thousandth time the answer came back: Williams, Kolenko, and Bugatti.

She flashed back to her introduction to the Enterprise—standing naked and shivering in front of the AD and the Sergeant while that grainy, green video played on the screen and she watched herself shoot a man twice in the head.

Hot tears filled her eyes, and she tried to wipe them away with the back of her hand. Her vision was so blurred that she had trouble finding her room, but finally there it was, several doors down the hall from the AD's.

Was Lee's room on this floor? Maybe. But maybe not. And she couldn't start banging on random doors to find out. She was alone, and that was just how it was going to be.

On what might be her last night on earth.... She sighed and unlocked the door.

CHAPTER TWENTY-FIVE

Entering the room, she flicked on the lights and saw her bag by the bed. There was no point in unpacking, so she took out only what she'd need that night and the uniform she'd wear the next day. She went into the bathroom and began filling the tub. She hung the uniform on the back of the bathroom door so that the steam would take out some of the wrinkles.

She wanted a drink, maybe a couple, but she hadn't brought anything and didn't feel like calling room service and waiting around while they brought her something. So she dimmed the lights in the bedroom and slipped out of her clothes, dropping the garments one by one onto the bed.

She left the lights off in the bathroom and slid into the tub. The water was very warm, almost as hot as she could stand, and felt good as it flowed over her skin, warming and relaxing her. She let the water run until it almost filled the tub, and then she turned off the faucet and lay back, letting the warm water lap over her and up to her chin.

She lay there in the near-darkness, letting her muscles loosen and trying to make her mind completely blank so she'd think of nothing at all except how good it felt to lie there. She succeeded for a while, imagining her brain as a blackboard with nothing written on it, but then she thought of Lee and wondered what he was doing.

Sleeping, probably. Well, that's what he needs to do. Maybe it's good that we're not together tonight. We'd just keep each other awake.

But she couldn't quite convince herself that it was better for them to be apart on the night before this obscene mission. She closed her eyes and saw Lee's face—the bright eyes, the strong chin, that little scar under his ear. She'd meant to ask him how he got that, but she hadn't.

Hadn't yet, she corrected. Hadn't yet. Then she thought of his mouth, how it looked when he smiled at her, how it felt when they kissed. Keeping her eyes closed in the warm, humid dimness, she moved a hand across her breasts, feeling the nipples stiffen. She let her hand linger there a while and then moved it lower, letting it drift down through the water until she was touching herself the way she loved for Lee to touch her.

She spread her legs slightly and moved her fingers a bit faster, feeling the warm, tingling sensation begin to spread outward. She heard the blood begin to sing in her ears and was surrendering herself to pleasure when she heard something else, something that made her snatch her hand away and open her eyes.

The AD was standing in the doorway and looking down at her. He was breathing harder than usual, and that was the sound she'd heard. She wondered why she hadn't heard him open the door to her room but then realized that the noise of the running water must have muffled the sound of the door.

"Get out!" She covered her breasts with her arm and closed her legs. "Get out or I'll yell for help!"

"No, you won't." He spoke softly to calm her. "First, you don't want any involvement with the authorities. Second, I can break your neck before you make enough noise to attract attention."

She knew he was right about the first point. "You won't kill me—you need me for the mission."

"I'd like to have you on the mission, but if I have to, I can do it without you." He paused, looking down at her. "Without Lee too, if it comes to that."

"Well, then what do you want? Did you forget to tell me something?"

He took a step inside the room. "You're a smart woman, Smith. Much too smart not to know what I want. What I've wanted for a long time."

With her suspicion confirmed, she felt her heart race but was determined not to show fear. "I guess I do. You sure picked a hell of a time to do something about it."

"What could be our last night alive? I'd say that was an excellent time."

"It's not going to do you any good. I mean, I won't, so—"

"Yes, you will."

"What makes you think so?"

"Because you want to live. You want Lee to live. And this is the only way you have any chance of that happening."

"You want me so much you'd kill us otherwise?"

"Yes. That much."

She closed her eyes and let her hand fall from her breasts to her side. She thought furiously, trying to figure a way out. There wasn't one. Even if she were willing to die now, she couldn't let him kill Lee. And she knew that he meant what he said. He always did.

She looked up at him. "You're not going to like it. I won't cooperate."

The AD smiled, and she wanted to shiver despite the warm water.

"We'll see." He stepped close to the tub, took a towel from the rack, and opened it. "Here. I'll dry you off."

She wished there were something she could do, some way out of this. Maybe if she had a gun, even a knife... but she didn't. She was trapped.

She remembered what he'd said to her once. "Smith, one day you and I will have to come to an understanding." She remembered how he'd looked when he said it, and she remembered the rest of it. "We'll have to find a suitable time and place so we won't be disturbed. Then I'll explain things to you in a way you'll understand—and never forget."

She even remembered her sarcastic reply. "Any time. Sir."

Well, this was the time and place. And now, despite all her best intentions never to be in this position again, here she was, and there was nothing she could do about it.

Slowly she stood, water dripping from her skin and hair. The AD reached toward her with the towel, and she shrank away from his hands.

"No, Smith. It's okay—here, I'm not going to hurt you." His voice was still soft, but now it carried an unfamiliar hint of tenderness. He reached toward her again, and this time she forced herself not to draw back. The towel was thick and soft and felt good on her skin.

She'd never seen him behave like this before, and his conduct confused her. Who was this man? The same one who'd barked at her countless times and threatened to kill her a few seconds earlier? Or someone she thought she knew but really didn't?

Maybe he was as much an actor as she was. Maybe living this life could make you that way. It hadn't affected Lee like that, but everyone was different. Maybe she had more in common with the AD than she'd realized. He'd suggested as much, but she hadn't believed him.

Still, even if that were true, she didn't want to be standing there naked in front of him, feeling his hands on her as he dried her body. Touching her everywhere, even her most intimate parts. Kneeling before her to dry her legs, then having her turn around so that he could dry her back and hips.

And she didn't want to think about what would come next.

He took another towel and gently rubbed her hair until it was merely damp. Then he tossed the towel aside and led her by the hand into the bedroom. The lights were low, as she had left them, and he threw back the covers on the bed.

"Get in." His voice had become thick, almost hoarse.

She looked at the bed, then at him. She tried again to think of a way out, but she knew there wasn't one. She remembered the way he'd stared at her sometimes when they were training in the desert, and she realized that this night would have come somewhere, sometime—maybe sooner, maybe later, but it would have come.

And here it was, and there was nothing she could do about it.

Slowly she got into bed and lay down, pulling the covers up to her chin. The AD looked at her with an unreadable expression. He began to undress, using quick, jerky movements. She had never seen him like this before. He seemed excited but almost... nervous now that he was so close to his goal.

She closed her eyes and thought of Lee. She thought of the night they'd sat in the hot tub, watching the bright stars wheel above them. She thought of him putting his hands on her.

Then she felt the touch of the AD as he slid naked into bed beside her. She tried to imagine herself a bird, a strong, broad-winged bird flying high above houses and fields and woods, flying far away. But what the AD was doing and saying, all without any response from her, at least no voluntary response, kept her grounded, and she could not escape the moment.

Just as she had not been able to escape in the desert. That moment and this one blended together until she thought she was back there again and the AD must be one of them. Or all three of them, the way he moved his hands over her, making her flinch, and the way he forced himself between her legs and then inside her, thrusting again and again as she squeezed her eyes tightly and vowed she would not cry, would not give in to the pain and humiliation and anger.

Would not—until finally she did, and the hot tears rolled down her cheeks. The AD whispered to her, gently, like a lover, but she could not stop crying. She cried for herself and Lee, for the people they'd killed, and for the entire fucked-up world that she'd never made, never wanted, but could not escape just as she could not escape this terrible moment.

By the time the AD had had enough of what he came for, her tears had slowed but not stopped. He didn't lie there long afterward but rather got up and got dressed in the darkness, occasionally speaking to her in a soft voice that she didn't answer. Before he left he put a hand to her face and wiped away some of the wetness there, but still she didn't respond.

Then he went, closing the door softly behind him, and she heard the lock click. The flat, metallic sound was as complete and final as that of chambering a cartridge before sighting down the barrel and squeezing the trigger.

She thought of taking another bath, of trying to wash herself clean, but then realized that she was long past that—she would never be clean again.

So she lay there in the still darkness, not trying to sleep but trying not to think. She didn't sleep, and she couldn't help herself from thinking. That night in the desert played itself like an endless loop in her head until it blended with this night, making a circle of horror that she knew she could never forget. Never escape. She didn't think even Lee could heal her now.

And she'd been close. So close.

She closed her eyes and wept again until all the tears were out of her and the black night gave way to gray dawn.

CHAPTER TWENTY-SIX

Smith slowed as her car approached the gate. The morning rush was over, so there wasn't a long line of cars waiting to get on the Dam Neck base. She lowered her window and held her military ID out so that the guard could see it easily. The last thing she wanted was to give the guard time to look her and the car over carefully while she fumbled for her ID.

The guard took her ID and examined both sides. Then he handed it back to her. "Welcome to Dam Neck. Drive safely."

"Thanks."

She put the ID back in her wallet and drove through the gate. She'd never been to this base before, but she'd memorized the map the AD had shown her, and the route to their rendezvous point wasn't hard to follow.

She wondered how Lee was doing on the nearby Oceana base. She wished she'd been able to see him that morning even if only briefly.

Crossing the hotel lobby, she'd looked around but hadn't spotted him anywhere. She'd entered the hotel's restaurant, but he hadn't been there among the people having breakfast. The normal people, a few in business attire but most more casually dressed, having their eggs and bacon or cereal or something else and drinking coffee while they glanced through newspapers or chatted with one another. The normal people who wouldn't have to kill anyone today.

She'd thought briefly about having breakfast herself and now regretted that she hadn't eaten something, both for energy and to calm her nerves. She badly wanted to descend from this high emotional cliff where she stood, jittery and alone. The memory of the night before combined with anticipation of the day ahead had her so keyed up that she had to grip the wheel hard to keep her hands from shaking.

Per the AD's orders, the four of them hadn't met at the hotel this morning, which was fine with her because she didn't want to see the AD again until she had to. Actually, she didn't want to see him at all, but she knew that it was unavoidable. But maybe it would be the last time. She hoped it would be, no matter how the mission ended.

She realized that if they were successful, completely successful, the AD would still be around, and she'd still be working for the Enterprise. But then a thought came into her head. The thought came unbidden, and she didn't know in what dark corner of her mind or soul it had lain sleeping.

The AD didn't have to survive the mission. Neither, for that matter, did Dietzler. And she could see to it that neither of them did. Then she'd be free. Free of the AD, the Enterprise, the endless killing. Everything except Lee—she didn't want to be free of him.

The two of them could go away somewhere, change their names again, and live normal lives. They might have to leave the country to do it, but she knew it could be done. At least she was willing to try, to take the chance. She deserved happiness, didn't she? Even after all she'd done. The first three had been for justice, and the rest—well, she'd just followed orders. She knew from history that "following orders" wasn't really a sufficient excuse, but it's the only one she had, so she told herself that it was enough.

So maybe this would be the last mission for the AD and Dietzler. She didn't have much time to think about it, and she didn't want to think any more. She just wanted to act. To let her training and experience and instincts take over and tell her what to do.

She drove slowly, staying under the base's low speed limit. She passed two groups of young sailors and Marines marching to class and tried to remember when she'd ever been that young, that naïve. It seemed like a long time ago, a time when she'd been someone else. Someone she liked much better than the person she was today.

She passed a base police car parked in a lot that adjoined the road. The officer inside was wearing dark glasses, so she couldn't see his eyes, but she saw his head swivel as she passed. Was he suspicious of her? Why would he be? He didn't know about the weapons in the trunk or what she was planning to do.

Suddenly she remembered the cop who'd looked so hard at her as she drove away from that hillside in California. She'd thought she was in danger then. If only she'd known what real danger was....

The police car didn't pull out to follow her. She let out the breath she'd unconsciously been holding and loosened her tight grip on the wheel. She was almost there.

Smith drove into the parking lot that the AD had designated for their rendezvous, a lot at the other end of the base from CID. She looked around for the car the AD had described. She didn't see it at first and started to worry, but then she spotted it off by itself at the far end of the lot. There were only a few other cars in the lot, none of them near that one.

She drove there and parked next to the car. The AD and Dietzler were inside. She'd wondered how she'd feel when she saw the AD again, and now she knew. A cold fury filled her, the anger great enough to act on when the time came but not hot enough to make her do anything foolish. She smiled to herself, gratified that the AD had put this emotional weapon in her hand.

She noticed that the AD and Dietzler were wearing dark glasses just as the cop had. The day wasn't that bright, so maybe it was some macho thing. Well, there was no time to think about that now.

She went over to the other car and got into the back seat. Both of the men turned to look at her. She couldn't read their expressions behind the dark glasses, and she wondered if the AD had said anything to Dietzler about last night. No, she decided, he wouldn't have. He was one of the most tight-lipped people she'd ever known, and he'd want to keep to himself what has passed between them.

She didn't expect any pleasantries at a time like this, and she didn't get any. "Ready?" the AD said, and she nodded slowly.

He picked up a small, handheld radio and pushed a button. "Lee?"

"Yes, sir." The radio's encryption process made Lee's voice sound strange, muffled, as though he were speaking through a blanket. But it would keep anyone else from listening in. The AD had told her that he'd gotten these radios from the Mossad and that neither the CIA nor NSA could monitor them.

"What's happening?"

"There's a Navy passenger van in front of the Oceana headquarters building. Navy driver inside. Two guys in dark suits standing on the sidewalk, one at the front of the van, one at the back."

"Just two? Good. Is the driver armed?"

"I don't know. He hasn't gotten out of the van since it pulled up fifteen minutes ago."

"Well, we can deal with him even if he is." The AD checked the time. "According to Peters' schedule, he and Captain Jorgensen should finish their courtesy call in five minutes. That will put him in front of CID in about half an hour."

"There's something else."

Even with the radio's distortion Smith could hear the strain in Lee's voice. Strain—or nervousness? It wasn't like Lee to be nervous. She must be imagining that.

"What?" The AD spoke sharply, clearly annoyed that something unforeseen might interfere with his careful plan.

"The Director is with them."

"Repeat!"

"I said *the Director* is with them."

"You're sure?"

"Yes. I'm parked where I'm supposed to be, fifty yards away, but these are good binoculars, and I'm sure it's him."

"Damn it." The AD's banged his fist on the dash. "He wasn't supposed to be here."

"Why is he?"

The AD glared at Smith. "I don't know. He's... unpredictable sometimes. As when he decided to recruit you." The AD waited a moment, but Smith didn't take the bait. "I suppose he's trying to persuade Peters not to shut us down. He sure picked a hell of a time to try to do it."

"Maybe he thought that on the plane ride he could speak to Peters alone. No staffers around, no one to remember the conversation but the two of them."

"Maybe." The AD thought for a moment. "Yes, that may be it. A good idea, actually, except that it interferes with our plans."

Smith sat back, pleased to learn that the Director didn't know about this mission. This must be all the AD's doing. Well, obviously they couldn't carry out the mission now, not with the Director present.

"So we have to call it off."

The AD replied instantly. "No, Smith, we don't."

"What? We can't hit Peters with the Director there!"

"Why not?"

"Are you crazy? We might kill him!"

The AD's expression told her that he didn't like her questioning his sanity. "Yes, we might. But if we carry out this mission, the Enterprise will endure. The Enterprise is indispensable—the Director is not."

Smith couldn't believe what she was hearing. Or rather she could, but she didn't want to believe it.

"What's the matter, Smith? Scared?" Dietzler spoke for the first time since she'd gotten into the car.

"Fuck you, Dietzler."

"Anytime, baby, anytime."

She wanted to knock the smirk right off his face, and she started to tell him that, but the AD interrupted.

"All right, that's enough. You two can insult each other after the mission—if you're both still around. Right now we need to focus on the job." He clicked the radio button. "Lee, any update?"

"No, not yet. They should be coming out very soon."

"We have to know whether the Director is coming over with them."

"Roger that. Wait—here they come now. Peters and the Director are coming out first. Captain Jorgensen is right behind them. The CIA guys are opening the van doors."

There was no sound in the car except the slight static from the radio. Smith realized she was holding her breath, and she thought the AD and Dietzler were also.

"Peters is getting in." Lee paused. "Yes, the Director is getting in too. And now Jorgensen. That's six people in the van, counting the Director."

"But maybe only two armed." The AD said it to them, not to Lee.

"Probably at least three," Smith said. "I'll bet the Director is armed, if for no other reason than to give Peters one more guard. And the driver may be too—we don't know. So maybe four."

"The Director doesn't matter."

You hope, Smith thought. Who knows what he'll do when the shooting starts? He's not in on this.

The AD thumbed the radio again. "Okay, Lee, you're done. Good job. We'll take it from here."

"Roger that. Uh, good luck, guys."

Again Smith heard something unfamiliar in Lee's voice, something she couldn't quite define. Well, she didn't have time to worry about that now. She had other things to worry about—like staying alive.

"Thanks. Out." The AD put the radio on the seat. He looked at Dietzler, then at Smith. "Ready?"

"Sure." Dietzler said it quickly and easily as though the AD had asked him if he wanted a cup of coffee. And that may be about all this means to him, Smith thought. If he had a conscience, she'd never seen any sign of it.

The AD cocked an eyebrow. "Smith?"

"I don't think we should do this, especially with the Director involved."

"Damn it, I didn't ask for your opinion—I asked if you're ready."

Smith thought about protesting some more but realized it wouldn't do any good. "Okay. I guess I'm as ready as I'll ever be."

"Just do your job, Smith. Just do your goddamn job."

"Yes, sir." She managed to say the words without expressing the sarcasm she felt. But it wasn't easy.

The AD nodded. "That's better. Now let's get our weapons."

Moving quickly and covering what she was doing as much as possible, Smith retrieved from the trunk of her car the small black bag that held her pistols. The AD and Dietzler got their guns from their own trunk. Each of them had two semiautomatics with full magazines—Glocks, Sig Sauers, one Colt, one Taurus.

Smith had asked the AD about the risk of bringing weapons onto the base this way, but he'd said the gate guards were unlikely to search cars driven by people with military IDs. "Getting the guns on base any other way would probably be riskier. Sometimes the boldest way is the safest way."

She'd also asked why they weren't using submachine guns—Uzis or something similar. The AD had said that Muslim terrorists in the United States weren't likely to have such weapons, so their team wouldn't either. "If we take the CIA security guys out first, this will be more than enough firepower."

He was probably right on both counts, Smith thought, but that "if" was a big one. She knew that CIA security officers were among the very best in the world. Three against two wasn't great odds, so they'd need some luck. She hoped they got it.

They were all back in the car in less than a minute. The AD checked the time. "Okay, we'll drive over to CID, get into position. They should be there in about fifteen minutes."

She didn't say anything, and neither did Dietzler, but she could practically smell the adrenaline pumping through all three of them.

The AD started the car and drove slowly out of the parking lot and down the street toward CID. They'd gone a couple of blocks before Smith remembered the cop who'd seen her drive up this street. When she saw his car, still parked in the same spot, she knew it was too late to duck.

"See that police car? He saw me drive by earlier."

The AD swore softly. "Did he look at you closely?"

"Yes. The way he's looking at me now."

"You might've thought of this before, Smith." The AD's voice was like the hiss of a snake.

"I know. My mistake. Sorry."

Dietzler half-turned his head toward her and spoke over his shoulder. "I just hope you didn't fuck us up."

Smith glared at him but said nothing. She was hoping the same thing.

"Okay," the AD said, "we'll just go by, nice and easy. Don't turn to look at him. Maybe he won't do anything."

They passed the police car. A few seconds later the AD turned his head toward the rear-view mirror.

"Did he pull out?" Smith almost whispered as though the cop might overhear her.

"No. Shit, yes, now he is. Coming this way."

Smith looked down at the bag beside her. She knew what she should do, but she didn't want to do it. After a moment she forced herself to unzip the bag, take out one of the pistols, flick off the safety, and rack a round into the chamber. She heard Dietzler doing the same thing. She put the gun on the seat and placed the bag over it.

When she looked up, she saw the AD watching her in the rear-view mirror. He didn't say anything—he just nodded slightly.

The police car's roof lights began flashing, and the cop whooped his siren for a few seconds. The AD pulled over, turned off the engine, and put both hands on the wheel where the officer could see them.

The AD watched the cop intently. "Good—he's getting out of the car. I don't think he radioed us in. He must just want to make sure nothing's going on."

"And to get a better look at Smith." Dietzler chuckled at his own wit.

"Shut up." The AD glanced at Dietzler and ran his window down as the cop walked up to their car.

"Yes, officer? Did I do something wrong?"

The policeman bent to look at the AD, then Dietzler, and finally Smith, letting his gaze linger on her. He was an older man, obviously nearing retirement. His belly sagged, stretching the polyester of his dark-blue uniform. But his eyes were bright and watchful.

"You weren't speeding, if that's what you mean. No, I just wondered why this young lady would be riding with you when she's got a car of her own."

"Oh, we're going to a change-of-command ceremony, and there's limited parking, so we're carpooling."

"I see." The officer straightened, apparently satisfied. Then he bent down again, glancing from Smith to Dietzler. "Wait a minute. You ain't going to a COC, not with them two in those working uniforms."

Barely moving his hand, Dietzler shot the cop between the eyes. The man dropped like a felled steer. The pistol shot boomed inside the car, but little of the sound escaped through the one open window.

"Quick! Throw him in the trunk. Dietzler, drive his car. Follow us but at a distance."

"Right." Moving as though electrified, Dietzler shoved his pistol in the bag and slid out of the car. Smith moved almost as quickly, and they had the officer's body in the car within seconds. Smith tried not to look at his face, but as Dietzler reached for the trunk lid, she glanced down. Immediately she wished she hadn't.

Then the lid slammed shut with a sharp metallic noise. It sounded like a hammer driving a nail, Smith thought. A coffin nail.

She glanced up and down the road. As far as she could tell, no one had seen them. Dietzler strode briskly toward the police car while she got into the front seat of the AD's car. She reached over the seat and retrieved her pistols.

The AD started the engine. As she put the bag beside her and fastened her seat belt, he looked at her and said, "Well, I didn't expect this little complication."

She didn't know what to say. The death of an innocent man—probably someone's husband, father, grandfather—had been reduced to a little complication. And she was complicit in it.

"I guess he just found you too attractive not to notice."

"Stop it!"

"What?" The AD was genuinely surprised.

"Stop talking like that. I don't want to be responsible for that man's death."

"But you are—we all are. It's part of the mission."

"Fuck this mission."

The AD gave her a searching look. After a long moment he put the car in gear and began to pull back onto the road.

"Okay, Smith, think what you want." His tone was as hard as she'd ever heard it. "Fuck the mission? Fine, if that's how you feel. But just don't mess up, okay? Try not to get any of us killed."

She wanted to shoot him then. She wanted to shoot him for that remark, for last night, for every shitty thing he'd ever done to her. She moved her hand toward the bag, fingers stiff from the anger that churned inside her.

He caught the movement from the corner of his eye. "Go ahead, Smith. Go ahead if you think you're brave enough. And fast enough."

Her fingertips touched the top of the unzipped bag.

He glanced at her hand and then looked back at the road. "But remember that you have to kill me before I kill you."

She knew he meant it. She also knew he could probably do it. But she wasn't sure she cared. She wasn't sure which scared her more—the thought of dying or the prospect of continuing to live this way.

He noticed her hesitation and chuckled. "Okay, Smith, you've made your decision. Now take your hand off that bag. Save it for the mission."

She let her fingers linger on the soft, smooth leather another few seconds. She didn't want to appear cowed by him. And she wasn't, but she knew he was right. She'd made her decision.

As Lee would say, the chips were on the table, and they'd see how the cards fell. She put her hand on her knee and squeezed. Squeezed hard until her fingers were white as bone.

CHAPTER TWENTY-SEVEN

They drove into the CID parking lot, Dietzler following, not too closely, in the police car. The AD found a spot fairly close to the entrance of the building, and Dietzler parked further away. Dietzler took his bag and the keys from the car, walked to the AD's car, and got in the back.

"Hi, Smith. How do you like riding with the AD?"

She looked at Dietzler, not sure whether he had a double meaning. His cocky grin told her nothing except that he was trying to psych himself up for the job.

"Fine. How do you like it? I mean, when he's the one doing the driving?"

His grin vanished, and he was about to snap back at her when the AD said, "Okay, you two. That's enough. Let's focus on our work."

Smith eyed Dietzler for another moment before she turned to look toward the entrance to the parking lot. "They should be here soon."

"We'll move as soon as we see them. Smith, you come with me. We'll walk toward the van. Dietzler, you circle around and come up from behind. We'll get them in a crossfire."

"But be careful not to shoot us," Smith said.

"Don't worry, sister. I'm always careful."

"Then how did you end up here?"

He opened his mouth to snap at her, but the AD spoke first. "Shut up, both of you. Look for the van."

They didn't have to wait long. In another minute or two the van turned into the parking lot and approached the main entrance to the building.

"Okay, let's go." The AD grabbed his bag and got out of the car. Smith and Dietzler did likewise.

"Walk quickly but don't run. Understand?" The AD looked at each of them.

"Right," Dietzler said. Smith just nodded.

The van was parked now, sitting in the space that had been reserved for it, the one closest to the building. The AD began walking briskly toward the van. Smith kept pace with him, but Dietzler headed off at an angle to go behind and then around the vehicle.

The front passenger door of the van opened, and one of the CIA security men got out. In his dark business suit he looked out of place on the Navy compound.

Smith couldn't see his eyes behind the sunglasses, but she knew he was scanning the area, checking for threats even though there should be none where they were. He looked at the AD and Smith for a few seconds but didn't seem to think there was anything unusual about them, especially with Smith in uniform and the AD, with his short haircut and fit body, looking like a retired military officer who now worked at CID as a civilian. From where the security man stood, the AD and Smith appeared to be headed for the building entrance, not necessarily the van.

The other security man opened the van's sliding door, got out, and jogged to and then up the steps of the building. He went through the revolving door and came out a few seconds later, satisfied that things looked normal on the quarterdeck. He nodded at his colleague, who turned to speak through the open door to the passengers in the van and then stepped back from the door.

Peters got out, followed by the Director and a Navy captain who had to be Jorgensen. As they emerged, Smith noticed a car coming into the lot the same way the van had come. Then she saw who was driving it.

"Lee." She barely breathed the word. The AD didn't say anything, so she thought he might not have heard her. "There's Lee. In that gray car."

"Yes, I see him."

"He wasn't supposed to come here. What's he doing?"

"Probably just trying to help."

Smith was surprised that the AD didn't seem bothered by Lee's unplanned appearance, and his remark made her wonder. Was Lee really trying to help? Coming to act as backup in case they needed him? Or had the presence of the Director prompted him to ignore orders and show up here? She wasn't sure.

They were getting close now, close enough to shoot with reasonable accuracy. Peters, the Director, and Jorgensen were walking toward the steps, flanked on each side by the security men. But Smith noticed that the men were making a mistake—they were looking at the people they were guarding and up at the front door of the building, but they weren't looking out toward the parking lot.

They're too relaxed, Smith thought. They glanced around, didn't see anything suspicious, and now they think there's no danger on this Navy base. But they're wrong. Dead wrong.

"Take the guard on this side. Dietzler will get the other one. I'll take Peters." The AD kept his voice low but enunciated clearly so that she could understand every word.

"And the rest?"

"We'll see."

"What?" Smith was incredulous. "You don't *know*?"

"I didn't know about the Director."

"Then call it off. Do it another time."

"No! We're here, and we'll take him. Now stop talking and do your job."

He pulled a small black radio from a pocket of his jacket and clicked a button on its side. Smith heard two soft clicks from the speaker, and the AD whispered into the radio. "Three minutes, maybe less."

The radio clicked twice again, and the AD slipped it back into his pocket. That's the escape route, Smith thought. Escape for those left alive. She wondered whether she'd be one of them. Well, she'd find out soon enough.

The AD opened his bag and took out a pistol. Sighing, Smith did the same. She knew things would move very quickly now.

They did.

The AD aimed and fired, hitting Peters in the back. Peters threw out both arms and fell forward onto the steps.

The security guards reacted instantly, whirling toward the sound of gunfire and pulling their own pistols from beneath their suit jackets. Smith shot the nearest man in the chest, but he was good enough to shoot back before falling.

A bullet slammed into Smith's left shoulder, and she stumbled into the AD, who cursed and pushed her away with the arm holding his pistol. She stumbled again and almost fell, but somehow she remained upright. The pain was excruciating, and, glancing down, she could see a red stain spreading on her uniform. She knew the odds of her getting away had just gotten a lot longer.

Dietzler was exchanging fire with the other security man, and she saw the man go down. The back of the van blocked Dietzler from her view, so she didn't know whether he'd been hit.

Jorgensen knelt to scoop up the pistol of the security man Smith had killed. As Jorgensen closed his hand on the gun, the AD shot him in the head, splattering his brains onto the sidewalk.

The Director watched the scene unfold, a horrified look on his face. He seemed rooted to the spot. Smith recalled that when the AD was training them for the mission in Japan, he'd said—boasted really—that he still went into the field occasionally but that the Director hadn't needed to go for a long time. Maybe the Director's reflexes had gotten dull. Or maybe he just couldn't believe what he was seeing.

The driver scrambled out his door, a pistol in his hand. The AD fired at him, but the driver, a young enlisted man, ducked back, and the bullet thunked into the metal door.

The man, who'd probably been hand-picked to drive these VIPs, edged around the door and snapped off a shot, hitting Smith in the stomach. She sank to her knees but managed to hold onto her pistol.

Then someone shot the driver from behind, and the young man sagged onto the pavement. Lee came around the front of the van, gun drawn, and looked down at the driver. Satisfied that the man was dead, Lee ran over to the Director and began dragging him toward Smith and the AD. The Director resisted at first, then let himself be pulled along, clearly still dazed.

The AD seemed relieved that Lee was there, gun in hand. As Lee approached, the AD said, "Dietzler?"

"Dead. But he got the CIA guy—they got each other."

A dark look came over the AD's face, but it was gone in a moment. "Okay." He glanced at the front door of the building. "I thought they might be swarming out now, but they've gone into lockdown." He paused, listening.

Smith heard the sirens. Faint now, but they'd get louder quickly.

"And they've called the cops," the AD said. "We have to move." Shading his eyes with his free hand, he looked to the east, toward the ocean that lay just over the dunes at the far end of the parking lot. "There it is."

Smith looked in the same direction and saw a small helicopter headed their way. Black, she thought. Of course it had to be black.

Lee reached them, and he let go of the Director to kneel by Smith. He saw the blood on her uniform and the blood oozing out beneath her hands as she clutched her stomach. He put a hand on her good shoulder, squeezed it gently, and said, "Come on. Let's get you out of here and to a doctor." He spoke so softly that the other two might not have heard it.

She saw him try to grin, but he couldn't quite manage it. She forced herself to smile, at least with her eyes. "Okay."

He began to pull Smith upright, but the AD put out a hand. "No, she's too badly hurt. You take the Director. I'll handle this."

Smith knew what the AD meant, what he planned to do. Despite her dread of prison she would have protested, but she knew it wouldn't do any good, and the pain was too great. Plus she didn't want him—or

Lee—to hear her plead.

The Director finally roused himself. "What—what are you doing? What is this?"

"Peters. We had to take him out. The rest of it is just collateral."

The sirens were louder now, but over them Smith heard the threshing of the helicopter. She looked up, and through the red mist that was beginning to blur her vision she saw its squat, dark body approaching. She wondered briefly which would win the race—the police or the helo. Then another wave of nausea hit, and the pain blotted out all thought.

The Director looked at Smith, at the bodies lying around the van. He turned to the AD, his eyes wide and his face red. "Peters? And collateral? What have you done? We had no orders!"

"Sometimes we have to act without orders. You know that. You've done it yourself."

"Yes, but...." His fists clenched, the Director sagged to his knees a few feet from Smith. She looked at him and saw him staring back at her, a terrible sorrow in his eyes. "Not like this. Not like this."

"Well, it's done, and there's no going back." The helo was very close now, coming in to land on the parking lot, and the rotor wash almost blew away the AD's words.

Smith turned her head to look at the road that led to the parking lot. She saw the flashing lights of the police cars that now were about five blocks away. If they were going to escape, they had to get aboard that helo now.

"Come on!" The AD tried to raise the Director to his feet, but the older man didn't cooperate.

"No, no," the Director said, barely audible over the helo and siren noise. "You've gone too far. We have to take responsibility for this."

"Goddamn it!" The AD dropped the Director's arm. "We did the right thing—the only thing."

"No, this was wrong... wrong." The Director closed his eyes, and Smith thought he suddenly looked like an old man. She touched his shoulder, and he put his hand on hers.

"We're out of time," the AD said. Before Smith could react, he raised his pistol and shot the Director in the face, spraying blood on Smith and Lee.

Ignoring the pain stabbing through her, Smith pointed her pistol at the AD. He caught the movement and whipped his gun toward her.

It was a Mexican standoff, just like that time in the barber shop. But this wasn't just an exercise, this was real, as real as anything could be.

Watching the AD's eyes, she tightened her finger on the trigger.

"Lee!" The AD's voice snapped like a whip, and Smith had to restrain herself from glancing at Lee.

She sensed movement at her side and wondered what Lee was doing, but she kept her pistol pointed at the AD.

"Lee, do it!"

"Look, we can bring her—"

"Do it! *Now!*"

The sound of the shot startled her, and something that felt like a hot knife slashed through her side. She dropped her pistol as she slumped to the ground. With her last ounce of strength, she turned to look at Lee.

He gazed back at her for a moment, his eyes wide with fear but also showing a terrible sadness. Then he looked at the ground. "I'm sorry! I'm so sorry! But he found Amy. He said they'd kill her if I didn't protect him, especially against you."

Smith felt the hot tears come, tears for Lee as much as for herself. Tears for what had been and for what would never be. And despite her pain and the darkness closing in on her, she couldn't help thinking of the irony of the situation. She was the one who'd suggested adding Lee to the team. One more mistake to add to the long list of others....

The police cars were very close, their sirens an incessant shriek. The AD reached down and took Lee by the arm. "Let's go! Hurry!"

Smith watched as Lee let the AD pull him to his feet. The two of them ran toward the helicopter, bending low as they neared the aircraft. As the AD scrambled aboard, Lee turned to look at her. He said something she couldn't hear, but his lips made it look like "forgive me."

Then he was aboard and the helo pilot dusted off. The front of the fuselage dipped low as the aircraft angled up and away, blowing dirt and scraps of paper over the bodies lying in the parking lot.

As she blinked her eyes against the grit, she felt herself slipping away. Images flashed through her mind, pictures of the desert, Laura, her family. Pictures of Lee... especially one of him lying beside her, his hands touching her gently.

And then herself as a little girl. Kneeling in that patch of dirt they'd called the back yard, shooting her brother's BB gun at the empty tin cans she'd placed in a row, knocking them over one by one. One by one.

Williams, Kolenko, Bugatti. Hernandez. The Japanese. That young woman who'd stood by the wall. And now this... all these people lying dead. For what? She didn't know.

The cars roared into the lot and skidded to a halt. Officers poured out and crab-walked toward the bodies, holding their guns out in front of them with both hands. Smith thought their shouted commands made them sound like barking dogs.

Smith closed her eyes. The pain wasn't so bad now, but she knew that was only because she was losing consciousness.

She heard one of the policeman kick her pistol away. She sensed him kneeling beside her.

"What happened?" The man's tone was urgent, insistent, reminding her of her drill instructor—her first teacher in the art of killing. "Who are you?"

She moved her mouth, struggling to speak before the darkness closed in completely.

"Who *are* you?"

"I'm Elizabeth," she whispered. "Elizabeth Grace Simmons."

The End